AUNT BESSIE YEARNS

AN ISLE OF MAN COZY MYSTERY

DIANA XARISSA

D1520723

For Chaad.

AUTHOR'S NOTE

And suddenly we're only one book away from Z and the end of the series. I never imagined, as I wrote Aunt Bessie Assumes, that I'd actually one day be writing the penultimate book in the series. As I've said before, this won't be the last you'll see of Bessie, though. A new series with many of the same characters will follow the last book.

I always suggest that you read the series in order, as the characters do change and sometimes references are made to events in earlier books. That's especially true in this title, although I've tried not to include any spoilers for those who haven't read the earlier books.

This is a work of fiction and all of the characters have been created by the author. Any resemblance that they may bear to real people, either living or dead, is entirely coincidental. The Isle of Man is a wonderful and very real place, but the businesses mentioned in this story are all fictional creations. Any resemblance that they may bear to any real businesses, on the island or elsewhere, is also coincidental.

As the setting is a UK crown dependency, I've used British (and Manx) English in the story. There is a glossary of terms and some other explanations at the back of the book for readers who find anything unfamiliar. The longer I live in the US, the greater the likelihood that American words, phrases, and spellings are sneaking into my books. I try to correct them when they are pointed out to me.

Please do get in touch. Hearing from readers always makes me smile. All of my contact information is available at the back of the book. Thanks for spending some time with Bessie and her friends.

CHAPTER 1

*B*essie opened her eyes and looked at the clock. It was quarter to six. Sighing deeply, she decided that that would have to do. Feeling as if she'd checked the clock at least a dozen times in the past four hours, she sat up in bed and then put her feet on the floor. Having been dreading this day for weeks, all she really wanted to do was go back to bed and sleep until it was over. Since sleep had proven elusive all night long, she knew she had to face the day, however much she was dreading it.

A hot shower made her feel slightly more awake, but no less grumpy. As she combed her short grey bob, she talked to herself in the mirror.

"You've been living on Laxey Beach since you were eighteen," she reminded her mirror image. "In all those years, however many that is, you've only ever found one dead body on the beach. The bodies in the holiday cottages don't count, as they weren't on the beach."

Bessie was aware that it had been a number of years since she'd been given her free bus pass at sixty, but there were still many years to go before she'd receive her first telegram from the Queen for her one-hundredth birthday. She felt that she was comfortably middle-aged and never bothered to actually count exactly how many years she'd lived on the beach.

The face in the mirror didn't look happy. "Yes, well, just because I found that body exactly two years ago today doesn't mean anything," she said to herself sternly. "Anyway, Doona has taken the day off to spend with me. She'll be here soon and then we'll do all sorts of interesting things and not give dead bodies a single thought."

Her reflection didn't seem at all convinced, but Bessie chose to ignore it. She applied some lipstick and then headed for the stairs. "I think I need coffee today," she said as she walked into the kitchen.

"You also need to stop talking to yourself," she added, shaking her head at her foolishness. She was definitely unsettled by her memories of the day two years earlier, but that was no excuse for having long conversations entirely by herself.

After starting the coffee maker, she dug around in the cupboards, looking for something interesting to have for breakfast. Wishing that she'd listened to Doona's suggestion that she stay in a hotel for the night, she finally decided that today of all days definitely called for pancakes. She had a small bottle of real maple syrup that had been an extravagance. She'd use the last of that on her pancakes after her walk, she decided.

Bessie had been walking on Laxey Beach nearly every morning since she'd first moved into her cottage, Treoghe Bwaane. She credited the exercise and fresh sea air for her continued good health. Her morning walks were one of her favourite things to do, even after she'd tripped over some driftwood and hurt her arm recently. Her arm was fine now, but today she felt reluctant to go out.

"You're being ridiculous," she told herself in a stern voice. "And you're talking to yourself again." This can't continue, she told herself silently as she put on her shoes and a jacket.

It was March. The skies were overcast and it looked as if it might rain at any moment. Bessie shivered as she remembered how cold and wet it had been two years earlier. Today was much better, almost unseasonably warm, she thought as she stepped outside.

As she nearly always did, Bessie first walked to the water's edge and then turned and walked along the sand. The long row of holiday cottages looked more lonely than normal as she went. It wouldn't be much longer before they were fully booked with families wanting a beach holiday, but for today they all sat dark and empty.

When she first spotted something on the sand, Bessie was certain that she was imagining things. She shut her eyes tightly. There is no way I'm seeing what I think I'm seeing, she told herself. When she opened her eyes, though, it was still there. For a moment, she was tempted to cross to it and feel it, just to make sure it was real, but she knew better. She'd been involved in far too many murder investigations over the past two years to make that sort of mistake.

Sighing, she pulled out her mobile phone. Two years ago today she'd first met Police Inspector John Rockwell. Now she had him on speed dial on her mobile.

"John Rockwell." It sounded as if she'd woken him.

She glanced at her watch. It was still a few minutes before seven. She probably had woken him. "I hope I didn't wake you," she said, wishing she'd simply rung the station. "It's Bessie. I'm on Laxey Beach. There's a body here."

"A body?" John echoed.

"Yes, a body. It's a man, or at least it looks as if it's a man from where I'm standing. I'm staying well back, of course, but the tide is coming in, so you'll probably want to get someone here fairly quickly."

"Where are you exactly?"

"Near the water's edge by the steps to Thie yn Traie," Bessie said, naming the huge mansion that was perched on the cliff above the beach.

John sighed. "I'll have someone there as quickly as possible. I'll be right behind them."

"I'll just stay with the body, then," Bessie said, swallowing a sigh.

"It won't be long," John promised. "I'm going to try to get Hugh. He's close by."

Bessie nodded, which was lost on John, of course. She slipped her phone back in her pocket and then began to pace back and forth slowly. What she really wanted to do was to get a better look at the body. There was something vaguely familiar about it, but she wasn't certain. Maybe she should go over and attempt to ascertain if the person was actually dead, she thought. But that would have simply have been an excuse to get closer to the body. There was no way anyone would be lying facedown on the beach on a cold March morning.

"Bessie? Are you okay?" Hugh Watterson called as he walked down the beach towards her.

"I'm fine," she said, frowning as her voice quavered slightly.

Hugh glanced at the body and then pulled Bessie into a hug. He'd been the first to arrive two years earlier as well. Bessie had known him since childhood and sometimes she still thought of him as much younger than his years. He still only looked fifteen to her, but he was in his mid-twenties now, a happily married man with a new baby. He was going back to school soon, too, to try to earn a university degree so that he could one day be promoted to inspector. Bessie was very proud of the young man, who'd worked very hard over the past two years.

"Maybe he just had a heart attack," he suggested.

"Maybe. What was he doing on Laxey Beach, though?"

Hugh shrugged. "We'll work it all out eventually. We always do."

Bessie sighed. "I was really hoping we were done with murder investigations."

"We've no reason to believe that this was murder," Hugh said flatly.

Bessie knew that Hugh was simply saying what was expected of him. There was very little doubt in Bessie's mind that the man on the beach had been murdered, and she knew that Hugh felt the same way.

"You got here quickly," Bessie said.

"I was up anyway. Aalish has started teething and she's very cross about it. Grace isn't very happy, either, because she loves Aalish's little toothless grin."

Bessie smiled. Grace, Hugh's wife, was a primary school teacher who was currently taking time off to bring up their baby. Aalish was nearly three months old. "Is that normal at that age?" Bessie asked.

4

"It's early, actually," Hugh said proudly. "Babies usually get their first tooth around six months old, but they can get it as early as two months or as late as their first birthday."

"That came right out of a book on child care," Bessie teased.

Hugh flushed. "I've been reading a lot of them. Grace bought about a dozen before we had Aalish and she leaves them all over the house. I feel as if the more I read, the more I'll know as we get to each new stage. The problem is, I just seem to realise that we're at a new stage and then she moves on again."

"Bessie, not again," a voice said from behind them.

Bessie and Hugh both spun around. Doona pulled Bessie into a hug. Her highlighted brown hair was pulled back into a messy pony-tail and she was wearing her glasses rather than the bright green contact lenses she often wore.

"Are you okay?" she demanded.

Doona Moore was Bessie's dearest friend, even though there was a sizeable difference in their ages. In her mid-forties, Doona was twice divorced. They'd become friends some years before Bessie had found that first body, and it was Doona that she'd rung that morning two years earlier. Doona worked at the front desk at the Laxey Constabulary, although she was working very little these days. When Doona's second husband had died, he'd left everything to Doona, even though the pair had been separated and Doona had filed for divorce.

The estate was tangled up in a huge UK court case, but Doona had already received settlements from some life insurance policies that her former husband had held. She didn't need to work any longer, which gave her time to help John with his two children, Thomas and Amy.

John had been unhappily married two years earlier. His wife, Sue, had been miserable on the island and had been doing everything in her power to convince their children that they hated it as well. Eventually John and Sue had divorced and she had remarried. On an extended honeymoon in Africa, where her new husband had been serving as a doctor on a humanitarian mission, Sue had contracted a fever and died. John was now left with two teenagers to raise on his own. He and

Doona were in some sort of relationship that seemed to make both them and the children happy. Bessie was doing her best not to pry.

"Did John ring you?" she asked as she hugged her friend.

"Um, yeah," Doona muttered. "He's on his way, but he had to stop at his office first. I didn't want to wait for him. I was planning to spend the day with you anyway."

"Starting somewhat later than this, though," Bessie pointed out.

Doona shrugged. "In hindsight, I should have insisted that we go away together for a few days. Someone else could have had the unpleasant experience of finding this body."

Bessie nodded. "Next year, I think I will go away," she said softly.

"Any idea who you've found?" Doona asked.

"He seems familiar somehow," Bessie replied. "I have my suspicions, but I can't imagine why he'd even be on the island, if it is who I think it is."

Doona raised an eyebrow. "Who do you think it is?"

"I'd rather not say as I could be completely wrong. Let's wait until John and the crime scene team get here. I can't be certain until I see the man's face, anyway."

"It does look as if it's a man, but it might not be," Hugh interjected.

"In which case, it definitely isn't who I think it might be," Bessie replied.

"It's chilly this morning," Doona said after a minute.

"Pop back to Treoghe Bwaane and get a heavier jacket," Bessie suggested, eyeing her friend's light coat.

"I didn't think about being outside in the weather when I threw this on," Doona admitted. "I probably do need something heavier if we're going to be out here for long."

"Why don't you both go back to Treoghe Bwaane," Hugh suggested. "John knows where to find you when he's ready to take your statement."

Bessie knew the idea was sensible, but part of her wanted to stay where she was. She felt an odd sense of responsibility for the dead man. A cold rush of air made her feel more willing to head for home.

As a light rain began to fall, she felt as if the decision had been taken out of her hands.

"I put coffee on before I left," she said. "It may not still be drinkable."

"I'll drink it anyway," Doona said. "And I'll bring a cup out for you, too," she told Hugh.

"I'll be forever grateful if you do," Hugh replied.

Doona laughed and then she and Bessie began their walk back along the beach. Back at her cottage, Bessie filled a large travel mug with coffee, adding a splash of milk and a few scoops of sugar.

"I'll just take this to Hugh before I have mine," Doona said.

After she left, Bessie got out the ingredients for pancakes. They no longer sounded good, but she needed to do something. She was just heating a pan when Doona got back.

"John's here," Doona told her. "He brought half the crime scene team with him, too. He said to tell you that he'll be here in the next half hour or so."

Bessie nodded. "If he manages that, he'll be able to have some pancakes."

"Is that what you're making?"

"They sounded good when I got up this morning. They don't now, but I need to keep busy."

"Are you okay?"

Bessie took a deep breath. "Not really. I was dreading today, dreading the anniversary of finding that first body. My life has been turned completely upside down in the last two years. I've found I don't know how many bodies, heard killers confess to murder, and been sought out by people who think they might be someone's next victim. Now, this day will forever be the day when I found two dead bodies, two years apart. There's another murdered man out there on the beach and I've no choice but to be right at the centre of another murder investigation. I just want my old life back, the one where I spent my days reading murder mysteries, not being caught at the centre of them."

Doona looked shocked. "I'm sorry," she said eventually. "I wish I could make it all go away."

Bessie sighed. "I don't mean to take it all out on you, but I've had quite enough of this. When we do find out who murdered that man out there, I'm going to demand an explanation as to why he killed him on my doorstep on the anniversary of another murder."

"Do you think they're connected?" Doona asked. "Maybe the victim has a connection to the Pierce family."

"We won't know for sure until he's identified. I suppose, if it is who I think it is, that there could be some connection."

"Who do you think it is?"

Bessie frowned. She didn't want to say until she'd seen the victim's face. A knock on the door saved her from having to answer.

"John, come in," she invited, stepping backwards to let him into the cottage.

John was a handsome man in his forties. His brown hair had a few grey streaks, but not many. He'd lost some weight during his former wife's lengthy illness, but he looked healthier now, and a smile crossed his face when his green eyes met Doona's.

"Good morning, again," he said softly to Doona.

"Good morning," she said, blushing and looking at the floor. "Bessie's making pancakes."

"I suppose, as I have to get her statement, that I have time for pancakes," he replied.

He took a seat at the table and, a moment later, Bessie put a plate of pancakes in front of him. While Doona got him some coffee, Bessie kept cooking. A few minutes later, they were all sitting together with their breakfasts.

"Are you okay?" John asked.

"Is that an official question?" Bessie replied.

"No, it's just from one friend to another," he said.

"In that case, no, I'm not okay. I ranted at Doona earlier about how tired I am of dealing with this, so I won't bore you with all of that, but I'm tired of dealing with this and I'm incredibly angry with whoever killed that man out there for ruining my day."

John nodded. "You've every right to be angry. These are delicious," he added, nodding towards his plate.

"I can make more," Bessie offered.

"No, I've been putting weight on at an alarming rate lately. Being happy seems to agree with me." He glanced at Doona and then smiled warmly.

"At least one good thing has come from all of these murders," she said.

"And Hugh met Grace. I don't know that she would have been so impressed with him if he hadn't been a part of solving a few murders by the time they'd met," Doona added.

Bessie nodded. Two years earlier, Hugh had had something of a reputation for being slightly dim and somewhat lazy. John had worked hard with him and with all of the young constables, teaching them investigative techniques and encouraging them to do everything they could to move up in their careers.

"Tell me about your day," John said after a moment. "Start with what time you woke up and go from there."

"What time I woke up or what time I got up?" Bessie asked. "I woke up just about every twenty minutes or so from midnight onwards. I was dreading today. I finally gave up on sleep a bit earlier than normal, maybe fifteen minutes or so before six."

John made a note in one of the notebooks he always carried before he took another bite. "Continue," he said around his mouthful.

Bessie frowned at him, causing him to blush. "I showered and started a pot of coffee. Then I decided that I'd have pancakes when I got back from my walk. It looked as if it wanted to rain, so I decided to get out and take a short walk before the rain started. Doona was supposed to be coming over around ten, so I thought I could have a short walk now and a longer one later."

John nodded. "And did you see anyone on your walk?"

Bessie shook her head. "The beach was empty, as it usually is in March. The holiday cottages are all empty. I didn't see Maggie or Thomas, either. Maggie is usually down here later in the day, painting and whatnot, but not this early."

9

Thomas and Maggie Shimmin owned the row of holiday cottages on the beach next to Bessie's cottage. Thomas had worked in banking for many years before he'd quit and he and Maggie had purchased the handful of cottages that ran along the beach next to Bessie's home. When they'd applied for planning permission for holiday cottages, Bessie had considered objecting. There was no doubt that having the cottages there had changed her life. Her summers were now spent surrounded by holidaymakers, some of whom didn't make for very good neighbours. For the most part, though, Bessie didn't mind the holiday cottages and she was happy for Thomas and Maggie that their business was such a success.

Thomas had been poorly for many months now, leaving most of the work at the cottages to Maggie. She was struggling to get them all ready for the new season on her own, but Bessie was sure that Maggie would manage it in the end.

"When did you first notice the body?" John asked.

"I saw something not long after I started walking. At first I thought it was just a large piece of driftwood or maybe someone's coat or something. It wasn't until I was fairly close that I realised that it was a dead body."

"You were certain that he was dead as soon as you saw him?"

"I wasn't certain, but I didn't want to get close enough to be certain, either. It was cold and windy. I can't imagine anyone choosing to sleep on the beach in this weather. The last thing I wanted to do was compromise a crime scene."

John nodded. "He is dead, just for the record. I checked when I arrived."

"Any idea what killed him?" Bessie asked.

John hesitated and then nodded. "We obviously don't have an official verdict yet, but I'm fairly confident that it was murder."

Bessie sighed. Although she'd known that it was almost definitely murder, a little bit of her had been hoping that the man had had a heart attack or maybe accidentally drowned.

"Anyway, I saw the body, realised it was a body, and rang you," Bessie said after a moment. "Then I waited for Hugh to arrive."

John nodded. "Did you hear anything unusual during the night?" he asked.

"Nothing, although it was a very windy night. The wind may well have masked a lot of odd noises," Bessie replied.

"Did you hear any cars drive past your cottage?"

"Not that I recall. I probably would have noticed, though, if I was awake, as cars down here at this time of year are unusual."

John nodded. "Did you notice a car in the car park for the holiday cottages this morning?"

Bessie frowned. "I didn't, but I didn't really look at the car park. It's mostly shielded from the beach by trees."

"It is, and the car was right in the corner, where the trees are at their thickest," John told her.

"Almost as if the driver didn't want anyone to notice the car," Doona suggested.

John nodded. "It might have driven past your cottage at some point yesterday or early this morning."

"Or the driver might have come down past Thie yn Traie. There is a back road through there, but it's narrow and easy to miss. If the driver knew the island well, though, he or she could have found it easily enough," Bessie replied.

John nodded. "I'm not sure I'd find it in the dark, but we've no idea when the driver arrived."

"I didn't notice any cars in the car park yesterday, either," Bessie said thoughtfully. "I wasn't looking for them, of course, and I took my last walk on the beach around midday. I spent my afternoon in Douglas."

John made a note. "What time did you get home yesterday, then?"

"I met a friend and we did some shopping and then had dinner," Bessie explained. "She drove me home around seven or half seven."

"Do you mind telling me which friend?" John asked. "I'll want to ask her if she saw any cars in the area."

"Of course I don't mind. It was Bahey Corlett. I hadn't seen her in several months. She's very busy with Howard, mostly."

Bahey had grown up in Laxey and was some ten years or so

younger than Bessie. They'd always been friendly, but had become much closer since Bahey had retired from a lifetime of service to the Pierce family, the same family that had once owned Thie yn Traie. The Pierces had sold the mansion after one of their own had been murdered on the beach, that first body that Bessie had discovered. Bahey had helped with the subsequent investigation, and she and Bessie had become good friends in the years since. Having never been involved with a man in her younger days, Bahey had been shocked when one of her neighbours, Howard Mayer, had first asked her to dinner.

The pair were an established couple now, even spending time together visiting Howard's daughter, who had given him his first grandchild. Over dinner the previous evening, Bahey had blushed and laughed when she'd told Bessie that Howard had recently proposed to her.

"Of course I said no," Bahey had told her. "We're too old to be getting married."

"Nonsense," Bessie had replied. "If you're happy together, why not get married?"

Bahey had shrugged. "I told him that I'd think about it," she'd admitted.

John made another note and then stretched in his chair. "Can you think of anything else to add to your statement?"

"I might know who he is," Bessie said.

John raised an eyebrow. "How close did you get to the body?"

"Not very close at all, but there was something familiar about him. I may be totally wrong, but I thought I should tell you. If it's who I think it is, you'll probably recognise him yourself."

"I did think that I recognised him, but I can't officially identify him. We're hoping to find identification on the body that will allow us to attempt to track down a relative. I'd rather not upset his family if I'm wrong about whom we've found."

"You're both terrible," Doona said. "Who do you think it is?" she demanded.

Bessie and John exchanged glances.

"Let me get you a photo," John suggested. "It won't take long. Once you've seen that, you may be more certain."

"Or I'll discover that I'm wrong," Bessie said.

John nodded. "I'll be back shortly with a photo," he promised.

Doona frowned as Bessie shut the door behind John.

"Who is it?"

"Did you want any more pancakes?"

"No, I just want to know who's dead."

Bessie began to pile dishes into the sink. "I'm not sure. You have to understand that I'm only going by his coat and shoes," she began. "They were familiar to me. The shape of the body seemed right, as well, at least as far as I could tell from what I could see."

"Right for whom?"

"Right for…" A loud knock interrupted.

"Miss Cubbon, the public have a right to know what's happening on Laxey Beach," Dan Ross, the obnoxious reporter for the *Isle of Man Times,* said when Bessie opened the door.

"No comment," Bessie said, trying to shut the door.

Dan slid a foot into the cottage. "It's the second anniversary of Daniel Pierce's death. Do you think there's a connection between that death and whatever is happening on the beach this morning?"

"No comment," Bessie said, holding the door as shut as she could.

"Did you find another body? The police aren't releasing any information, but I know a crime scene team when I see one. You found another body, didn't you?"

"Doona, can I have him arrested for something?" Bessie asked her friend.

Doona came and stood next to Bessie. "Harassment, maybe," Doona said, staring at the reporter.

"Ah, Mrs. Moore, this is an unexpected pleasure. I've been wanting to talk to you for ages. Do you think it's appropriate for you to be spending nights with your lover, seeing as his wife has only been dead for a few weeks?"

Doona pressed her lips together and then took a step backwards. Bessie pulled out her mobile phone. "You have two seconds to remove your foot and get away from my cottage before I ring the police," she told Dan.

He shrugged. "I'm just trying to do my job."

Bessie didn't reply. She simply began to punch in numbers on her phone. After a moment, Dan pulled his foot out of the door. Bessie slammed it in his face.

Doona was still pale as Bessie pushed her back into her chair. "You can't let him get to you," Bessie said firmly.

"I know, but it's difficult. What John and I do isn't any of his business."

"Absolutely not," Bessie agreed, thinking that Doona could share more with her closest friend, though.

Another knock on the door had Bessie pulling out her phone once more. "If that's Dan again, I'm ringing Hugh," she told Doona.

John looked surprised when Bessie opened the door a crack. "I did say I'd be back," he said.

"Dan Ross was just here," Bessie explained as she let him into the cottage. "He was incredibly rude to both Doona and me."

John took Doona's hand and waited until she was looking at him to speak. "Are you okay?"

Doona shrugged. "We'll talk about it later," she replied.

John looked as if he wanted to argue, but instead he reached into his pocket and pulled out a photograph, one of those instant type photos that had been popular for a while years earlier. "It's not a good picture, but it's the best we could get at the moment. I just want to know if you agree with me as to the dead man's identity."

Bessie glanced at the picture and shuddered. Anyone seeing the picture would instantly know that the subject was dead. He looked lifeless as his eyes gazed, unseeingly, past the photographer.

"It's who I thought it was," Bessie said softly. "It's Harrison Parker. But he'd gone across. What was he doing back on the island?"

CHAPTER 2

"*H*arrison Parker?" Doona repeated. "That really annoying reporter who made Dan Ross seem reasonable? Is it really him?"

Bessie handed her the photograph.

Doona looked at it and sighed. "I didn't like him, but I didn't want him to be dead. I was quite happy that he'd left the island, though."

"And he did leave the island," John said. "He'd managed to get himself a job with one of the London papers. An inspector there actually rang Pete for an informal chat about the man."

"What does that mean?" Bessie asked.

"It means Harrison was already sticking his nose into things and annoying people in London," Doona told her. "So much so that the police were notified."

John shrugged. "Pete told me about the conversation. I don't think Harrison was doing anything wrong, exactly, but he'd managed to annoy a few people. At least one of those people had a friend with the police and made an informal complaint."

"Surely no one would have followed him from London to kill him," Bessie said. "We have to find out what he was doing on the island."

"I'm going to have to talk to Dan Ross," John sighed. "If anyone will know what Harrison was investigating while he was here, it should be Dan."

"Maybe he was here because of something he was investigating across," Bessie said thoughtfully.

"Also a possibility. I'm going to have to get in touch with whoever he was working for in London to find out what he was currently investigating," John said.

"Maybe it was personal," Doona suggested. "I'm sure he was just as annoying with his friends and family as he was with strangers."

John chuckled. "That is also a possibility. We'll be taking a close look at his personal life, too."

"Could he have been doing any follow-up reporting on the case that got him the job in London in the first place?" Bessie asked. "That would explain what he was doing on the beach near the last holiday cottage."

A man had recently been murdered in that last holiday cottage, and Harrison had broken the story when the murderer had been discovered. As far as Bessie knew, the murderer was still behind bars.

"I'll be checking on everyone associated with that case," John told her. "Do you know if there's anything happening at Thie yn Traie at the moment?"

Bessie frowned. After the murder two years ago, the Pierce family had sold Thie yn Traie to George and Mary Quayle. George was a loud, exuberant man who'd made his living selling everything from cars to insurance. His wife, Mary, was quiet and shy, preferring to spend her time with her children and grandchildren while George went to every event the island offered. Bessie and Mary had become friends over the years, and Bessie hated the idea that this latest murder might be connected to Thie yn Traie.

There had been more than one other case involving the mansion and its residents over the past twenty-four months. The last thing Bessie wanted was for George and Mary to decide to sell their Laxey home. They still owned an even larger home in Douglas, and Bessie knew that George preferred that house to Thie yn Traie. It was Mary who loved the house on the beach, and Bessie liked having her friend so close to her own home.

"Actually, now that you mention it, George has some visitors at the moment," Bessie said. "Remember a year ago, when he and Alastair Farthington broke ground on that new retail park in Douglas? Apparently Alastair has lost interest in the idea, so George is trying to find a new partner to buy Alastair out. Nothing has been done with the site since the groundbreaking and, from what Mary said, George is very eager to get things moving this spring."

"I wondered what was happening with that retail park," Doona said. "I just assumed it was moving forward very slowly. I suppose I don't blame Alastair for losing interest. His wife was murdered here, after all."

Bessie nodded. "That's a part of it, anyway. He's also been buying up properties in the US and spending more time there. I believe he has half a dozen shopping malls in New York and Pennsylvania now."

"I didn't realise you were keeping such a close eye on Alastair," Doona said.

"He rings me once in a while," Bessie replied, blushing. "He tells me what he's doing and he asks for my advice. He knows I won't tell him what I think he wants to hear. Apparently I'm the only person who's happy to stand up to him."

"What sort of advice do you give him?" Doona asked.

"Last month when he rang he was thinking about getting married again," Bessie told her. "The woman in question was twenty-seven. I suggested that she might be more interested in his money than in him. He already knew that, of course, but he said it helped, hearing it from someone else. He ended things with her shortly thereafter and then discovered that she'd been stealing from his home and sleeping with his gardener."

Doona shook her head. "The poor man, although he certainly isn't poor."

"Not financially, but he is lacking in friends or family who care about him," Bessie said. "I feel quite sorry for him every time he rings me. We barely know one another and yet he feels I'm the only person with whom he can really talk."

"Is he on the island now?" John asked.

"No, he's already told George he isn't coming back here. Apparently the memories are too painful."

"I didn't think he cared that much about Vikki," Doona remarked.

"He did care about her, and also about the person who killed her," Bessie replied. "Whatever, he isn't here and he isn't coming back. George is trying to find someone to buy his share of the retail park project."

"So he has a potential partner staying with him?" John asked.

"Mary said something about half a dozen dull businessmen coming to stay for a fortnight. I don't know if she was exaggerating or not, but they were due to start arriving yesterday, I believe."

"We're still trying to work out when Harrison arrived on the island," John said "I think I need to go and talk to Mary."

"I'd hate to think that one of George's associates is a killer," Bessie said.

John raised an eyebrow. "He hasn't had the best track record when it came to selecting his associates in the past."

Bessie nodded. "But we've nothing to connect Harrison with Thie yn Traie, at least not yet."

"Exactly. For now I'll just be taking statements from everyone there regarding what they may or may not have heard last night," John said.

"Maybe Harrison was trying to sneak up the stairs and slipped and fell," Bessie suggested. "Those stairs aren't safe."

"I won't disagree about the stairs, but if he did slip off the steps, the fall didn't kill him," John told her. "He was some distance from the stairs when you found him, anyway."

"I just don't want it to have been murder," Bessie sighed. "I want it to have been a tragic accident or suicide or anything other than murder."

"He was probably too young to have had a heart attack," Doona said. "Although young people do die of natural causes sometimes."

"Maybe he had pneumonia or a brain tumour or something. Maybe he was meant to be in hospital, but he came over here and then just died."

John shook his head. "I'm reasonably certain that Harrison was murdered. While I wait for an official verdict, I intend to treat it as a murder investigation, anyway."

"I'm never going to want to walk on that beach again," Bessie sighed.

John got to his feet. "I'm going to go and talk to everyone at Thie yn Traie. I think you should take another walk later today. The longer you leave it, the less you're going to want to go back out there."

Too late, Bessie thought. I already never want to go back out there. She walked John to the door and gave him a hug.

"You're spending the day with Bessie, aren't you?" he asked Doona.

"That was the plan. Do you need me to collect the children or take them anywhere?" she asked.

He shook his head. "We'll be fine tonight. They both have practice after school, and I know they can both get rides home with friends. I'll pick up a pizza when I finish for the day and I'll probably get home before they do, murder investigation or not."

"Ring me if you need me," Doona said.

"I will," he replied, winking at her.

"Isn't it exhausting, keeping up with John and the children?" Bessie asked after she'd shut the door.

"Yes, but it's also wonderful. I never really wanted children, but teenagers are very different to babies. Oh, don't get me wrong, they're hard work, but they're also interesting people in their own right. I'm really enjoying getting to know them and I'd be happy to help John with all of the driving them around even if he and I weren't, well, whatever it is that we are."

Bessie laughed. "Whatever it is?"

"We're trying not to take things too seriously, at least not in a hurry. John was badly hurt by Sue and I have two failed marriages in my past. Neither one of us wants to rush into things only to see it all fall apart."

"What do the children think?"

"They seem happy enough. They're both keeping themselves really busy, mostly so they don't have to think about their mother, I believe. It seems to be working, for the most part, anyway. We're all just muddling through as best we can at the moment."

"Which is all we ever can do, really."

"But what do you want to do with your day?" Doona asked. "I took the day off to spend it with you so that you wouldn't be alone on this anniversary. Things haven't exactly gone to plan thus far, though, have they?"

"I was going to suggest a trip into Ramsey for some shopping, but I'm not sure I want to go out now. I feel as if I should be here, but I don't know why."

"There isn't anything you can do for Harrison just sitting around the house all day," Doona pointed out.

"It just seems disrespectful to go out shopping right after finding a dead body," Bessie tried to explain.

"Does that mean you want to stay in, then?"

Bessie sighed. "No, I really want to go shopping. I just don't want to feel guilty for doing so."

"You shouldn't feel guilty. You found the body and you rang the police. That's all you can do, isn't it?"

"I could investigate."

"At the moment, you've no idea why Harrison was even on the island. Until the police work that out, I'm not sure where you'd even start an investigation."

"You're right, of course," Bessie sighed. "If I were going to investigate, and I really shouldn't, anyway, I'd want to start at Thie yn Traie. That's where John has gone, though. I don't think he'd be very happy with me if I turned up there now."

"He would definitely not be happy," Doona said firmly. "Let's go to Ramsey and see if the bookshop has anything new."

"I'm never going to say no to a trip to the bookshop," Bessie replied. It only took her a few minutes to touch up her makeup and brush her hair. When she came back down the stairs, Doona was using her mobile.

"I just texted John about our plans," she told Bessie, dropping her phone back in her bag. "He said to let you know that Mary is going to ring soon."

"I never switched the ringer back on," Bessie exclaimed. She'd decided, some years earlier, that there was little point in trying to race down the stairs if the phone rang in the middle of the night. Switching off the ringer on the device was now part of her evening routine. She kept her mobile with her, next to her bed, so if one of her closest friends needed her, he or she could reach her. Otherwise, she was quite happy for calls to go to her answering machine until morning. Now she turned the ringer back on and checked her messages.

"Five messages, all from people who'd heard about the dead body already," she sighed after she'd listened to the messages. "News travels too fast on the island."

The phone rang before Doona could reply.

"Hello?"

"Bessie? It's Mary. I was wondering if I could come over later today, maybe around three? I wouldn't normally invite myself anywhere, but under the circumstances…" she trailed off.

"You're more than welcome here any time," Bessie replied. "Doona and I are just going into Ramsey for some shopping. I'll make sure to get some nice chocolate biscuits for your visit."

"Yes, I may need something sweet," Mary muttered. "I'll see you later, then."

Bessie put the phone down. "She's coming to see me this afternoon."

"Would you rather I wasn't here when she came?"

"If you have other things to do, you don't have to stay, but you're more than welcome. I know Mary likes you and I'm sure she'll happily talk in front of you."

The pair headed for Doona's car. Bessie told herself not to look at the beach as she climbed into the car, but she couldn't help herself. From where she was, it looked as if a small tent had been erected around the body. No doubt the police were trying to protect any evidence from the rain that was still falling.

She was silent on the drive into Ramsey, lost in thought about Harrison Parker and who might have killed him. When Doona pulled into the car park for the bookshop, Bessie started. "That was quick," she remarked.

"I thought we should park here as you're more likely to want things from the bookshop than anywhere else. Do you need to go to ShopFast, too?"

"I promised Mary some chocolate biscuits, so I'll need a quick trip around ShopFast. You can leave the car here, though. I can carry a box or two of biscuits from ShopFast back to here."

"Let's see what the rain does," Doona suggested.

The rain was still light, but the wind was picking up as the friends made their way into the shop.

"Bessie, we were just packing a box for you," the shop assistant behind the desk said. "Do you want to take it with you?"

Bessie nodded. The bookshop kept a list of her favourite authors and once or twice a month they sent her any new books by the authors on her list. It saved her from having to carry too many books around Ramsey when she came on her regular shopping days. "My friend parked right outside today, so I don't mind having a few books to carry," she explained.

"Take a quick look at what I've put in the box," the girl suggested. "There's the first in a new series by one of your favourites and a new book in an old series, but by a new author."

Bessie frowned. "Someone has started writing another author's books?"

"Something like that," the shop assistant told her. "He's doing so with the full support of the original author's estate. I haven't read the book yet, but it's getting good reviews."

It only took Bessie a few minutes to go through the box. "I'll keep this one," she said after she'd read the back of the book by the new author. "It sounds as if he's managed to capture the characters reasonably successfully. We'll see. I don't want this one," she added, handing the girl the first book in a new series by an old favourite author. "The main character is a young man who drinks and smokes and chases women. I much prefer female protagonists."

"I'll make a note not to include that series in your boxes going forward," the shop assistant told her. "Let me know if you want any more in the other series."

"Yes, I will," Bessie promised. "I'm looking forward to trying this one, anyway. It's been years since the original author died and I've really missed the characters."

Bessie spent a happy half hour browsing through the mystery section, adding a few more books to her pile at the tills. Doona selected a handful of cookbooks.

"Now that I'm cooking for John and the kids at least a few nights each week, I need ideas," she told Bessie as they paid for their purchases. "I could just do spaghetti every week as everyone enjoys that, but I feel as if I have to put in more effort than that."

"Don't feel as if you're competing with Sue," Bessie cautioned her. "The children are probably going to remember her as wonderful at everything. You can't compete with their memories."

"She did cook more than I do," Doona sighed. "She also used to bake amazing cakes, apparently."

"You could make amazing cakes if you weren't busy working and running the children everywhere," Bessie replied. "You can't do everything."

Doona nodded, but Bessie could tell that her friend wasn't really listening to her. Sighing, she followed Doona out of the shop. They dropped their bags into Doona's boot and then headed up the street. There were shops along both sides of the road, and the pair went into several charity shops as they walked.

Bessie loved to buy secondhand books from charity shops, but today she couldn't seem to find anything she wanted. Doona had better luck, buying another half-dozen cookbooks from the various shops. Bessie just bit her tongue as her friend kept buying more.

They walked through the town, eventually reaching the large ShopFast grocery shop where Bessie did her weekly shop. It only took her a few minutes to find the biscuits she wanted. Doona bought bars of chocolate.

"One for me and one for Amy," she told Bessie. "It's an addiction that we share."

Bessie laughed. "I thought everyone in the world loved chocolate."

"Thomas isn't that interested in it, really. When he was very young he was allergic to milk, so he couldn't have chocolate, not milk chocolate, anyway. He outgrew the allergy but never really developed a taste for chocolate. I mean, he'll eat it, but he doesn't crave it the way that Amy and I do."

"All this talk about chocolate has made me hungry," Bessie said as they walked back to the car.

"Let's get lunch somewhere nice," Doona suggested.

"What about the café in Lonan?" Bessie replied. "I think Jasmina has taken over there now. I miss Dan and Carol and Dan's amazing sample plates, but I'm interested in seeing what Jasmina has done with the place."

"When does Dan's new restaurant in Onchan open?"

"Not for another month or two. Mary was telling me that they've found a few minor issues with the building that they weren't expecting. While they are all small concerns, each one will take time to repair, and apparently they have to be done in a particular order, as well. Luckily, Dan and Carol saved quite a bit of money to help carry them through until the new restaurant opens. I'm sure Mary is doing what she can to help them, too. And I know just about everyone on the island is looking forward to when they'll be open in the new location."

"I know I am. John and I were just talking the other day about going there as soon as we can. He wants to buy me dinner somewhere to thank me for everything I've been doing for him and the kids. I told him that I wanted to eat at Dan's new place, so he'll just have to wait for that dinner."

"They never took bookings at their old location, but they may have to at the new one."

"Let's go and see how Jasmina is getting on, then," Doona said when they reached her car.

The drive to Lonan didn't take long. The small car park was about half-full when they arrived. As they made their way towards the café, a couple walked out.

"Don't waste your time," the male half of the couple snapped at Bessie. "It's under new management. No more sample plates, just an ordinary menu."

Bessie laughed. "I know the new owner and I've followed her here from her old location. She may not do sample plates, but she does delicious food."

The man shrugged. "Whatever."

"I hope Jasmina isn't getting that reaction very often," Bessie said in a low voice as she and Doona crossed the road.

"Dan had signs up for weeks letting everyone know that he was selling the place. And it isn't as if Jasmina's trying to hide it, either," Doona remarked, waving at the large sign across the front of the building that read "Under New Management."

The door buzzed as Doona opened it.

"Oh, Bessie and Doona, hello," Jasmina said, smiling happily at them. "You already knew I was here. You won't be disappointed to see me."

Bessie glanced around the room. There were people at about half of the tables. It had always been packed when Dan had owned it.

"Give people time to get used to the change," Bessie told her. "Once people try your food, they'll start telling their friends. You'll soon find yourself having to turn people away again."

When Jasmina had first moved to the island, she'd run a café in a tiny building near the Laxey Wheel. It had just enough room for three tables, with four chairs at each table. Word had quickly spread through Laxey about the delicious food that Jasmina was producing, and those three tables were nearly always full whenever Bessie had wanted to visit the café.

Jasmina shrugged. "I don't mind if it's a bit slow for the first month or two. Having my own place has been my dream forever, and I still have to keep pinching myself every time I look around this room. This place is truly mine, aside from the large mortgage. The last one was rented and not even in my name."

She showed Bessie and Doona to a table in the corner and then handed them menus.

Bessie read the note on the front out loud. "Welcome to my café. If you came in expecting the incredible sample plates that Dan used to produce here, I'm sorry. While Dan made it look easy, that sort of cooking takes a great deal of time and effort. My cooking is simpler, using fresh ingredients and recipes that I inherited from my mother and her mother before her. I appreciate you giving me a try. If you don't enjoy your meal, you don't have to pay for it. Thank you for coming in today."

"How many people don't pay?" Doona asked Jasmina.

"So far, none of them. Well, I've had a few people ask, but when I explained that I was happy for them to not pay, but that I didn't expect them to come back again if they were unhappy, they all changed their minds."

"So they were just hoping for a free meal?" Bessie asked.

"I suppose so. When I said that they shouldn't come back, they all insisted that they were prepared to give me a second chance. I said they could refuse to pay on their second trip, then."

Bessie and Doona both laughed. "Good for you," Bessie said.

Jasmina shrugged. "I don't want anyone to think that I'm trying to take advantage of Dan's success. He did very well in this space, but he did very different things to what I do. I was making sandwiches, mostly, at the café in Laxey. I'm not even sure that some of my recipes are any good."

"I've had your beef stew and it was excellent," Bessie said as she looked down the menu. "Chicken and leek pie sounds wonderful for today."

Doona looked at her menu. "It all sounds wonderful. I think I'll have the steak and kidney pie, no, the shepherd's pie."

"Are you sure?" Jasmina asked.

Doona looked at the menu again and then nodded. "Cottage pie, I'm sure."

Jasmina laughed. "Cottage pie? Okay, then. And chicken and leek for Bessie. I'll have that right out. I made a chocolate cake for my pudding special today."

"That, too, then," Bessie said quickly.

"Yes, please," Doona agreed.

True to her word, Jasmina delivered their food a short while later. It was every bit as delicious as Bessie had expected it to be.

"I can't imagine anyone complaining about this food," she told Jasmina as the woman cleared their empty plates.

"I don't think it's so much that they don't like my food as that they're disappointed it isn't Dan's food," Jasmina explained. "If I could cook the way Dan does, I'd do it, but I don't have enough creativity to keep coming up with new ideas and themes every day."

"Maybe you could just work with what you have," Bessie suggested. "You have half a dozen different savoury pies on the menu. You could offer them in pairs of half-sized portions, or even trios. People could choose their favourites and have a little bit of each. It's similar to what Dan does, but it doesn't require you to do anything more than serve differently sized portions."

Jasmina looked thoughtful. "I could do that, but I wouldn't want Dan to think that I was trying to steal his idea."

"So talk to him first," Bessie suggested. "I can't see him minding, though. He'll still be doing daily samplers, which is a completely different thing."

"That was a great idea," Doona said as Jasmina walked away. "I wish she was already doing it, because I really did want three different things."

"Chocolate cake," Jasmina said a moment later, putting a generous slice of cake in front of each of them. "And before you say it, yes, I should offer some sort of pudding sampler, too. I have a few puddings that will always be on the menu. I could easily combine small portions of them with the day's special on a plate."

"If you need someone to test the theory, Bessie and I can come back tomorrow," Doona offered.

Jasmina laughed. "You're both more than welcome any time. The next time you come in, I promise you an assortment of puddings, anyway."

The chocolate cake was delicious. "I'm glad this was all that I got today," Bessie said as she pushed her empty plate away. "I enjoyed every single mouthful and I wouldn't have wanted any less of it."

"But imagine how nice it would have been to have a bit of something else, too," Doona replied.

"No, not today, not with that cake. That cake was amazing," Bessie said stoutly.

When Jasmina gave them the bill, Bessie checked it over. "You haven't charged us for the puddings," she told the woman.

"Because you gave me such a wonderful idea for my restaurant," Jasmina replied. "I considered not charging you for anything, but I thought you'd probably object."

Bessie nodded. She certainly would have. As it was, she left a generous tip to cover the cost of the cake slices, sliding the notes under her plate so that Jasmina wouldn't find them until they were gone.

"And now we should get back to Treoghe Bwaane," Doona said as they crossed back to the car.

"Must we?" Bessie sighed.

"Yes, and we're going to take a walk on the beach, too," Doona said firmly. "It's your home and you love it. I understand why you're reluctant to go back, but you can't let a dead body put you off."

"If it were just one dead body, I probably wouldn't," Bessie muttered as she got into the car.

The drive didn't take anywhere near long enough, in Bessie's opinion. Doona parked the car and then looked at Bessie. "We should walk off some of that cake," she suggested.

Bessie knew that Doona was right. She'd eaten a huge slice of cake. A long walk on the beach was exactly what she needed.

They put their handbags inside and then Doona set off down the

28

beach, with Bessie following. It wasn't long before they ran into the first constable.

"Hello, Doona," he said. "And Miss Cubbon," he added as Bessie reached them.

"Is this as far as we're allowed to go?" Doona asked.

The constable shrugged. "I was told to stand here and turn away the nosy. You two aren't just being nosy, though. I can ring the inspector and see what he says."

Bessie looked past the constable at the beach, which was swarming with police constables and crime scene investigators. She shook her head. "We don't want to get in the way. We'll walk in the other direction."

They turned around and walked back the way they'd come. Once they were past Treoghe Bwaane, Bessie sighed. "I never walk this way because there's very little beach to walk on in this direction."

"And the tide is coming in," Doona pointed out.

"We'd better turn back before we get caught by the tide."

They walked back to Bessie's cottage and then settled on the large rock on the beach behind her house.

"At least we can get some fresh air out here," Doona said, determinedly cheerful.

Bessie gave her a wry smile. "Or we could go inside and open a bottle of wine. I don't usually drink much, but today seems to be a good day for drinking more than I should."

They were still sitting on the rock, staring out at the sea, when Mary's limousine pulled into the parking area next to Bessie's cottage.

CHAPTER 3

"I'm terribly sorry for inviting myself over," Mary said as Bessie greeted her with a hug. "That was incredibly rude of me."

"Not at all," Bessie replied.

"I didn't know what else to do. I wanted to talk to you, but I couldn't invite you to Thie yn Traie. We have guests, you understand."

"I do understand, and you are always welcome here, under any circumstances."

"I would have asked to go out for a meal somewhere, but I'd rather not risk being overheard."

"Stop fretting," Bessie said firmly. "You are welcome here any time, under any circumstances. You don't even have to ring first. You can simply turn up on my doorstep at any time, day or night."

Mary flushed. "You really mean that, don't you? I've never truly had a friend that wouldn't mind my simply appearing on her doorstep."

"I'm quite used to guests just appearing at my door," Bessie said. "Years ago I used to have teenagers here nearly every night."

Never having married or had children of her own, for decades Bessie had enjoyed being something of an honorary aunt to the children in Laxey. Nearly every child who'd grown up in the village had spent a night or two in Bessie's spare room to escape parents who simply didn't understand whatever teenaged drama was happening in his or her life. Bessie didn't try to understand. She simply offered tea, biscuits, and sympathy. Sometimes she had cake. Usually she had some words of wisdom to share that helped the teen see things in a different light.

Some children spent more than an occasional night at Bessie's. Hugh was one of the ones who'd stayed with Bessie for weeks on end after disagreements with his parents about his plans for the future. His mother and father hadn't agreed with his decision to join the constabulary right out of school. They were incredibly proud of him now, though.

"Let's go inside," Doona suggested as a cold wind blew past them.

"I'll put the kettle on," Bessie said as Mary and Doona took seats at the kitchen table.

She filled a plate with the chocolate biscuits she'd just purchased and put that in the centre of the table. A short while later, after passing around tea, she joined the others.

"I don't have to stay, if you want privacy," Doona said after a sip of tea. "I'll just have one biscuit and then go quietly."

Mary laughed. "You can't possibly only have just one of these biscuits. They're too nice. Anyway, you're more than welcome to stay. Nothing I have to say to Bessie is at all private or personal."

Doona grinned. "I was afraid I might have to try to sneak a few biscuits out in my handbag."

"I would have put some into a bag for you," Bessie said.

"This is much nicer, though," Doona replied, taking another sip of tea.

"So what can I do for you?" Bessie asked Mary.

Mary sighed. "I heard about the body on the beach. George rang the Chief Constable. Was it really Harrison Parker?"

Bessie glanced at Doona, who shrugged. If Mary and George were getting their information directly from the Chief Constable, it seemed pointless to deny what they'd been told.

"It was," Bessie said.

"Do you know why he was on the island?" Mary asked.

Bessie shook her head. "The last I knew, he'd moved to London to work for a newspaper there. I've no idea what might have brought him back here."

"He had to have been working on a story," Doona said. "I can't imagine he had any friends here."

Bessie grinned. "Just because you didn't care for him doesn't mean that he didn't have any friends."

"I'm with Doona on that, actually," Mary said. "He was thoroughly unlikeable. I can't imagine anyone spending time with him voluntarily. Anyway, he was only on the island for a few months, maybe more like six weeks. He probably didn't have time to make any friends."

"Maybe he was doing a follow-up to his story about Phillip Tyler's murder," Bessie suggested.

"That would explain why he was outside the last holiday cottage," Doona added.

"Unless he was there because he was investigating someone at Thie yn Traie," Mary said.

"What's happening at Thie yn Traie that might warrant an investigation by a nosy reporter?" Doona asked.

"George has some guests at the moment. There are four of them, and I don't care for any of them."

"You said they were all potential new partners in the retail park project, didn't you?" Bessie checked.

"They are. I've been doing everything in my power to persuade George to simply forget all about the retail park. I've suggested that we simply sell the land and let someone else decide what to build there, but he's adamant that he wants to build a retail park."

"I thought he was meant to be retired," Bessie said.

Mary laughed bitterly. "He is meant to be retired, but he can't stop working. He tried working with small companies, helping them grow their businesses, but apparently that got boring. This retail park project is one of the biggest projects upon which he's ever worked.

He's enjoying the challenge and he has both of our sons working with him on it, which is the first time that's happened."

"What about Elizabeth?" Bessie had to ask. George and Mary's only daughter, Elizabeth, had dropped out of several universities, unable to decide what she wanted to do with her life. She'd recently started her own party and event planning business that seemed to be doing very well, but Bessie wasn't certain how her parents felt about the girl's new career.

"She's going to get a suite of offices in the new retail park. The business is growing so quickly that it's getting more difficult for her to run it out of Thie yn Traie, so George has promised her office space there. She'll be able to meet with potential customers and showcase some of the events she's done in the past there."

"Good for her," Bessie said.

"She's excited, but she may need to find a temporary office space in the meantime. The retail park is probably two years away from being ready to use. She's probably only a few months away from needing a proper office."

"Do you have any reason to believe that Harrison was here to investigate any of your guests?" Bessie asked.

Mary shrugged. "I don't know what to think. As I said, I'm not fond of any of them. I'd hate to suggest that any of them might be behind a murder, though."

"Why don't you tell me about them," Bessie suggested.

"Inspector Rockwell has met them all," Mary said. "He interviewed them when he came to Thie yn Traie earlier. I know he's very good at his job, but I just feel as if it would help if you knew about them, too."

"You said there were four of them?" Bessie asked. Mary seemed reluctant to talk about the men. Bessie realised she was probably going to have to ask many questions in order to get Mary talking.

"Yes, there are four of them. They all arrived the day before yester-day. Two flew in from London. They were on the same plane, but didn't know one another until they'd arrived here. Another arrived from Manchester, and the fourth came in from Liverpool on the ferry."

"Let's start with names," Doona suggested.

Mary flushed. "I'm not very good at this, am I? I want to tell you everything because I'm worried that one of them might be behind Mr. Parker's death, but I don't want to talk out of turn about my husband's guests and business associates."

"Nothing you say here will go any further," Bessie promised. "If you say something that I feel the police need to know, I'll tell John, but strictly in confidence and off the record."

Mary nodded. "I'd hate for any of the men to think that I've been discussing them behind their backs. Business deals are built on trust, to some extent, anyway. They need to feel that they can trust both George and me."

Bessie looked at Doona. She looked as if she was losing patience with Mary's waffling.

"Surely there's no harm in giving me their names," Bessie said.

Mary chuckled, but it sounded forced. "I'm sure I'm making this much more complicated than it needs to be. Of course I can tell you their names. Let's start there, anyway."

Bessie took a sip of her tea and then ate a biscuit while Mary sat back in her seat and drank some tea.

"Right, in no particular order, the first guest is Ted Pearson. He's American, which surprised me, but his mother was British, so he's actually a citizen of both the US and the UK. He grew up in California and he almost looks as if he just stepped out of a Hollywood movie. He has blond hair and blue eyes and I'm sure he surfs in his spare time."

"How old is he?" Doona asked.

"Oh, early fifties, maybe, although he'd probably be happier if I said late forties," Mary replied.

"What makes him interested in owning part of a retail park on the Isle of Man?" Bessie asked.

"He already owns what he calls strip plazas in several cities in California," Mary replied. "He also owns a retail chain that has a prime location in every one of his plazas. I believe he's hoping to get his chain into the UK by buying into retail parks here. He's been looking at some properties in Bolton and in Bath, apparently, in addition to the project here."

"Is there that much money to be made from a retail park on the island?" Doona asked. "We've a fairly small population, I'd have thought, for an international company to be interested."

"I believe some of his interest has to do with the TT and Manx Grand Prix fortnights," Mary replied. "The island's population doubles during the TT and it grows significantly during MGP. People come from all over the world for them, as well, which means he might have a chance to get international exposure for his brand. That was what he told me, anyway."

Bessie nodded. "I suppose it makes sense. I've no idea how successful or otherwise a new retail park will be on the island, but if he's done this before, presumably he's done his research."

"He has a team for that," Mary told her. "They ring him at odd hours, all through the day and night. His mobile has one of the most annoying ringtones I've ever heard and it goes off almost constantly. We've yet to get through a meal without someone ringing him at least a few times. I swear I can hear his ringtone in the middle of the night, too, even though his suite is on the opposite side of the house from my room."

"Oh, dear," Bessie said.

"I've tried politely suggesting that he ask his staff to ring a bit less frequently, but apparently they only ring when it's absolutely critical, and everything that happens is critical," Mary added.

"How did he arrive?"

"How did he arrive?" Mary repeated, looking confused. "Oh, he was one of the ones who came over from London," she said after a moment. "He and Owen Oliver flew in from London."

"Tell us about Owen Oliver, then," Bessie said.

"He's in his sixties. He's about my height, so not very tall. His hair is grey and his eyes are brown. That has to be the most boring description of anyone ever," Mary said with a laugh.

"Is he boring, then?" Bessie wondered.

"Yes and no," Mary replied, making a face. "He's not interesting to

35

speak with, certainly, but he can be quite snappish and difficult, which keeps him from being forgotten in the corner."

"What makes him interested in a retail park on the island?" Doona asked.

"His business is building retail parks and other commercial spaces. He isn't interested in retaining ownership once the park is built, but he's happy to own half of the property during the building stage, assuming that his company gets the contract to build the park, of course."

"Is that something that happens regularly?" Bessie asked.

"I'm not sure. George didn't seem surprised by the idea, so it can't be that unusual, I suppose, but I don't really know anything about George's business."

"Tell me about the other two men," Bessie said. "I want to talk more about the retail park at the end, though."

Mary nodded. "The one who flew in from Manchester is Nicholas Taylor. He's also in his sixties. He owns shares in just about every shopping mall in the UK. He really wants to build a mall over here, but it seems unlikely that the population would support an entire mall. I believe he sees the retail park as a way to get a presence on the island upon which he might be able to expand one day."

"I don't think the island needs a mall," Bessie said.

"As much as I love to shop, I'm inclined to agree with you," Doona said.

Mary nodded. "I'm not convinced that we need another retail park, actually, but don't tell George that. He's very excited that the project might get off the ground this time. He was extremely disappointed when Alastair told him that he was no longer interested in pursuing it."

"Alastair doesn't want to come back to the island," Bessie said. "And he can't stand the idea of being involved in a project that he can't drop in on without warning."

Mary laughed. "That sounds like Alastair, actually."

"Who is the last man, then?" Doona asked.

"His name is Edmund Rhodes. He's probably in his fifties, as well.

He came over on the ferry, because he's thinking of submitting a bid for the island's ferry service the next time the contract comes due. He wasn't impressed with what he saw on the ferry. Pretty much all he's done since he arrived is complain about his journey."

"What did he find to complain about?" Doona wondered.

"It might be easier to tell you what he didn't complain about, which was nothing at all. He had to wait in a very long queue at the docks before he could drive his car onto the ferry. Then he had to squeeze his car into a very small space, right next to other cars that weren't nearly as nice as his. Once he'd left his car, he had to stand in another queue in order to get the key to the private cabin that he'd booked for the crossing. The cabin was too small. It was either too hot or too cold, I forget which. The crossing was rough and he felt quite unwell." She stopped and sighed. "I could continue, but I'm boring myself. Suffice to say that he wasn't impressed and that he's convinced that he can do it better and make more of a profit whilst doing so."

"Good luck to him," Bessie said. "I don't mind the ferry, but if he can improve on it without charging higher prices, I think everyone in the island would be grateful."

"I'm sure, knowing him, that the prices would go up," Mary said. "But he may not even bother, as now he's very interested in investing in the retail park instead. My concern with him is that he has a short attention span. I'm afraid he'll sign all the contracts and then change his mind next week."

"Which would you choose if you had to select one to be George's partner, then?" Bessie asked.

Mary frowned. "That's a difficult question. I don't like any of them. Not Edmund, he's my least favourite of the four. Owen is better, but I don't like the idea of him selling his share as soon as the construction is finished. I don't trust Nicholas. I can see him leaving the retail park project half-completed if he were to suddenly get permission to build something bigger on the island. That leaves Ted." She sighed. "He just wants a place to put one of his shops. I suspect he's working on a number of locations across and that the island is a last resort. I think

37

he'll drop the entire project if a space comes through in a big city across."

"Maybe George needs some new friends," Doona said.

Mary smiled. "They aren't his friends, though. They're simply business associates. He's known some of them for years, even worked with Owen and Edmund before. Ted is the only one about whom George knew nothing before last week. Ted is here because Alastair recommended him. Alastair is eager to sell his share, but George has to agree to the purchaser, so Alastair is doing what he can to facilitate the deal."

"What's the purpose of having them all here at once?" Doona asked. "Surely they're in competition with one another?"

"Not really, although maybe," Mary replied. "That's about as clear as mud, I know, but I don't totally understand it myself. George has been talking to several different people about the park and these four were the best candidates. I should say that George found three of them and Alastair found Ted. Anyway, after dozens of phone conversations and probably hundreds of emails, George finally decided that he needed to meet everyone, preferably at the same time and in the same place. He invited them all here for a week so that he can get to know them all and they can get to know the island. To the best of my knowledge, none of them have ever been here before."

"But they're all competing for the same deal, aren't they?" Bessie wondered.

"Not necessarily. George and Alastair are prepared to consider a number of different options, or so I've been told. For example, it was suggested that Owen buy into the partnership for the building stage, with a contracted agreement to sell his share to one of the others as soon as the construction is complete. Owen suggested the other night that he might be interested in buying half of Alastair's share if one of the others wanted to buy the other half. I'm sure there are other possibilities as well."

"It all sounds incredibly complicated," Bessie sighed.

"It was complicated, and now someone has been murdered. That's an extra complication," Mary said.

"The murder might not have anything to do with the retail park deal," Doona said.

"I really hope it doesn't, but the Chief Constable told George that the police believe that Harrison was interested in something or someone at Thie yn Traie," Mary told her.

"Based on what?" Bessie demanded.

"He wouldn't tell George anything else. He simply warned him that the police would be asking both us and our guests a great many questions."

"Could Harrison have been interested in the retail park deal?" Doona wondered.

"I can't imagine why," Mary replied. "I can't see why his newspaper in London would want an article about a retail park on the Isle of Man, no matter who ends up being George's new partner."

"If he wasn't here because of the retail park deal, then why was he interested in your guests?" Bessie said, thinking out loud.

"I'm sure they all have secrets," Mary said.

"Any idea what any of them might be hiding?" Bessie asked.

Mary shrugged. "I know there were some problems on one of Owen's last big projects. I don't know the whole story, but there were some issues with safety violations and a man got badly hurt. There were fines imposed, I believe, but no one went to prison or anything."

"Interesting," Bessie said. "Do any of the others have similar things in their pasts?"

"I'm sure George said something about Ted's father being involved in some unpleasantness in California. It was rather more personal than Owen's problem, I believe. George said there were several young women involved and a great deal of alcohol, but I'm not clear on what actually happened."

"My goodness, that doesn't sound good, but I can't see why it would bring Harrison to the island. Surely Ted's father isn't of interest to the UK press," Bessie said.

"Unless Harrison was already looking to move again, maybe to the US this time," Doona suggested.

"He'd only just moved to London," Bessie protested.

Doona shrugged. "Do you know anything about the other two men that might have brought Harrison here?" she asked Mary.

"I don't, but it wouldn't surprise me if George did. He's the one who knows the men, after all. I generally try to avoid getting involved in George's work."

"I'm sure the police will be looking very closely at all four of them," Bessie said, "and everyone else staying at Thie yn Traie at the moment."

Mary frowned. "I would like to think that George and Elizabeth and I won't appear on the list of suspects, but that's probably wishful thinking."

"I'm sure you'll be at the bottom of the list," Bessie assured her.

"What about the staff?" Doona asked. "Any reason to believe that any of them have deep, dark secrets?"

"Most of our staff have been with us for many years," Mary replied. "Some of them came across with us when we moved from the UK, and most of the others worked for us in Douglas before we bought Thie yn Traie. The cook hasn't been with us for very long, and we aren't terribly happy with her, either, but I can't see her killing anyone. Otherwise, it's just the butler who's new."

"Jack? There's no way Jack's behind any of this," Bessie said firmly. She'd known Jack Hooper as a small child, long before he'd moved across and gone to school to train as a butler. At Thie yn Traie, he was always called Jonathan, but to Bessie he would always be Jack.

"Jonathan is in London at the moment," Mary told her. "We used an agency to find a temporary replacement. Geoffrey Scott has been with us for a few weeks now."

"I knew Jack, er, Jonathan was going across, but I didn't realise he'd already gone," Bessie said. "Tell me about Geoffrey."

"He's very good, really, but I miss Jonathan. Jonathan is formal and proper without being stiff and I always feel as if he truly enjoys working with us. Geoffrey is, well, stiff and almost condescending. He's held positions in noble households, and I rather feel as if he doesn't quite approve of George and me."

"Why isn't he still working in noble households, then?" Bessie asked.

"As I understand it, he had some health issues. He had to leave his last position because of ill health and he's only just now back to being well enough to work full-time. This assignment is sort of a test for him, to see if he truly can manage the demands of the job."

"How is he doing?"

"As far as I can tell, he's doing well. He does take breaks sometimes during the day, but that's not really a problem. With only the three of us in the house, we don't really need a full-time butler, but George wants one and I can't be bothered to argue."

"You don't think he has any secrets he'd kill to keep, do you?" Doona asked.

"Don't we all?" Mary replied.

Bessie was sure she looked shocked, but Mary just laughed and waved a hand.

"I barely know the man, really. His references were impressive. George rang his last employer and they spoke very highly of him. The agency vets its people very carefully. None of that proves anything, of course. He could have secrets."

"He seems less likely than the other four men, anyway," Bessie said.

Mary nodded. "I don't like or trust any of them," she said. "You should come to lunch tomorrow and meet them. Maybe you'll be able to work out which one of them killed Harrison Parker once you've met them all."

"I don't think that's very likely, but I'm happy to have lunch with you anyway," Bessie said. "Do you expect them all to be at lunch tomorrow?"

"That's part of the problem, actually," Mary replied. "They're always underfoot. None of them have any interest in seeing the island, aside from the site where the retail park is going to be built. Mostly they all just sit around Thie yn Traie, talking on their mobiles about other deals they want to make. George invited them all to stay for a week, and I'm already counting down the days."

"If the police really do think that Harrison's death is tied to Thie yn Traie, they may not let the men leave," Bessie told her.

Mary made a face. "What a horrible thought."

"I must admit that I'm curious to meet them all now," Bessie said.

"I'm going to see if I can get Andy to make lunch for us," Mary told her. "Our chef has been working overtime since the men arrived. She'd probably appreciate a free afternoon, and I know I'd much rather have Andy's cooking than hers."

"I'd love to see him. He never seems to find the time to visit me," Bessie said.

Andy Caine had just finished culinary school in the UK. He'd grown up on the island dreaming of having his own restaurant, but had never been able to afford to chase that dream. An unexpected inheritance had left him with enough money that he didn't actually have to work, but instead of living a life of leisure, he'd put himself through culinary school and was now planning to open his own restaurant. He and Elizabeth Quayle were seeing one another, but Bessie was unsure how serious the relationship was.

"He's been trying to find a location for the restaurant he wants to open. He and George have been talking about putting it in the retail park, but he isn't sure that's what he wants to do. He has all sorts of great ideas, but he seems to be struggling to focus on any one of them," Mary told her. "He's also spending a lot of time with Elizabeth, helping her with her business. She's going to miss him when he finally does get his restaurant open."

"He and Elizabeth seem well-suited," Bessie said.

Mary nodded, but she looked uncertain. "I'm not sure Elizabeth is ready to settle down. I'll feel terrible if she breaks Andy's heart. He's such a lovely person."

"He is, but he's old enough to make his own mistakes," Bessie replied.

Mary nodded. "Anyway, he's nearly always at Thie yn Traie these days. I'll see if he'd be willing to make us lunch tomorrow."

"If he can't manage lunch, maybe he could just make pudding,"

Bessie suggested, her mouth watering when she thought about some of Andy's delicious puddings.

Mary laughed. "Maybe he could just make several puddings and we could forget about having lunch first."

"If you do that, I want to come," Doona said.

"You're more than welcome, whatever we do," Mary told her.

Doona shook her head. "I have to work tomorrow, actually. I was only supposed to work in the morning, but they need me all day now. Things usually get busier during a murder investigation, and we're a bit short-handed anyway."

The conversation moved on to other topics, including the weather, Mary's grandchildren, and the price of the local paper. Eventually, Mary glanced at her watch and gasped.

"My goodness, is that the time? I've been here for over two hours. Bessie, you should have told me to go. I'm sure you have better things to do than chat with me all afternoon," she said as she got to her feet, pulling out her mobile phone.

"We didn't have any plans for today," Bessie assured her. "You're always welcome and you may stay for as long as you like."

Mary flushed and then tapped something on her phone. "Thank you, but I must get back to Thie yn Traie. Our guests will think I'm terrible, leaving them alone all this time. George is probably out and I'm sure Elizabeth won't have given the guests a single thought. Poor Geoffrey will be dealing with them, which has probably made him grumpy."

"Surely that's part of his job," Bessie said as she followed Mary to the door.

"Yes, of course, but that doesn't mean that he enjoys it," Mary replied. She opened the door and she and Bessie watched as her car rolled into the parking area.

"Midday tomorrow," she told Bessie. "I'll plan lunch for half twelve. You're welcome to come over earlier, if you'd like."

"I'll plan on being there around midday," Bessie replied. "Ring me if anything changes."

Mary nodded before she walked out to the car. The driver had her

43

door open for her before she reached it. She waved to Bessie as she climbed inside.

"All this talk about pudding has made me hungry," Doona said when Bessie turned back around. "Where can we go for dinner that has good puddings?"

After several minutes of debate, they agreed on a favourite restaurant in Ramsey. They washed up the dishes from tea together.

"How about another walk on the beach?" Doona asked when they were done. "Maybe we'll be able to walk a bit further this time."

"Or we might be able to walk in the other direction. I think the tide is out."

The beach was slightly less busy. They walked a bit further than they had earlier and then turned and walked back past Bessie's cottage and on in the other direction.

"It's lovely this way," Doona said as they made their way along the thin strip of sand at the bottom edge of the cliff.

"But there's only sand here when the tide is out. We don't want to go too far and risk getting caught with nowhere to go but up the cliff."

Doona nodded. After a few more minutes, the pair reluctantly turned back. Bessie just needed time to brush her hair before she was ready to go and have dinner in Ramsey.

CHAPTER 4

*a*fter a delicious dinner and an even better pudding, Doona drove Bessie home.

"I'll just come in and check that everything is okay," she said as she parked her car.

"Everything will be fine," Bessie told her. "I hate when you fuss."

Doona didn't bother to reply. If Bessie was honest with herself, she didn't truly mind Doona's fussing as much as she had previously. Some months earlier, her cottage had been broken into, and now Bessie was somewhat more cautious when coming home after dark.

It only took Doona a few minutes to walk through the small cottage. "Everything looks perfectly normal," she told Bessie when she walked back into the kitchen.

"I knew it would be," Bessie retorted.

Doona laughed. "At the risk of being accused of fussing even more, are you going to be okay on your own tonight? I can stay, if you'd feel better having company."

Bessie shook her head. "I'm fine. I truly appreciate the offer, but I feel quite safe here, no matter what's happened on the beach." She could tell that Doona wanted to argue, but Bessie was telling the truth. While this latest murder was upsetting, she didn't feel as if she was in any danger. Whatever Harrison Parker had been doing on the island, it was nothing to do with her.

"I wonder if Hugh would come and stay for a night or two again," Doona said thoughtfully.

After Bessie had found that first body, Hugh had moved into her spare room, staying with her until the murderer was safely behind bars. "He has a wife and a child now. He needs to be at home with them. I'll be perfectly fine. You get home and get some rest, or are you going to John's?"

Doona blushed. "I'm going to pop over to John's for a short while. I promised Amy that I'd help her with some homework tonight. I won't be out late, but if you need me, ring my mobile. That way you're sure to get me."

"Thank you for spending the day with me," Bessie said, hugging her friend. "It didn't quite go the way I'd hoped it might, but it's over, anyway."

She watched Doona's car as it disappeared down the road, before shutting and locking the door. Feeling as if she had far too much evening to fill, Bessie sat down with her box of new books and tried to read. Her brain refused to focus, though, and after she'd read the same page six times and still didn't know what was happening, she shut the book. Pacing around the house held little appeal. It was too late and too dark to take another walk on the beach. She'd given up walking after dark after the break-in.

Instead she let herself out her back door and settled on the large rock behind her cottage. The sound of the waves was calming and Bessie was certain that sea air had medicinal qualities. She breathed in deeply and let herself relax. A few tears slid down her cheeks, tears for Daniel Pierce, for his wife, Vikki, who'd also died on the island, and for Harrison Parker, the latest victim she'd been unfortunate enough to discover. For a few minutes, she let herself remember all of the men and women whose murder investigations she'd been a part of in the past two years. Then she wiped her tears and went back inside Treoghe Bwaane.

When she opened her eyes at two minutes past six the next

morning she realised that her dreams had been about Matthew. It had been a long time since she could remember dreaming about the man she'd almost married.

Matthew Saunders had courted her when she'd lived in the US with her parents and her older sister. When her parents had made the decision to return to the island, they'd insisted that Bessie, still only seventeen, return with them. She'd had no interest in returning to the place she'd left at the age of two, but her parents wouldn't allow her to remain behind with Matthew, a man they barely knew. Bessie's sister had remained in Ohio, marrying the man she'd been seeing for several years. Bessie had practically had to be dragged onto the boat for the journey back to the island.

Months later, she'd received word that Matthew was coming to get her. Bessie had been thrilled, only to see her hopes dashed when word was sent that he'd passed away on the sea crossing. Before he'd left the US, he'd written a will, leaving everything he had to Bessie. The small sum that she'd received had been enough to allow her to buy her tiny cottage by the sea. She'd been desperate to move out of her parents' home, as she'd blamed them for Matthew's death. By that time, she'd been eighteen, so they could do nothing to stop her.

Bessie's advocate had invested wisely the money left over after the purchase of the cottage. By living frugally, she'd been able to live off of those funds for her entire life, never having to find employment. Those clever investments had left her quite comfortable in recent years. She enjoyed using her money to help others, generally only indulging herself with more books. As Bessie nearly always donated anonymously, there were very few people on the island who knew the extent of her fortune or her generosity.

Dreaming about Matthew always unsettled Bessie. After a shower, she patted on the rose-scented dusting powder that always reminded her of him. Today the memories were more bittersweet than normal as he'd been so alive to her in her dream. Feeling as if she deserved a treat, she spread honey on her toast and added an extra spoonful of sugar to her tea. Still feeling somewhat out of sorts, she headed out for her walk with her mind elsewhere.

The beach was as empty this morning as it had been the previous day. The difference today was the strips of police tape that blocked off a huge area of sand. Someone had pushed stakes into the sand to make a large rectangle, with police tape marking its boundaries. Bessie walked along the water's edge for as long as she could, stopping when she reached the tape. From where she was standing, she couldn't tell if she would be able to go around the enclosed area or not. The stakes at the water's edge were buried in several inches of water. She wasn't about to wade through the cold water to keep going.

Sighing, she turned and headed for home. Maybe she'd walk back and then repeat the exercise, she thought as she slowed her steps. Perhaps a walk to the small shop that was just up the hill from her would be a better way to spend some time. She'd only gone a few steps when she heard her name being called.

"Bessie? Hello."

Turning around, she smiled brightly at Maggie Shimmin, who'd appeared on the patio behind one of the holiday cottages. Maggie waved. "Come on over," she called.

Feeling as if that was the last thing she wanted to do, Bessie kept smiling as she crossed the sand.

"Hello," she said when she reached Maggie.

"Thomas is here, painting, and I need to keep an eye on him," Maggie told her in a low voice. "The doctors don't want him over-doing anything. He's only just starting to recover, really, but he will insist on helping."

"I'm glad he's feeling up to helping. It must mean less work for you, too," Bessie suggested.

Maggie shrugged. "You know I never complain, but he isn't much help, really. He gets tired very quickly and then he needs to rest, which means I have to take him home, because the furniture in the cottages isn't very comfortable, really. For the last few days, I feel as if I've been driving Thomas back and forth more than anything else."

"Oh, dear."

"The painting is moving along, but slowly. We still have three more cottages to paint, and we need to replace the flooring in one of the cottages, as well. There's a leaky roof in another one, but we're going to have someone else deal with that. I'm not climbing on a roof and I've managed to persuade Thomas that he shouldn't be doing so, either."

"I should think not."

"My back has been giving me terrible grief, as well," Maggie continued. "My doctor told me not to do any more painting, but Thomas can't manage it on his own, and when we tried to hire someone, well, that was a disaster, really. Anyway, the season starts next month. We actually have some bookings for April and I believe we're nearly full in May, so we need to get the work done."

"What about the last cottage?"

Maggie made a face. "We were all set to pull it down and now the police have the entire beach blocked off because of yet another murder. Even you must admit now that Thie yn Traie is cursed."

"I'll do no such thing. No one died at Thie yn Traie."

Maggie waved a hand. "No, but someone from Thie yn Traie killed Harrison Parker. It's the only thing that makes sense."

"I don't see it that way at all."

"Ladies, why don't you come inside?" Thomas asked from the doorway.

Maggie glanced at Bessie and then nodded at her husband. "We didn't want to be in your way."

"But it's the perfect time for me to take a break," he told her. "I can chat with Bessie, too."

Bessie followed Thomas, who was looking slightly better, although he was still gaunt and pale, into the cottage.

"Have a seat," he said, waving a hand at the couch in the small sitting area.

Bessie sat down. Maggie dropped heavily into the chair next to her. Thomas sat at the opposite end of the couch, frowning as he did so.

"We should have bought better furniture," he said to Maggie. "I'm surprised we don't get more complaints about these couches. They're not very comfortable."

"It was affordable. With the amount of furniture we had to buy, our guests are lucky they get a couch and two chairs. If it had been up to me, we would have only put one chair in each cottage," she told Bessie.

"But that would look unbalanced," Thomas argued.

Maggie shrugged. "We could have saved a lot of money."

"That was years ago," Thomas said. "Let's not argue about it now. How are you?" he asked Bessie.

"I'm fine," she replied.

Thomas leaned over and touched her arm. When Bessie looked at him, he stared into her eyes.

"How are you really, though? I'm sure finding another body was upsetting for you," he said.

"Yes, it was, but I'm certain the police will work out what happened quickly," Bessie replied.

"It was someone from Thie yn Traie," Maggie said firmly. "They've half a dozen guests at the moment, all from across. Harrison must have followed one of them over here, chasing a big story."

"Who's staying at Thie yn Traie, then?" Thomas asked.

"Some of George Quayle's top-secret investors," Maggie replied in a loud whisper. Bessie wondered who she thought might overhear them.

"Top-secret investors?" Thomas repeated.

"I heard that he's trying to find someone to buy out Alastair Farthington's share of the retail park," Maggie told him. "Alastair's son was supposed to move over here to look after his father's interests, but he's in the middle of a messy divorce. Alastair won't come back, not after what happened the last time he was here."

"I can't say as I blame him," Thomas said.

"Whatever, he's trying to sell his share of the retail park business, but George has to agree. As I understand it, there are six or seven men staying at Thie yn Traie right now, all trying to win George's support for them to buy Alastair's share," Maggie continued.

"Six or seven men?" Thomas echoed. "I'm surprised that many people even know about the island."

Bessie laughed, but Maggie was undeterred.

"One of them is an American," she said. "His father got caught supplying girls to his business associates for, um, well, you know what I mean."

Thomas caught Bessie's eye. For a moment she thought he was going to ask Maggie to explain, but then he laughed. "Are you suggesting that George is doing something similar?" he asked after a moment.

"Not George Quayle. He wouldn't do something like that. But that doesn't mean that this American man didn't come over here expecting it. Maybe that's how deals are made in America."

"If his father was arrested for it, that seems unlikely," Bessie said.

Maggie shrugged. "Anyway, George has a lot of business associates staying with him, and I'm sure they all have secrets they didn't want Harrison Parker finding out about."

"That's one possibility," Thomas said.

"What other possibilities are there?" Maggie demanded.

"Maybe Harrison was on the island following up on his investigation into Phillip Tyler's death," Thomas replied. "Maybe the police arrested the wrong man for that murder."

Bessie shook her head. "I'm quite certain they have the right man for that murder," she said.

"Then maybe he had an accomplice," Maggie interjected. "I can believe that, actually. Maybe Harrison had found his accomplice."

"That doesn't explain what Harrison was doing on the beach in the middle of the night," Thomas said. "Surely he wasn't dumb enough to agree to meet anyone on a deserted beach after dark."

"He must have done, though," Maggie said. "Bessie, did you see or hear anything?"

"Not a thing. It was quite far from my cottage, of course."

"And you didn't notice the car?" Maggie asked.

"No, not that night and not the next morning, either. What about you? Did you see the car?" Bessie asked.

Maggie glanced at Thomas. "We did some painting earlier in the day, but we were done by one or two o'clock. Thomas was tired and my back was bothering me, so we gave ourselves the afternoon, or what was left of it, off. We didn't come back down until after we'd heard about your latest find."

"And the car wasn't there when you left?" Bessie checked.

"No, definitely not. We were parked in that car park. Ours was the only car there when we arrived and the only car there when we left," Maggie told her.

Bessie shrugged. "Let's hope the police can work out what happened fairly quickly."

"They won't get any answers from that lot at Thie yn Traie," Maggie said darkly.

"What do you mean?" Bessie asked.

"They'll all lie and cover for one another. That's how the wealthy are, you know. All they have to do is insist that everyone was locked in for the night and the police will never be able to prove otherwise," Maggie told her.

"I'd like to believe that George and Mary will tell the truth," Bessie said.

"They might, but then it will be the other seven or eight men against them. I'm sure they're probably already leaving the island, actually. They'll all have expensive solicitors on speed dial, ready to come over and rescue them if the police try to stop them from leaving," Maggie replied.

Bessie thought about arguing, but decided it wasn't worth it. Maggie loved to complain and she loved to gossip. Anything Bessie said would be spread around the island within hours, and much of it would probably be reinterpreted before it was repeated.

"What do you think of this paint colour, then?" Thomas asked, waving a hand at the wall.

Bessie smiled. "It's very neutral," she said. It was not quite white and incredibly dull, but Bessie knew that was probably best for rental properties.

"It's meant to be extra durable," Maggie said. "We're trying it in two of the cottages. It costs nearly twice as much as regular paint, but if it means we could start painting every other year instead of yearly, it will be worth it."

"Good luck," Bessie said, getting to her feet. "I should let you get back to work, then."

"What were you and Mary talking about yesterday?" Maggie asked.

Bessie frowned. "I think she just needed to get away from all of their houseguests for an hour," she said after a moment.

"She was at your cottage for closer to two hours," Maggie replied. "I was surprised that she'd leave her guests on their own for that long, especially in the middle of a police investigation."

"I'm sure she has plenty of staff to make sure that her guests don't miss her," Thomas said. "They were probably all in meetings with George all afternoon. No one probably even noticed that she was gone."

Bessie gave Thomas a grateful smile. "I really must get out of your way," she said as she walked towards the door.

"I understand Doona is living with John Rockwell now," Maggie said. "I'm not sure that's setting the best example for the children."

"You seem to know more than I do, then," Bessie said. "Good luck with the painting." She pushed the sliding door open and made her way out into the fresh air. It smelled especially good after the paint fumes in the cottage. Feeling as if Maggie had pushed things too far this time, Bessie stomped back to Treoghe Bwaane and opened the door. Her phone was ringing, and she grabbed it without thinking about who it might be.

"Miss Cubbon, it's Dan Ross. Please don't put the phone down. This could be a matter of life or death."

"What do you want?" Bessie asked.

"Harrison Parker. Why was he on the island? What was he investigating?"

"I've absolutely no idea," Bessie snapped.

"It was something to do with Thie yn Traie. We know that."

"Do we?"

"That's what my sources tell me, and I have complete faith in my sources."

"Mr. Ross, this is a police investigation. It has nothing to do with me."

"You say that, but Harrison Parker knew the island well enough to know that you're the best source for everything that happens in Laxey. I'd bet my life that he came to see you the night before he died, before he walked off down the beach to Thie yn Traie."

"You'd be dead if you did so," Bessie retorted. "I met the man exactly once, the day after your car accident in January. I never saw him again."

"Maybe he tried to visit you but you weren't home," Dan suggested.

"I suppose that's remotely possible, but I was home for much of the evening."

"What's going on at Thie yn Traie now, then? I understand that George has some houseguests."

Bessie opened her mouth to reply and then snapped it shut again. Dan had actually managed to get her chatting so much that she'd nearly forgotten who he was. "No comment," she said eventually.

"Miss Cubbon, Aunt Bessie, even, don't do this to me. There's every chance that there's a madman out there randomly killing newspaper reporters. My life could be in danger. I'm not looking for headlines, I'm just trying to stay alive."

"No comment."

He made an impatient noise. "Look, I want to investigate Harrison's murder. If I'm honest, I'd love to solve it. Imagine the headlines I could get. I might even be able to get his job across, the one that's suddenly available."

Bessie gasped. "What a horrible thing to say," she scolded him.

"Not horrible, just realistic. The thing is, though, as much as I want that job, I want to stay alive more. I'm afraid if I investigate, I'll draw the killer's attention. That's the last thing I want to do."

"I'm sure there are plenty of other things you could report about for the local paper," Bessie said.

"Yes, of course there are, boring, ordinary things. I want to write about murder, and about Harrison's murder, at that. I just want to stay alive to enjoy the headlines, not turn up in them myself."

"If I were you, I'd steer clear of this murder investigation, then," Bessie said, really wanting the man to stay away from her.

"I was thinking, you know George and Mary Quayle. Maybe you could talk to them, find out about the men who are staying with them. If you give me a list of their names, maybe I could dig into their backgrounds very, very quietly, without any of them knowing what I'm doing."

"I have to go," Bessie said.

"I'd give you full credit in the paper," Dan offered. "Or you could be listed as an anonymous source. How does that sound?"

Bessie simply put the phone down. She didn't enjoy being rude, but she'd had quite enough of that particular conversation. When the phone rang again, she ignored it, heading up the stairs to her office.

Bessie's friend at the Manx Museum, Marjorie Stevens, who was the librarian and archivist there, had sent a large packet of letters to Bessie for her to transcribe. Having been an amateur historian for years, Bessie had welcomed the new challenge. She'd recently taken a class in reading old handwriting, which had focussed on the script of the sixteenth and seventeenth centuries. These letters, though, were considerably more modern, the earliest dating from the nineteen-twenties, but the writer's handwriting was as challenging to decipher as anything centuries old.

Onnee had grown up on the island. When she'd been eighteen, a distant cousin from America had visited, bringing along a friend, Clarence. Onnee and Clarence had fallen in love and married just weeks before he and the cousin were due to return to the US. Onnee had started writing to her mother on her journey to the US with her cousin and her new husband, and Bessie knew that there were fifty years' worth of letters at the museum.

Thus far, Bessie had read about how the cousin had died on the difficult ocean crossing, and how Onnee had been shocked when she and Clarence had reached Wisconsin and she'd learned that he'd left behind a fiancée called Faith. The first years of marriage had been difficult for the couple. Onnee had fallen pregnant, only to lose the baby. She'd fallen pregnant again almost immediately, this time giving birth to a baby girl, Alice. There had been complications with the delivery and Onnee had been told that Alice would likely not survive for long, but thus far she'd been thriving, at least according to Onnee's letters.

Onnee had fallen pregnant again in short order. In the meantime, she and Clarence were struggling financially, but had finally found an affordable house to buy. Faith was still in the picture. She'd been staying with Clarence's parents while he'd travelled and now, years later, she was still living with them. Faith had health issues, some of which Onnee suspected might have been miscarried pregnancies, as she was convinced that Clarence was still involved with Faith.

Now Bessie sat down to transcribe another month or two of letters. For the most part, Onnee had written every single month, but occasionally she'd missed a month. She'd missed one when she'd had Alice and Bessie suspected she'd miss another when she gave birth to her second child.

The work was difficult and tiring. She had to transcribe a word at a time, which meant she couldn't really read the letters until she'd finished a page. An hour later, she sat back and stretched.

After all of the upset in her own life over the past day, Bessie could only hope that things were going well for Onnee and her little family in Wisconsin. Sighing, as she anticipated trouble, Bessie began to read. When she put her transcription down a short while later, she felt better.

The pregnancy was going well and Onnee was starting to feel more at home in Wisconsin. The new house was larger than their flat had been, so little Alice had her own room and they already had a nursery set up for the baby. Alice was still progressing, in spite of what the doctors continued to say. Onnee reckoned that she was meeting all of her milestones on schedule and that the doctors were simply wrong.

She and Faith had been spending more time together, and Onnee admitted to her mother that she may have misjudged the other woman. From what Onnee could determine, Faith had truly loved Clarence and had been heartbroken when he'd come home with Onnee. Clarence's parents were like parents to her. She'd lived with them for an entire year while Clarence had been travelling. During that year, her own parents had died, leaving her alone in the world. Onnee wrote of feeling terribly guilty about how Clarence had treated the girl, even though it wasn't her fault in any way.

Onnee had concluded the letter by asking for prayers for a safe delivery of a healthy baby, and Bessie found herself almost desperate to read the next letter. Of course, she knew Onnee would survive. There were many more years of letters waiting for Bessie. But what about the baby? A glance at the clock made Bessie frown. Her head hurt and her eyes were tired. She knew she needed a break, but if she hadn't been expected for lunch at Thie yn Traie, she might well have started on the next letter anyway.

As it was, she stood up and stretched and then went to her bedroom to get ready. Mary was always impeccably dressed and perfectly made-up, so Bessie felt as if she had to make some effort with her appearance. She changed into a simple blue dress and matching flats. After combing her hair, she powdered her nose and added lipstick to her lips.

"That will have to do," she told her reflection.

The woman in the mirror simply shrugged.

Bessie walked down to the kitchen and grabbed her handbag. She was heading for the door when she remembered the police tape. Her plan had been to walk to Thie yn Traie. It wasn't far, after all, but the police tape was probably blocking her access to the stairs that led to the mansion.

Sighing, she reached for the phone. It was probably too late to ring for a taxi, but she'd have to try. Feeling annoyed with herself for forgetting about the tape and getting lost in Onnee's world for so long, her hand hesitated over the phone.

The message light on the answering machine was blinking frantically. No doubt Dan Ross had rung back repeatedly, she thought as she pressed play.

The first message was from Dan. It was a long and rambling message about how certain he was that he was in danger and about how much Bessie could help simply by asking a few questions and then sharing the answers with him. Bessie deleted it when it finally ended. The second message was from Mary.

"I'm sure you're planning on walking over here, but with the police tape on the beach, I'm not certain that you can. I'll send a car for you at midday or just before. Ring me back if that's a problem," Mary had said.

Bessie grinned. It was a good thing she'd listened to her messages before she'd rung for that taxi. A moment later someone knocked on her door.

"Elizabeth? This is a surprise," she greeted the girl.

"Mum was going to send her car and driver, but I offered to come. I didn't think you'd mind," the pretty blonde replied as she gave Bessie a hug.

"Of course I don't mind. I'm delighted, actually. I feel as if I haven't seen you in ages."

"I've been busy with lots of events. Actually, I've been busy with Andy, mostly. It's wonderful having him here all the time, but neither of us seems to get anything done. We go out to look at possible sites for his restaurant and end up just driving around, talking. He had a horrible childhood, especially compared to mine. He's really made me appreciate how fortunate I've been."

"That's good to hear," Bessie told the girl. She'd always thought Elizabeth was a good person who'd been spoiled a bit too much by her loving parents.

"Anyway, we've agreed not to see each other for a few days so that we can both concentrate on work. We'll still go out in the evenings, of course, but no more long lunches or late breakfasts or any of the other things we've been indulging in since Andy finished school."

"I'm glad things are going so well for you both."

"I'm almost frightened by how well things are going," Elizabeth admitted. "I've never been very good at relationships. I like Andy a lot and I'm afraid that he's going to break my heart. I'm also afraid that I

58

might break his. We're trying to take things slowly as we've only really been together in the same place for a month and a half, but it's hard. He's looking for a house, and I know I shouldn't have any say in what he buys, but it's hard not to offer my opinions."

"You need to stop worrying so much and try to enjoy the relationship as it develops," Bessie advised. "There's nothing wrong with you offering your thoughts on houses when Andy looks at them. You'd do the same for any of your friends if they asked, wouldn't you?"

"Yes, of course, but with Andy I keep picturing myself moving into the houses, and that complicates things." Elizabeth waved a hand. "But we need to go. Mum will be waiting. She's so happy that you're coming over this afternoon so that she doesn't have to endure another meal with Daddy's guests on her own again."

"Your father won't be there?"

"Oh, no. Daddy is at work, all day, every day. He has dinner with us and the guests, but not lunch."

"Why aren't his guests at his office with him?" Bessie asked as she followed Elizabeth out to the girl's shiny red sports car.

"Daddy has lots of other business concerns, none of which have anything to do with the retail park. The four men staying with us are only interested in the retail park and nothing else. He should have invited them over one at a time, had a meeting with each in turn, and then selected which one he wants to work with, but he thought it would be better to get them all here at once for an entire week. Mum is beside herself trying to keep them entertained, and now it looks as if they may have to stay even longer, seeing as how they're all suspects in a murder investigation."

Bessie fastened her seatbelt and Elizabeth turned the key. A moment later they were driving far too quickly down the short road between Treoghe Bwaane and Thie yn Traie.

59

CHAPTER 5

*E*lizabeth parked in the huge garage and led Bessie through the side door and into the mansion.

"Miss Elizabeth, your mother is waiting for you and your guest in the great room," the man standing in the corridor told her.

Elizabeth nodded. "Bessie, this is Geoffrey Scott, our temporary butler while Jonathan is in London. Geoffrey, this is Bessie Cubbon. She's a dear friend of the family and an island institution."

Bessie smiled at him. He was probably in his mid-forties. His dark brown hair was sprinkled with grey that made him look distinguished. His accent was proper Received Pronunciation, which made quite a contrast to Elizabeth's casual speech. His suit was perfectly tailored and his shoes shone.

"I'm not sure I want to be an institution," Bessie laughed.

Geoffrey nodded solemnly. "It is a great pleasure to welcome you to Thie yn Traie," he said. "Mr. Hooper was kind enough to share some details about the family and their friends before he left. He told me that he'd known you since his childhood and that you were the person to ask if I had any questions about Laxey or the island."

Bessie flushed. "Jack, er, Jonathan grew up in Laxey. It's been my home for a great many years. If you do have any questions, my cottage is just down the beach from here."

"Down the beach? I thought the cottages on the beach were all holiday rentals," he replied.

"Most of them are holiday rentals. I still live in my little cottage all year-round, though," Bessie told him.

"It must be nice to be on the beach all the time, but surely it gets quite cold at this time of year?"

"My cottage is very cosy," Bessie replied. "I had central heating put in years ago, when I had it extended."

"Very good," he said, bowing again. "Mrs. Quayle is in the great room."

"Yes, Mum's probably afraid we forgot to come back," Elizabeth laughed. "We'd better get in there."

Bessie smiled again at the butler and then followed Elizabeth down the long corridor to the huge great room. The wall of windows that showcased the sea always took Bessie's breath away. She stood and watched the waves for a moment before crossing the room to Mary, who was standing next to a long table that had been set up as a bar.

"Is it too early for wine?" Mary asked Bessie when she joined her.

"Not if you don't have to drive anywhere later," Bessie said.

"In that case, shall I open a bottle of something?"

Bessie hesitated and then shook her head. "I'd really rather have tea or coffee, if you don't mind."

Mary sighed. "I don't mind. I shouldn't be drinking, really, it's just been a long day already."

"What's gone wrong?"

Mary glanced around the room and then led Bessie to a small cluster of chairs in one corner. As they sat down, Elizabeth called across the room.

"Since no one is here yet, I'm going to go and help Andy in the kitchen."

She disappeared before Mary could reply.

"So much for not seeing one another during the day," Bessie laughed.

Mary smiled indulgently. "They are trying to see less of each other, but they're falling in love and are rather obsessed with one another at the moment. It's incredibly sweet, but I do worry that one or the other of them is going to get hurt. I'd love to think they'll end up together forever, but they both seem incredibly young."

"How old were you when you got married?"

Mary flushed. "Younger than Elizabeth is now, but I was years older in other ways. She's been very sheltered, really. The problem is, I like Andy a great deal. I'm more worried about Elizabeth hurting him than him hurting Elizabeth. He seems ready to settle down, but I'm not sure the same is true for my daughter."

"Is that what's made today so long already?"

Mary shook her head. "Unfortunately, no. Our guests have been incredibly difficult today. Not all of them, just most of them. They all came prepared to stay for a week, but now, with the police telling them that they can't leave, they're all suddenly desperate to get away. They've been ringing solicitors and Manx advocates and every connection they have with police elsewhere. George finally had to ring the Chief Constable to get an official statement, but I'm not sure that's actually helped."

"What did the Chief Constable say?"

"That the police have hard evidence that the murder on the beach has some connection to Thie yn Traie and that no one will be permitted to leave the island for the next forty-eight hours at a minimum."

"Oh, dear."

"He wouldn't elaborate on the connection between the dead man and Thie yn Traie, and he wouldn't guarantee that people would be able to leave after the forty-eight hours, either. All four of our guests were upset, and I'm not even sure if any of them will be coming down for lunch."

"Have they never had Andy's cooking before?" Bessie asked

Mary laughed. "They haven't, actually, and I don't think any of them have been very impressed with what our chef has been producing. She prefers to cook for smaller numbers. Having to make three meals a day for groups of eight has caused no end of trouble."

"Maybe she'll quit."

"I certainly hope so," Mary said.

"Are we having lunch in here today?" a voice said from the doorway.

Mary got to her feet and Bessie followed suit. They walked towards the man, who hadn't moved.

"I've invited a friend to join us for lunch, and I brought in an outside chef to make something special," Mary explained as she walked. "We'll be eating in the dining room, but I thought maybe people would want a drink first."

The short, grey-haired man nodded and then walked further into the room.

"Bessie Cubbon, this is Owen Oliver," Mary said quickly. "Owen is a builder who specialises in retail and commercial spaces. Bessie is a very dear friend."

Owen nodded at Bessie and then crossed to the bar. He poured himself a drink as Mary and Bessie followed behind him. There was a large coffee pot on the bar. Mary poured a cup for Bessie and then one for herself.

"Thank you," Bessie said.

"I don't suppose the police have said any more about us leaving," Owen snapped.

"I haven't spoken to anyone, but I doubt they'll say anything further until after they've had more time to investigate," Mary said.

He shook his head. "I'm sorry that someone died, but it's nothing to do with me. I'm quite certain I didn't know the dead man, Parker something, wasn't it?"

"It was Harrison Parker," Bessie said. "He was a reporter for a London newspaper."

Owen shrugged. "I can't imagine why I'd want to murder a London reporter, but then, I also can't imagine why a London reporter would be wasting his time on the Isle of Man. I've never been anywhere where less happens than this island."

"You've been here for just a few days and already someone has been murdered," Bessie pointed out.

His laugh was a sharp bark. "Touché. You're right, of course. I've only ever been involved in one other murder investigation and that was, what, twenty years ago? A girl I went out with once or twice managed to get herself murdered by some man she'd met in a pub. The police questioned everyone she'd ever been involved with, however briefly, but, luckily for me, I had an alibi."

"That poor girl," Bessie said, certain that the man had never given the girl a single thought.

He blinked at her and then shrugged. "Yes, of course, but it was inconvenient for me. I had to answer all manner of unpleasant questions, and then they dragged the girl I was seeing into things as well. She had to swear that we'd been together that night, which was awkward, because she was supposed to have been somewhere else altogether." He took a sip of his drink and then laughed heartily. "She lost her job because of it, actually. She worked for my competition and when her employer found out she was, er, fraternising with the enemy, he let her go."

"I hope you helped her out," Bessie snapped.

"Oh, I gave her a job in one of my companies," he replied. "She'd been hoping for the job of Mrs. Oliver, but that wasn't going to happen. I'm not the marrying kind."

And women everywhere are grateful, Bessie thought but didn't say.

He finished his drink and then glanced around the room. "Where is everyone?" he demanded.

"The butler is busy scaring us up," a voice said from the doorway.

Bessie immediately guessed that the newcomer was Ted Pearson. He looked, as Mary had suggested, like her mental image of a California surfer.

"Ted, come and meet Mary's friend," Owen called. "She's called Betsy and she's fascinating."

Bessie felt herself flush as she turned to greet the new arrival.

"Ted, this is Bessie Cubbon. Bessie, this is Ted Pearson. You've something in common as he's American," Mary said.

"You're American?" Ted asked.

"In a way. My family moved to America when I was two, and once my parents naturalized, I became an American citizen, but we moved back to the island when I was seventeen and I haven't been back since," Bessie explained.

"You have an American passport, though, right?" he asked.

Bessie nodded. "I even renew it every ten years, even though I've never used it for anything."

"It's lovely to meet another American. I was starting to feel entirely outnumbered," Ted said excitedly. He offered his hand and shook Bessie's enthusiastically. "You said you moved back when you were seventeen. Why didn't you ever go back to the US?"

Bessie shrugged. "I thought I would once I'd turned eighteen, but things didn't work out the way I'd hoped. I ended up buying a small house on the island and then finding that I loved living on my own by the sea."

Ted looked out the window. "The views here are amazing," he agreed. "It's the one thing that tempts me to buy property here. I don't think I could stand living here, though. There's nothing to do."

"Have you explored any of the island's historical sites?" Bessie asked.

Ted laughed. "History was never my thing. It's all dates and battles and whatever. Not for me."

Bessie shrugged. "The island has some wonderful historical sites. It has shops and restaurants, theatres, art galleries, clubs, and pubs. What would you be doing if you were in London or back in the US?" she asked.

Ted frowned. "Making million-dollar deals during the day and clubbing at night," he told her. "The clubs here are far too tame for my taste, and I haven't been able to make a single deal since I arrived. George is playing his cards very close to his chest, not letting anyone know what he's thinking. I didn't realise, when he invited me here, that things were going to be like this."

"I'm sorry if George didn't explain the situation properly," Mary said.

Ted waved a hand. "He told me that he was having a bunch of business associates come to stay for a week. I just expected it to be more like a party and less like one long business meeting. I was expecting social evenings with drinks and girls, you know?" He addressed the question to Owen, who laughed.

"A social evening would be nice, but I think that the murder on the beach has eliminated any chance of anything like that happening this week," Oliver replied.

Ted sighed. "I'm not even sure who died," he said. "The police asked me a million questions, but I couldn't really follow them. Who died?"

"A reporter from a London paper. A man called Harrison Parker," Bessie told him.

"And the police are keeping me here why, exactly?" Ted asked. "I've never even heard of the man. They can't honestly suspect that I had anything to do with his death."

"But they do," Owen told him. "They think one of us killed him. That's why we can't leave."

"Why would I kill a random London reporter?" Ted demanded.

"A better question might be what a random London reporter was doing on the island," another man said as he walked into the room.

"Bessie, this is Nicholas Taylor," Mary said. "Nicholas, this is my friend, Bessie Cubbon."

"It's a pleasure to meet you," Nicholas said, taking Bessie's hand and giving it a squeeze. "I don't suppose you have any idea what that reporter was doing on the island."

Bessie looked at him in surprise. "How would I know?" she asked.

He laughed. "Haven't you ever watched those police dramas on telly? The police always ask random questions like that in the hopes of tripping up the killer."

"Well, I didn't kill Harrison Parker, and I've no idea who did, either. I didn't know he was on the island and I don't know why he was here," Bessie replied.

"You say that as if you knew the man," Nicholas said.

Bessie shrugged. "We'd met."

"Really?" Nicholas said. All three men suddenly looked a good deal more interested in Bessie.

"Tell us more," Ted demanded. "Where and when did you meet him?"

"I met him some months ago when he was working on the island," Bessie replied. "He stumbled across a big story the same day I met him and left the island almost immediately after that."

"Well, that wasn't very interesting," Ted complained. "You could have at least tried to make it interesting."

Bessie looked at Mary, who shrugged. "Does anyone else want a drink?" she asked.

"Yes, please," Ted replied.

Mary moved towards the bar, but she was interrupted by another new arrival.

"I'm late for lunch," the man in the doorway said loudly. "I do apologise. I've been ringing everyone I know all morning trying to find a way off this miserable island, and I nearly forgot about eating."

"Edmund, come and meet Mary's friend," Ted called. "She's called Bessie and she's terribly interesting."

"Really?" Edmund replied as he walked into the room.

"Well, interesting if you want to learn more about the island and its history. She's part of it, I believe, since she's lived here for, like, forever," Ted said.

Mary flushed. "I'd prefer it if you didn't insult my friends in front of both them and me," she said tartly.

Ted shrugged. "I didn't mean it as an insult," he said carelessly.

Bessie mentally moved him up her list of suspects, which made her feel better.

"Edmund Rhodes, this is Bessie Cubbon," Mary said. "She's a dear family friend."

"Oh, no," Ted said. "Does she know George? Is she going to tell him not to do business with me now because I was rude?"

Mary gave him a level stare. "She may not, but I certainly will," she said coolly.

Ted sighed dramatically. "There goes my last chance of getting anything out of this miserable week. I must get my lawyers to get me out of here."

"Lunch is ready," Geoffrey said from the doorway.

Mary nodded. "Let's move into the dining room, then, shall we?" she said.

Bessie could hear the tension in her friend's voice. As she was already tired of George's business associates, and she'd only spent a few minutes with them, she felt tremendous sympathy for her friend.

"You can stay in my spare room for a few days," she whispered as she took Mary's arm and walked with her out of the room.

Mary laughed. "If only," she replied.

The dining room was only a few steps away. There were two tuxe-doed waiters standing ready as they walked into the room.

Mary took a seat at the head of the table and motioned for Bessie to sit beside her. Ted flopped into a chair on the opposite side of the table, keeping his eyes on the glass in his hand.

The other three men took seats seemingly at random, with Edmund ending up in the seat on Bessie's other side. Elizabeth walked in as the waiters began to fill glasses with water for everyone. She smiled at her mother and then took a seat between Ted and Owen.

Ted immediately sat up and put his hand on her arm.

"Hello, beautiful," he said.

"Not interested," she told him.

Ted laughed. "You can't keep fighting me forever. Sooner or later you're going to succumb to my charms."

"While I'm sure you're charming, I have a boyfriend," Elizabeth replied.

"A boyfriend," Ted repeated, putting the emphasis on the first syllable. "I'm a man."

Elizabeth shrugged. "And far too old for me, really."

Ted flushed as the other men laughed.

"Give it up," Nicholas suggested. "She's too smart to get involved with you. Anyway, she has plenty of her own money, and your money is the only thing charming about you."

Ted sat back in his seat. "Just trying to break up the boredom a little bit," he said.

"Our first course is potato and leek soup," Geoffrey announced.

The waiters delivered the soup, and Bessie was grateful that for several minutes everyone was focussed on their food.

"Delicious," Edmund said. "This wasn't made by the same woman who's been cooking every day since we arrived," he said to Mary.

"No, I asked a friend to cook for us today," Mary replied. "Our regular chef needed an afternoon off."

"Get rid of her and hire your friend," Owen advised. "This is excellent, and your regular chef's cooking is very ordinary. Offer your friend double. He or she is worth it."

"Our regular chef isn't used to preparing food for more than the immediate family. Having so many guests has been an adjustment for her. Andy, our friend who cooked today, has just finished culinary school."

"Would he be interested in working in London?" Nicholas asked. "I've never bothered with a personal chef, but I might be prepared to consider it."

"I believe he's planning to stay on the island for the foreseeable future," Mary replied.

"Why?" Ted demanded. "He could have a first-class restaurant in London. I'll back him financially if he wants to open his own place in any big city in the UK or the US."

"I'll pass the offer along," Mary said.

"I'd rather talk to him myself," Ted said.

"Maybe we should wait until we've finished the meal," Edmund suggested. "He might just be good at soup."

Ted laughed. "Good point."

"Our second course is chicken with white wine sauce, crispy roast potatoes, and roasted vegetables," Geoffrey announced as one waiter cleared plates and the other began to deliver the main course.

"Wonderful," Bessie said with a sigh after her first bite.

Elizabeth beamed at her. "He's been playing with sauces for weeks," she told Bessie across the table. "This is one of my favourites."

"It's very good," Owen said. "It's a bit heavier than I'd like, but I'll forgive him because the potatoes are perfect."

Elizabeth looked as if she wanted to argue, but Bessie caught her eye and shook her head.

"How long have you known Mary and George, then?" Edmund asked Bessie.

"I met George not long after he and Mary moved to the island," Bessie replied. "He was kind enough to write a large cheque to a charity with which I was involved, and we all got to meet him in order to thank him. Some weeks later, the charity had a dinner party and George and Mary were the guests of honour."

"George is very generous, then?" Edmund asked.

Bessie shrugged. "He's been very good to the island's charities since he's been on the island. I believe that Mary is the driving force behind his generosity, though."

Edmund laughed. "That sounds about right. All three of my wives always nagged me to help out more good causes."

"Three wives," Bessie echoed.

"I get bored easily. I've had, I don't know, maybe a dozen fiancées in between the various wives."

"Goodness."

"No children," he said. "My second wife would have lasted longer if she hadn't wanted children so badly. I cared about her, and she was an interesting person, too, but after six months of hearing about how desperately she wanted children, I'd had enough. Last I'd heard, she'd found another man and they'd had six children in eight years. Good luck to them both."

Bessie took a bite of carrot, trying to work out an appropriate reply.

"Do you have kids?" he asked.

"No, I never married," Bessie told her.

"You're smarter than I am, then," he laughed. "Marriage is for fools and romantics. I'm neither, even though I've made that mistake three times. I won't make it again, anyway."

"No?"

"Not going to happen, not even if I met the perfect woman. The thing is, I've enough money to buy myself companionship when I get lonely. That's a lot cheaper than another ex-wife, I can tell you that for sure."

Bessie nodded, wishing that someone would interrupt the uncomfortable conversation

"You know the island, though. What do you know about the man who died?" Edmund asked abruptly.

"Next to nothing."

"Really? Someone must know why he was here. Who were his friends when he lived here?"

Bessie shook her head. "I met him once, and from what I could see, he wasn't the type to have many friends. He was very focussed on his career and he wasn't interested in staying on the island for any length of time."

"Smart, then."

Bessie opened her mouth and then shut it again to give the words some thought. "He did seem smart when I met him," she admitted. "He'd done some research and he knew who I was and how he thought I could help him."

"But he was dumb enough to meet someone he suspected of something criminal on a deserted beach," Edmund argued.

Bessie shrugged. "He used lock picks to get into an empty building so that he could overhear a conversation," she said. "I think his desire for a story overrode his worries about potential dangers."

"So if he thought he was going to get a good story, he would have arranged to meet someone on an empty beach."

"Maybe. Maybe he didn't realise just how empty that stretch of beach would be at that hour on that night. In the summer there are people on the beach nearly all the time and guests staying in the holiday cottages, as well."

Edmund nodded. "So he might have expected there to be someone around, if he didn't realise that the cottages were only holiday rentals."

Bessie shrugged. "Maybe he didn't arrange to meet anyone. Maybe he was looking for someone or something and got caught by the killer."

"I understand the police have tied the death to someone at Thie yn Traie. That's worrying. I'd hate to think that one of these other men is a killer." Edmund looked around the table. Everyone was looking at him, clearly listening to his conversation with Bessie.

"Everyone is capable of murder, under the right circumstances," Ted said.

"I believe you mean the wrong circumstances," Owen corrected him.

Ted inclined his head. "Of course."

"So which one of us was driven to kill the nosy reporter?" Nicholas asked.

"I do beg your pardon, but the kitchen is ready with the pudding course," Geoffrey interrupted. "For pudding, the chef has prepared a warm shortbread biscuit bowl filled with vanilla ice cream and topped with warm caramel sauce."

"Wonderful," Bessie said.

The waiters quickly cleared the empty plates, replacing them with the promised pudding. Bessie took a bite and smiled. "Delicious."

"I want to hire the chef," Ted said. "I'll pay him double whatever you're paying him," he told Mary.

"I'm not paying him," Mary laughed. "He's a personal friend who hasn't found the right location for his restaurant yet. I don't believe he's interested in working for anyone other than himself."

"Nonsense. He just needs to be offered enough money," Ted replied. "I'll talk to him after lunch."

Mary shrugged. "You're welcome to try."

"He probably won't want to agree to anything until you've been cleared of murder," Owen suggested.

Ted laughed. "That almost sounds as if it's an accusation."

"Not at all," Owen replied quickly. "We're all suspects, of course. Unless anyone has an alibi that I've not heard?"

"We were all in bed, in our suites, dreaming of making million-dollar deals," Ted said. "I assume we weren't being watched during the night, though."

Mary shook her head. "We have security on site, but they only monitor the main exterior doors and windows. Anyone could have gone out through one of the back doors and walked down to the beach relatively unnoticed."

"Relatively?" Edmund repeated.

"They may have been spotted on camera, but not watched. The security team is tasked with checking people coming up the stairs, but not going down them," Mary explained.

"So they would have noticed when the killer came back to the house," Owen suggested.

"Perhaps," Mary replied. She sighed. "There are a number of ways to get into or out of Thie yn Traie unnoticed. George and I have been talking about installing better security, but it's a huge undertaking."

"What do you mean by ways to get in or out unnoticed?" Ted asked.

"There are secret passages and hidden staircases," Mary told him. "We've found a few sliding doors, including one to a room that we didn't know we had. There's at least one tunnel from inside the house to a spot about halfway down the cliff face."

"You're suggesting that the killer knew about these hidden exits?" Ted asked. "Because this is all news to me."

"Of course, you'd say that even if you knew about the tunnel and whatnot," Nicholas pointed out. "The killer has to pretend ignorance lest he give himself away."

"How would I have learned about such things?" Ted demanded.

"I believe you're familiar with at least one member of the Pierce family," Edmund said.

Ted frowned. "I knew Daniel Pierce, but only slightly. He was working on a project with a colleague of mine just before his untimely death. What does that have to do with anything?"

"This house used to belong to the Pierce family," Mary told him. "Daniel died here on the island."

"I suppose I knew that," Ted replied. "I remember hearing that he'd died, but I don't really remember the details. Anyway, I barely knew Daniel. We never talked about his house on the Isle of Man and its secrets. We hardly spoke at all the one or two times we did meet."

"Does anyone else know anyone from the Pierce family?" Bessie asked.

"I know the whole family, but only slightly," Edmund replied. "We have mutual friends, and I used to see them at charity events, but they've rather disappeared over the past two years."

"I knew Daniel, too," Nicholas admitted. "Rather well, actually. We did a few deals together over the years. I remember him talking about the island and about having a summer home here, but we never spoke in any detail about the house. Until right now, I didn't even realise that this was their old house."

"Which you'd say, even if he'd given you blueprints for the place," Ted said.

Nicholas shrugged. "Of course."

"That makes me the odd man out," Owen said. "I don't believe I ever met any of the Pierce family, although I did build a small retail shop for their company many years ago."

"You must have met someone from the family, then," Ted argued.

Owen shrugged. "I suppose I may have done, but I don't recall doing so. As I said, it was years ago. This house may not have even been built at that point."

"Considering the secret exits and whatever, none of us have an alibi, is that correct?" Ted said.

The four men exchanged glances. "Or a motive," Nicholas interjected. "None of us knew the dead man, did we?"

"I certainly didn't," Owen said.

"Perhaps he brought his trouble with him from the UK, and Thie yn Traie isn't actually involved," Ted said. "Let's hope the police can work it all out quickly, anyway. I'm eager to get back to London as quickly as possible."

Bessie opened her mouth to ask another question, but she was interrupted by Geoffrey.

"Ladies and gentlemen, may I introduce today's chef, Andy Caine," he said from the doorway.

The next several minutes were chaotic as all four of the men threw offers at Andy. Bessie lost track of how many times Andy politely refused to discuss the topic. Eventually, Ted gave up and stomped out of the room. Owen and Nicholas weren't far behind him. Edmund took a few extra minutes of persuasion, but he finally conceded defeat.

"If you change your mind, ring me," he told Andy, handing him a business card before he walked out of the room.

Andy looked at Bessie and shrugged. "I hope you enjoyed lunch," he said. "Everyone else seems to have been satisfied."

"It was delicious, as always," Bessie replied, getting to her feet and walking around the table to give Andy a hug. "It's even better to see you, though."

The pair talked for several minutes before Elizabeth interrupted.

"We have a meeting at three," she reminded Andy.

He nodded and then gave Bessie another hug. "I'm catering an event for Elizabeth," he explained. "After we meet with the organisers, we're going to look at a house that just might work for my restaurant. I'm trying not to get my hopes up, but on paper it looks good."

"I'll keep my fingers crossed," Bessie told him. "You know I can't wait for you to open."

He laughed. "If this is the place, I probably won't be open for a year or more. It's going to need to be gutted and completely redone inside."

Bessie watched as the young couple left the room, chatting happily together about the event Elizabeth was planning.

"Thank you for coming," Mary said. "Let me get someone to take you home."

CHAPTER 6

"Geoffrey, can you arrange for a car to take Bessie home, please," Mary asked the butler, whom they found in the corridor outside the dining room.

He nodded and then cleared his throat. "I could take her home," he suggested. "I need to go out and get a few things and I thought this might be a good time for me to go. Unless I'm mistaken, everyone has had lunch and no one has plans for the afternoon."

"Elizabeth has gone out, but I don't believe any of the guests have any plans for the rest of the day. I didn't realise you needed anything. Of course you can go. If you can take Bessie home along the way, that would be most helpful."

"Thank you, madam," he said. "Miss Cubbon, if you wouldn't mind waiting here for a few moments, I'll just get my coat and the keys to my car."

"I don't mind, but you must call me Bessie."

He nodded. "Thank you."

He disappeared down the hall, leaving Bessie with Mary.

"Do you miss Jonathan?" Bessie had to ask.

Mary nodded. "I can't complain about Geoffrey. He does the job well, but I do miss Jonathan. Geoffrey is very formal, while Jonathan is always proper, but also good company. I'm not even sure what I'm saying, really, except that I truly like Jonathan and I'm still not comfortable with Geoffrey."

"I can't imagine feeling uncomfortable in my own home."

Mary shrugged. "When you have staff, it becomes increasingly difficult to feel truly relaxed. We have a butler and a housekeeper and two or three women who help with the cleaning. We have two drivers, one for George and another for anyone else who needs one. We have our cook, and she has two assistants, as well. At any given time, there could be half a dozen people in the house, most of whom are essentially strangers to me. It's exactly the way George wants it to be, but it does sometimes make me uncomfortable."

"I think I'll stick to living alone."

"It's worse at the moment because of the houseguests, of course. I find them difficult to spend time with, and they're keeping our staff extra busy, too. I hope the police find the killer quickly so that everyone can go home on schedule."

"If you're ready, Miss Cubbon," Geoffrey said as he rejoined them.

"I am, but you really must call me Bessie," she replied.

He nodded. "I'll try to remember."

She followed him through the house to the garage. He led her to a small car with UK plates.

"You brought your own car with you?" she asked.

"I did. I've had this car for a number of years. I didn't want to leave it in the UK where it wouldn't have been driven for months, so I came across on the ferry with it. Although Mr. and Mrs. Quayle kindly offered me the use of any of their vehicles during my stay, I've found having my own car here quite handy."

Bessie gave him directions to her cottage. The drive only took a few minutes.

"What an adorable cottage," he said as he pulled to a stop next to it.

"Thank you. It's been my home for many years."

"Do you mind if I get out and take a walk around it?" he asked.

"Of course not. The beach is public, anyway, so even if I did mind, I couldn't stop you."

He chuckled. "How unfortunate for you."

"I'm quite used to it, really. In the summer months, the beach is full of guests in the holiday cottages. I've grown accustomed to people running up and down behind my cottage at all hours of the day and night."

Geoffrey followed Bessie out of the car and then walked with her around the cottage.

"So many windows at the back, facing the sea, but none on either side of the cottage," he remarked.

"There used to be windows on the sides, but I had the cottage extended twice and ended up removing the windows from the ends. I get more than enough natural light from the windows at the back of the cottage, and now that the holiday cottages are there, I'm quite glad I can't see anything in that direction when I'm inside."

Geoffrey chuckled. "I'm sure I wouldn't want to watch a bunch of holidaymakers lying on the beach all day, either." He walked Bessie to her door.

"Thank you for the ride home," she told him.

"It was my pleasure. I haven't spent much time on the beach since I've been here, but now I've realised what I've been missing. I'm going to have to start trying to get out more."

"Mary was saying that there are hidden passages and tunnels throughout Thie yn Traie. You could probably sneak out without anyone even noticing."

He gave her a rueful grin. "It's my job to be available when the family or their guests need me. Sneaking out isn't something I'm able to do, I'm afraid." He bowed and then turned and walked back to his car. As he drove away, Bessie let herself into Treoghe Bwaane.

The answering machine light blinked at her as she hung up her coat. The first three calls were all from nosy friends who wanted to talk about the latest murder. Bessie deleted them without bothering to take note of who had rung. There was no doubt in her mind that all of the callers would ring again, maybe even when she was home and willing to chat. The fourth call was from Doona.

"John thought it might be helpful to get everyone together tonight to talk about the case," she'd said. "We'll bring dinner and pudding. Ring me back if there's a problem, otherwise we'll be there around six."

Bessie glanced at the clock. She had a couple of hours to fill. Onnee's letters were waiting, but instead of going up the stairs, Bessie headed for the sitting room. She dug out a new book from the box from the bookshop and curled up in her favourite chair. When someone knocked some hours later, Bessie blinked and reluctantly returned to the real world.

"You looked surprised to see us," Doona said when Bessie opened the door

"I was in California, tracking a killer through Los Angeles," Bessie told her. "I feel rather as if I crash-landed back on the Isle of Man without warning."

Doona nodded. "I want to read that one when you're done."

"I'll probably finish it tonight. It was difficult to put down."

"Even though we have a real-life murder to solve?" John asked.

"You know I'd rather not deal with any more real-life murders," Bessie countered.

John nodded. "If you'd rather not be involved, we don't have to have this conversation."

"Oh, I'm already involved, whether I want to be or not. I'd prefer to help you solve the case as quickly as possible, under the circumstances."

While they'd been talking, John had been busy unpacking the large box he'd carried in from the car.

"Something smells wonderful," Bessie said. "What did you bring?"

"A new restaurant just opened across from the station," Doona told her.

"Again?" Bessie asked.

Doona shrugged. "No one ever seems to stay there for more than a few weeks. I don't know if the businesses keep failing, or if the owners end up deciding that they really don't want to own restaurants, or what."

"I'd have thought it would take more than a few weeks for a business to fail," Bessie replied.

"But maybe not for someone to realise that they hate owning a restaurant," Doona suggested.

"What's the new place called, then?" Bessie asked.

"Mama's Italian Kitchen," Doona told her. "They do pasta and pizza, and I've heard nothing but good things about them so far."

"I'm almost afraid I'm going to like it," Bessie said. "Even if it's delicious, the place probably won't still be there next month."

Another knock on the door had Bessie letting Hugh into the cottage.

"I brought pudding," he said. "Just fairy cakes from the bakery in Ramsey. That seemed easy, and I got several flavours."

"That sounds good, too," Bessie said. "I'm almost sorry I ate so much lunch, but as Andy Caine cooked it, I'm not really sorry at all."

"Where did you have lunch?" John asked.

"At Thie yn Traie."

"I was hoping you were going to say that Andy suddenly got his restaurant up and running," Doona sighed. "Don't tell me that Andy is going to be Thie yn Traie's private chef? That isn't fair to the rest of us."

Bessie laughed. "He just agreed to make lunch today to help Mary. Her chef has been working overtime because of the houseguests, and Mary wanted to give her an afternoon off. Andy cooked, and Mary was kind enough to invite me along."

"So you've met all of George's potential business partners now?" John asked.

"I have, yes."

"Good, we'll have lots to discuss later, then," John said with a smile.

Doona began to open containers as Bessie got down plates. They all filled their plates with pasta and garlic bread before sitting down at the table.

"How's the baby?" Bessie asked Hugh.

"She's good. Aside from the teething, of course. Although we aren't sure now that she actually is teething. She might just have a cold. She's certainly very grumpy. I was really happy when John said we were having a gathering tonight."

"Poor Grace," Doona said.

"She's going out with her friends tomorrow night," Hugh replied. "I've been trying to get her to go out more often, without Aalish, but she hates being away from her. One of Grace's friends from school is getting married, though, so they're having a girls' night out tomorrow night."

"That should be fun for her," Bessie said.

"Knowing Grace, she'll only stay for an hour and then rush home," Hugh said. "Especially with Aalish being poorly. Her mother is coming up to spend the night so that I'm not on my own with the baby, even though I'm perfectly capable of looking after her for a few hours."

"You could just tell Grace's mother not to come," Doona suggested.

Hugh flushed. "I can't do that. Grace's mother loves to be involved, and besides, we're in the middle of a murder investigation. What if I'm needed for something to do with the case?"

"You aren't on call tomorrow night," John told him.

"I know, but you'll still ring me if something comes up with the case, won't you?" Hugh replied.

"Are you sure you think you're perfectly capable of looking after Aalish on your own?" Bessie asked.

"I am, but I don't mind the extra help," Hugh muttered before taking a big bite of bread.

Bessie grinned. "I'm sure, as she gets older, you'll find yourself alone with her quite regularly. Enjoy the extra help while you have it."

"How are Thomas and Amy?" Hugh asked, obviously changing the subject.

"They're okay," John said, looking questioningly at Doona.

"I think they're both coping remarkably well," she replied. "They've been through a lot, but they're both working hard at school, and at their after-school activities as well. Amy is struggling a bit with maths, but Thomas has been able to help her. It's all beyond me."

John laughed. "I'm glad I'm not the only one who feels that way about her maths homework. The other day she tried to explain it to me and we both ended up with pounding headaches."

"Thomas seems to understand it, anyway," Doona said.

"Grace will have to help Aalish with her homework," Hugh said. "At least with her maths homework."

Bessie knew that Hugh was hoping to go back to school to earn a university degree so that he could eventually move up to inspector. She also knew that he'd failed the maths portion of the entrance exam for the course he wanted to pursue. The last she'd heard, Grace was tutoring him in the subject. She shot him a questioning look.

He shrugged. "Later," he mouthed at her.

Bessie was sure that Doona saw the exchange, but she didn't question it. John was focussed on his dinner.

"That was very good," Bessie said when she'd cleared her plate.

"It was good, but not great," John replied.

"I liked it," Hugh said.

"You like everything," Doona retorted. "It was better than I was expecting, though. If they stay in business, I'd get their food again."

"I hope they stay in business," Bessie said. "If only for a bit of continuity for a while."

"The fairy cakes should be good," Hugh said as he got up to get the bakery box. "I've never had a bad thing from this bakery."

Bessie got everyone clean plates for their cakes and then put the kettle on. She made tea and then rejoined the others.

"They've been trying different flavours," Hugh said as he opened the box. "Strawberry and lemon are new. The vanilla and chocolate haven't changed."

"Vanilla and chocolate for me," Doona said, taking one of each.

"Lemon sounds interesting," Bessie said cautiously. "I may have to have a different one to get rid of the flavour if it isn't good."

John took a chocolate while Hugh took one of each.

"I promised the shop assistant that I'd try them all and report back," he said as he shut the box.

"That was awfully good of you," Bessie teased.

Hugh shrugged. "Just trying to help."

Doona chuckled and then bit into her vanilla cake. "So good," she said after she'd swallowed.

"The lemon is delicious," Bessie said, aware that she sounded surprised. "The flavour is very light and refreshing. I think it would be especially nice on a hot summer day."

"I like it," Hugh said, "but it doesn't feel very indulgent."

Bessie laughed. "Four fairy cakes is indulgent, whatever their flavours."

After her lemon cake, Bessie gave in to temptation and had a chocolate one as well. Hugh enjoyed all four of his cakes, which surprised no one.

"Right, should we talk about murder, then?" John asked after a sip of tea.

"Must we?" Bessie sighed. "There's no chance that Harrison had a heart attack or met with an unfortunate accident, then?"

"He was murdered," John told her. "I won't say any more than that at this point, but we are quite certain that it was murder."

"Mary said that the Chief Constable told George that the police have evidence that connects Thie yn Traie to the murder," Bessie said.

John nodded. "The Chief Constable has also given a statement to Dan Ross with the same information. In his defense, the man is doing everything he can to keep George's four business associates on the island for as long as possible. All four of them seem to have high-priced solicitors on call. Luckily for me, the Chief Constable's office is dealing with them."

"You can't tell us what ties Harrison to Thie yn Traie, though?" Bessie asked.

John hesitated. "I suspect Dan Ross will have the information before too much longer. He has sources within the police force. Until the news becomes public knowledge, though, I can't share it."

"But you can confirm that there is something that connects Harrison with Thie yn Traie?" Bessie checked.

"Yes, I can confirm that," John replied.

"And that has to make George's visitors the main suspects, doesn't it?" Doona demanded.

"At this point, everyone at Thie yn Traie is a suspect," John told her.

"Well, you can cross George, Mary, and Elizabeth off the list," Bessie said. "I know you can't officially do that, but they aren't on my list and we've no need to discuss them in relation to the case."

"How well do you really know George?" John asked.

Bessie raised an eyebrow. "Well enough," she said firmly.

"We never could tie him to anything criminal, even though we found plenty of evidence that his former partner was breaking quite a few laws," John said. "Some of the men staying at Thie yn Traie at the moment had connections to Grant Robertson before he went missing. There's a real possibility that Harrison was chasing those connections."

Bessie frowned. The police had spent many months trying to link George to his former partner's activities and had failed to find any evidence of any wrongdoing on George's part. If he was guilty of anything, it was of being too trusting and a bit naïve. It had never occurred to her that any of George's guests might have had ties to Grant, though. Now she could only regret that she hadn't had a chance to bring him into the conversation over lunch.

"Surely Harrison's employers knew why he was on the island," Doona said.

"Unfortunately, Harrison was apparently doing his own investigations outside of the stories he was being asked to research for the paper. He'd requested a few days of annual leave and came over to the island without telling anyone where he was going. They were as surprised that he was here as we were," John told her.

"He was chasing his own stories," Bessie said. "Why doesn't that surprise me?"

"His editor at the paper said that he kept all of his notes in a small notebook. The notebook wasn't found with the body or in the man's hire car. He had a hotel booked for three nights, but he never actually checked in."

"Which hotel?" Bessie asked.

John named a small and inexpensive property on the Douglas

promenade. It was one of the few places that remained open during the winter months when visitors were few and far between.

"So he wasn't worried about staying near Laxey," Bessie said thoughtfully.

"Or he couldn't find anywhere to stay near Laxey," Hugh replied. "The Seaview in Ramsey is closer, but it's a lot more expensive."

Bessie nodded. "And very little else is open this time of year. I wonder if he tried to book a holiday cottage. You should talk to Maggie or Thomas," she told John.

"We already did," he replied. "All of their bookings are handled by an estate agency in Douglas now. The woman there told me that if anyone rings to book a cottage in the off-season, she simply tells them that nothing will be available until mid-April. She doesn't take names or any other information from people who ask about dates that are unavailable. She also doesn't specifically recall anyone asking recently, but admits that she may have forgotten all about a call or two."

Doona sighed. "So there goes that lead."

"Harrison probably knew that the cottages were empty, though," Bessie said. "I'm sure he did some digging into their use when he was investigating Phillip Tyler's murder."

"Perhaps," John said. "At this point, all we can say for certain is that no one seems to know why Harrison was on the island, but there seem to be a number of possibilities."

"Such as?" Doona asked.

"Such as follow-up on the Tyler case, for one thing," John said. "But that doesn't tie into Thie yn Traie, and we know he was interested in Thie yn Traie. It seems more likely that he was interested in George's guests, but we've no idea why."

"They're interesting men," Bessie said. "I'm sure they all have things they want to hide from the press and the police."

"I heard what Mary said about all of them," Doona said. "But I'm much more interested in what you thought when you met them."

Bessie chuckled. "John, I'm sure you've met them all. Hugh, have you met the men in question?"

"No. I was busy at the crime scene while John was interviewing the sus, er, witnesses," Hugh replied. "Pretend I know nothing about them, although I have read their witness statements."

"None of them were very forthcoming in their interviews with me," John said. "I'm hoping you managed to learn more than I did," he told Bessie.

They all looked at her expectantly. She took a deep breath and then sighed. "My goodness, I'm sure that I'm going to disappoint you all. I barely spoke to them, really, although Mary did give me some background on them, as well."

"Start with Edmund Rhodes," John said.

"He was the last to arrive in the great room for lunch. He sat next to me at lunch and asked me several questions about George and Mary and the dead man. He complains a great deal, according to Mary, although he didn't complain at all about lunch today. He was the most difficult to persuade that Andy wouldn't come to work for him."

John was taking notes. "Did Mary tell you anything about why he's interested in being George's partner?"

"She said that he's interested in bidding on the ferry service to the island, as well, but that he has a short attention span. She's afraid that he'll sign the deal and then lose interest, in the same way that Alastair has done," Bessie replied.

"Anything else?" John asked.

"He's been married three times and engaged at least a dozen more, but he doesn't plan to get married again," Bessie said.

"He does have a short attention span, doesn't he?" Doona asked. "Unless he's very old."

"I think he's probably about fifty, give or take a year on either side," Bessie said.

John nodded. "He's fifty-one, actually."

"Oh, and he admitted to knowing the Pierce family, but only slightly."

"Really? How did they come up in the conversation?"

"Someone asked about alibis for the night of the murder, and Mary mentioned that the house has several hidden passages and a tunnel that apparently opens halfway up the cliff face. I assume it opens onto the stairs."

"Yes, it does," John said. "It's very cleverly done, and if you didn't know it was there, you'd probably never find it. The door is small and covered in stone on the outside. Mary took me down the tunnel and through the door after the murder to show me how someone could have left Thie yn Traie and returned unnoticed."

"Someone suggested that anyone who knew the Pierce family could have known about the tunnel," Bessie explained. "And nearly everyone knew at least someone in the Pierce family."

"Nearly everyone?" Doona asked.

"Owen claimed to have never met any of the family, even though he did a building project for them many years ago," Bessie replied.

"I've forgotten Owen's surname," Doona said.

"Owen Oliver," Bessie said. "He's in his sixties. He's a builder and he only wants to buy into the project to get it built using his company. Once that's completed, he plans to sell his share."

"That doesn't seem as if it would be good for George," Doona said.

Bessie shrugged. "Apparently it isn't unusual."

"What else did you learn about him?" John asked.

"Not much, really. He didn't know the Pierce family, or if he did, he doesn't remember them. He really didn't say much over lunch."

"What about Nicholas Taylor?" John asked as he flipped to a new page in his notebook.

"He's also in his sixties, I believe. He wants to build a mall, but for the moment he's considering buying into the retail park instead," Bessie replied.

"I can't see the island supporting a mall," John said.

"I agree," Bessie said. "He admitted to having known Daniel Pierce quite well, but claimed that they never discussed Thie yn Traie."

"And why would they if they were business associates?" Doona wondered.

"I don't know. If I had a summer house that was full of tunnels and secret doors, I think I'd tell everyone I met," Hugh said.

John nodded. "If they were talking about a building project, I can imagine it coming up, actually. Of course, whether it did or not, Nicholas won't admit to it now."

"Who's the last man, then?" Doona asked. "He's American, right?"

"Yes, Ted Pearson," Bessie said. "He's the one Mary described as looking like a California surfer, which was accurate. He's in his fifties, and I didn't care for him one bit. I must admit to hoping that he killed Harrison Parker. I'd quite enjoy seeing him arrested."

"What was wrong with him?" Doona demanded.

"He doesn't like the island. He thinks it's boring and he didn't want to hear about the many interesting historical sites we have. He was rude and loud and opinionated and he made a very clumsy play for Elizabeth, as well."

Doona laughed. "My goodness, you could have just said 'everything' and been done with it."

Bessie grinned. "I simply didn't care for him. George didn't know him before he arrived. He's Alastair's candidate, apparently. Maybe I should ring Alastair and ask him some questions about the man."

"Don't do that just yet," John said. "I may need to question Alastair myself and I'd rather do that before he's spoken to you."

"What else can you tell us about Ted?" Hugh asked.

"He knew Daniel Pierce too, although he claimed he didn't know him well. He was the one who suggested that no one had an alibi for the murder," Bessie said.

"And he's right. At the moment, we can't rule out anyone from Thie yn Traie," John told her.

"I suppose I'm a suspect, as well, since I live close to where the body was found," Bessie said.

John shrugged. "Technically, yes, but as I said, we're fairly certain that Harrison's death is tied to Thie yn Traie."

"One of the men did suggest that none of them had a motive for killing a random London reporter," Bessie said. "I didn't get a chance to ask anyone any questions about possible motives."

"Mary said something about one or two of them, though," Doona said. "Wasn't one of them involved in some sort of industrial accident or something?"

"Mary mentioned that there had been an accident on one of Owen's building sites," Bessie replied. "Whether that was something that Harrison might have been interested in investigating or not, I don't know."

"Was it recent?" John asked.

Bessie and Doona exchanged glances. "Mary didn't say exactly when it happened, but I don't think it was very recent. She said something about fines being imposed, so it sounds as if it was all settled, as well."

"That doesn't mean that Harrison hadn't found a new angle or some new information, but it makes it seem less likely," John said. "From what I'm learning about Harrison, he preferred to break new stories rather than rehash old ones, even if there was something new in his reports."

"Mary said something about Ted's father being involved in some trouble in California, but I can't see that raising Harrison's interest, either," Bessie said.

"I'll check into it, but I'd be surprised if that was why Harrison was on the island," John said.

"What was he working on back in London?" Bessie asked.

"He was investigating a number of business deals that seem to be interconnected in some way, even though they aren't meant to be," John told her. "None of the men at Thie yn Traie are involved in any of those deals, though."

"And George isn't involved?" Bessie asked.

John shook his head. "It's all to do with London property. Harrison's editor told me that they suspect that someone is buying up properties throughout a particular area of London, with plans for something big."

"Something big?" Doona echoed.

"Apparently, large corporations sometimes buy up land using a number of shell companies to hide their intentions so that prices don't go up," John explained. "Someone might be planning a large shopping mall, for example. They'd need to purchase a lot of land and then, once they had what they needed, they'd have to apply for planning permission. Perhaps a more likely scenario is that someone wants to take down a number of older homes in an area and build new and much more expensive properties in their place."

Doona nodded. "And you're sure that none of the men at Thie yn Traie are involved?"

"As sure as we can be," John told her.

"So all four men had the means and opportunity to kill Harrison Parker," Hugh summarised. "What we need now is a solid motive for any one of them."

"What about the staff at the mansion?" Doona asked. "I mean, I'm sure that George and Mary are very careful when they hire staff, but the staff have to be on the list of suspects, too, don't they?"

"We're looking at all of them," John told her. "Most of them have been with George and Mary for years, though."

"They have a new, temporary butler," Bessie said. "I met Geoffrey Scott today. He seems to be good at his job, but I didn't warm to him. That may just be because he isn't Jonathan, of course."

John nodded. "We're looking at him as well. He came from an agency and they spoke very highly of him, but everyone has to be considered."

"I can't imagine why he'd want to kill Harrison Parker," Bessie said. "I mean, we have to assume that Harrison had discovered something about someone at Thie yn Traie. It must have been something serious to lead to murder."

The foursome talked for a while longer, but they could only guess at possible motives for Harrison's murder. After a while, Hugh began to yawn every other minute.

"Sorry, the baby still isn't sleeping through the night consistently," he said. "She's doing better, but we're up at least once between ten and seven almost every night."

"Go home and get some rest," Bessie told him. "We're done here anyway, I think."

"We are," John agreed. "I have to go and make my kids go to bed, anyway. They stay up too late every night."

Doona had been doing the washing-up. Now she walked with John to the door. "You can drop me off at home, right?" she asked. "Since I came with you."

He laughed. "I can certainly do that. I wouldn't just abandon you here."

"Thanks," she grinned.

Bessie let them out and then gave Hugh a hug as he reached the door.

"I have my second attempt at the maths exam tomorrow," he told Bessie in a whisper. "I don't think I'm ready, but Grace wanted me to see how far I've come. If I don't get a seventy-five or better, I can take it again in another month. I still have plenty of time to keep trying."

"Well, good luck tomorrow, then," Bessie said. "You don't need it, though. I know you've been working hard."

"I have, and I plan to keep working, too. Even if I pass, I'm still not all that good at maths. I want to get good enough to help Aalish with her homework when she gets older."

"Judging from what Doona and John were saying earlier, you may have a lot of work ahead of you."

Hugh laughed and then disappeared out the door. Bessie shut it behind him and then locked it. It was late, but she didn't feel tired.

CHAPTER 7

*B*essie headed up the stairs, telling herself that she ought to go to bed, but when she reached the first floor, she changed her mind. She had just enough time to transcribe another of Onnee's letters before she needed to get some sleep.

An hour later, she sat back and read through her transcription. The baby had arrived safely, a little boy. Onnee wrote that Clarence had wanted to call the baby after himself, but that she wanted to call him William, after her father. They'd settled on William Clarence, Onnee told her mother happily. It was very early days yet, but Onnee seemed confident that Alice would adjust to her new role as an older sister fairly easily. Onnee also confided that Alice had stayed with Faith at Clarence's parents' house for an entire week when she'd first brought the baby home from hospital.

"Faith truly seemed to enjoy the experience and has offered to have Alice again whenever I need a break. Clarence seems slightly confused by the friendship that is growing between myself and Faith, but I can't tell you how much more pleasant life has become now that I have a friend who is close to my age," Onnee had concluded her letter.

Bessie put the paperwork away, her thoughts very much on Onnee and baby William. She was relieved that Onnee's second delivery had been easier than her first, although it seemed as if Alice was doing much better than everyone had expected. As Bessie crawled into bed, she wondered about Onnee and Faith's new friendship. She could only hope that it would continue, as it sounded as if Onnee truly needed a friend.

The skies were grey and overcast the next morning. It was cooler than it had been lately, as well. Before her walk, Bessie made herself a second cup of tea to go with her cereal. While she enjoyed her morning walks, this morning the beach didn't appeal to her. Expecting that it would probably rain later, though, she forced herself to put on a coat and shoes and head out.

A brisk wind was blowing, pushing Bessie down the beach at a pace that was a bit faster than she might have liked. It didn't take her long to reach the police tape, which was being buffeted by the wind. There was no one in sight and for a moment Bessie was tempted to duck under the tape and continue her walk. Suspecting that someone would catch her if she tried it, Bessie sighed and turned back towards home. She was just passing the very last holiday cottage when she heard her name.

"Miss Cubbon? Bessie," a voice called in an odd whisper.

She looked around and spotted Dan Ross standing beside the cottage, looking around in a furtive fashion.

"Mr. Ross?" she replied.

"Shhhh," he hissed. "Is there anyone around?"

Bessie looked up and down the beach and then shook her head. "I don't see anyone."

He nodded and then quickly walked over to join her. "Invite me in for a coffee," he said, his eyes darting back and forth as he scanned the beach.

"I beg your pardon?"

"Please, you don't have to actually give me coffee, but I want to talk to you and I don't want to do it standing out in the open."

Bessie would normally have argued, but she was too curious about what Dan wanted to refuse. "I didn't make coffee this morning," she said as she continued on her way home. "You're welcome to a cup of tea, though."

"Tea will do nicely," Dan said, dashing after her, nearly tripping as he tried to watch behind himself as he walked.

He stood off to the side of Treoghe Bwaane, in the house's shadow, as Bessie unlocked her door. She stepped inside. A moment later, Dan rushed in and slammed the door behind him.

"Was that really necessary?" Bessie asked.

He shrugged. "I'm trying to be extra careful. Someone murdered Harrison Parker. The killer could be targeting journalists."

Bessie thought about arguing, but there seemed little point. Ultimately, she didn't care if Dan thought his life was in danger or not. She refilled the kettle and switched it on. Feeling slightly put out, she piled some biscuits onto a plate and put it on the table. "Have a seat," she suggested.

Dan dropped into a chair and looked around. "You need to update your kitchen."

"I like my kitchen just the way it is."

He shrugged. "The appliances are older than I am."

"They work better than you do, too," Bessie shot back.

Dan stared at her for a minute and then laughed. "You're probably right about that, at the moment, anyway. I'm not getting anything done right now. I'm not sleeping. I'm not eating. I'm not writing stories. I really just want to run away."

"So take a holiday," Bessie suggested. The kettle boiled and she focussed on making tea. A few minutes later she joined Dan at the table, passing him his cup of tea as she sat down with hers.

"I was thinking I might take a holiday," he said around a mouthful of biscuit. "But that feels disloyal to Harrison and his memory."

"You didn't like Harrison," Bessie pointed out.

Dan winced. "I didn't like competing with Harrison for stories, but it isn't fair to say that I didn't like him. We were something close to friends while he was here."

"That's good to know. The police have been looking for Harrison's friends."

"I know. I had a long conversation with Inspector Rockwell, all about Harrison. Unfortunately, I couldn't really help him."

"You didn't know what Harrison was on the island investigating?"

"We hadn't spoken in some time, not since he'd left the island, actually. We didn't exactly part on good terms, after he stole my biggest-ever story out from under me."

"You were unconscious and incapable of writing the story," Bessie reminded him.

"Yes, well, he should have at least shared the byline with me. I would have shared it with him if he'd been the one attacked by a crazy murderer."

"Really?" Bessie asked.

Dan flushed and then took a sip of his tea. "Anyway, none of that matters now. I want to know what you learned about the four men at Thie yn Traie when you had lunch there yesterday."

Bessie stared at him for a full minute. "No comment," she said eventually.

"It can all be off the record. I'm not interested in getting a story right now. I just want to stay alive. You've talked to a lot of murderers in the past two years. Which one of the four seemed most like a killer to you?"

"No comment."

"I'm not going to quote you or anything. I just want your gut instinct. You know people and you know murderers. I'm sure you have your suspicions."

"No comment," Bessie said, picking up her teacup.

"I'm going over to Thie yn Traie later today. George wants me to write an article about the retail park. He's going to give me an interview and introduce me to all four of his potential partners. I need to know which one I should be most worried about. What if I say the wrong thing to one of them? You'll feel terrible if you find my body on the beach tomorrow morning."

"I suggest you avoid meeting anyone on the beach after dark," Bessie replied.

"Maybe Harrison didn't meet anyone on the beach. Maybe he was at Thie yn Traie when he got killed. Maybe the killer just pushed the body off the cliff."

Bessie thought back to where she'd found the body. There was no way it would have landed where she'd found it if it had been pushed from the top of the stairs to Thie yn Traie. "I don't think that's possible."

"But maybe that will be what happens to me," Dan said, sounding slightly hysterical.

"If you're that worried, you shouldn't go this afternoon."

"I don't have a choice, do I? My editor isn't going to accept any excuses. I have to do my job. George Quayle doesn't give interviews very often and he hasn't said a single word about that retail park since the groundbreaking a year ago. This is real news that the island needs to know."

"So you'll just have to be careful about what you say to everyone," Bessie suggested.

Dan sighed. "I should be asking tough questions. This is my chance to interview the four main suspects in a murder investigation, and I'm too terrified to do my job correctly. My editor told me that I'm to limit my questions to the retail park project, but he's not worried about keeping me alive. He just doesn't want to upset George."

"If you do as your editor asked, you should be perfectly safe."

"Unless I accidentally say something that I don't know is the wrong thing."

"Which is true every day with every conversation you have," Bessie replied. "You never know what secrets people possess or what they might be willing to do to protect those secrets. Yours is a dangerous business."

"I suppose so. It's never felt dangerous before, though."

"Someone did try to kill you not that long ago."

"But he didn't do a very good job of it. Harrison is dead."

"If you're that concerned, stay away from Thie yn Traie."

"I can't do that. I have to be there at one o'clock today. Once I'm finished there, I'm going to come here, though. I'm going to tell you everything that was said, word for word. Even if you can't help me work out who killed Harrison, I want you to know everything that I know. That will keep me safe."

"I have plans for this afternoon," Bessie said, stretching the truth, as she hadn't had any plans until Dan had said he was coming back. Now her plans were to be out of the house so that he couldn't return.

"Change them," Dan said flatly. "My life is at stake here."

"You keep saying that, but I don't think there's any evidence to support that theory."

"Harrison was investigating something to do with one of those four men. He's dead. If I ask the wrong questions today, the killer might decide that I know something, even though I don't. He could target me next."

"No one knows for certain what Harrison was investigating," Bessie pointed out.

"But the police have tied it to Thie yn Traie. They're pretty definite on that."

"They could be wrong. I've no idea what evidence they've found to link the two."

Dan glanced around the room and then leaned in close to Bessie, as if concerned that he might be overheard. "Harrison kept all of his notes in a notebook. The notebook wasn't found with the body. They did find his wallet, though, and inside his wallet was a sheet of paper that had been taken from a notebook like the ones that Harrison always used. It had 'Thie yn Traie, Laxey,' written on it in Harrison's handwriting."

"How did you find that out?" Bessie demanded.

"I have sources inside the constabulary. They give me information, sometimes for publication, but not always. One of my sources shared that with me, as long as I promised not to publish it until the police are ready to release it. He told me because he knows how worried I am about my safety."

Bessie made a mental note to ring John and let him know about the leak in the department. "The note in his wallet doesn't necessarily prove anything," she said thoughtfully.

"Maybe not, but it's certainly a starting point for the police. If they disregard it, they'd have to question everyone on the island."

"Even assuming that Harrison was investigating something to do with Thie yn Traie, the killer doesn't have to be one of the four men visiting George."

"You aren't suggesting that George is the killer, are you?"

"Of course not," Bessie snapped. "George, Mary, and Elizabeth are all above suspicion. That still leaves a considerable number of staff, though."

"And it leaves Andy Caine. I understand he's been staying there more nights than not. Maybe Harrison found out something about Andy's parentage. Maybe the fortune he inherited isn't really his, after all."

Bessie shook her head. "Andy is also above suspicion. I've known him since he was a small child. He'd never kill anyone."

"Not even if there was a lot of money at stake? His money that he'd already spent a chunk of on a costly training course? His money that he's hoping will be enough to buy him a big house and a restaurant space, and keep a certain spoiled young woman satisfied, as well?"

"You can speculate about Andy all you like. I know he didn't have anything to do with Harrison's death," Bessie said dismissively.

"But you don't trust the staff at Thie yn Traie," Dan said thoughtfully. "That's interesting, as they've all been carefully selected by Mary Quayle herself. It almost seems as if you're doubting her ability to choose her own staff."

"Murderers often seem to be perfectly ordinary people when you meet them," Bessie said. "Most of them probably thought of themselves as perfectly ordinary, until some circumstance led them to murder."

"So I need to watch what I say to the staff, as well as to the four men this afternoon. Which member of staff do you suspect?"

"I don't suspect anyone," Bessie said tightly.

"Maybe after I've spoken to them all, you'll get a clearer picture of them," Dan said thoughtfully. "I don't suppose you want to come with me this afternoon? I can tell everyone that you're my assistant or something."

"Not in a million years."

"I know you don't care for me, but surely you'll be sad if I end up dead."

Bessie swallowed a dozen different replies. "Did you want more tea?" she asked eventually, having given up on finding a more appropriate response.

Dan glanced at the clock. "It's still hours before one and I don't know what to do with myself. What do you do all day?"

"I enjoy reading, doing historical research, visiting friends, shopping..."

Dan held up a hand. "Never mind. I'm too upset to go into my office right now. If I promise to stay out of the way, can I simply sit here until one?"

Bessie looked at the clock. There was no way she wanted Dan in her home for another five hours. "Sit there?" she echoed, trying to think of a way to politely refuse.

"Or somewhere else, if you don't want me in here. I understand you have a guest bedroom. I could go up there so that I'm out of the way. Maybe I could even try to sleep for an hour or two. I haven't slept in days."

Now that he'd mentioned it, Bessie noticed that he did look quite tired. Feeling certain that she'd regret it, she nodded slowly. "If you'd like to try getting some sleep, you're welcome to stay in my guest room for a few hours," she said.

"Thank you," Dan said, jumping to his feet. "Just tell me how to get there." He headed out of the room with Bessie on his heels.

As he raced up the stairs, Bessie called after him. "Turn left at the top."

He did as instructed and was standing in the middle of the guest room when Bessie got there a moment later.

"I don't know that any bed has ever looked as comfortable to me as that one does," he said with a crooked grin. "I'm going to be in your debt forever."

"What time shall I wake you?" she asked, hoping that he would decide to set his own alarm.

"Oh, if I'm not up, please knock on the door at midday. That should give me enough time to wake up properly before I have to be at Thie yn Traie."

Bessie nodded and then left, shutting the bedroom door behind her. For a moment she was tempted to lock it to prevent him from doing any snooping if he couldn't sleep, but she settled for shutting the other doors on the floor, aside from the loo. He was welcome to use that if he needed it.

Back downstairs, Bessie washed up the dishes. It felt odd suddenly having a houseguest, and she wasn't sure what to do with herself while Dan was in bed. She certainly wasn't prepared to leave him alone in the cottage. Having told him that she had plans for the afternoon, she felt as if she should make some, but couldn't come up with anything that appealed to her, at least not more than staying home and hearing from Dan about his visit to Thie yn Traie.

"You're just nosy, that's all," she told herself as she admitted to herself that she wanted to hear what he'd thought of the four men.

Not wanting to go upstairs and risk waking Dan, Bessie finished tidying the kitchen and then curled up in the sitting room with a book. Her mind was elsewhere, but she kept at it, turning pages periodically, even though she knew she wasn't really following the story. Just before midday, she went into the kitchen to see what she could offer Dan for lunch.

A quick search through her cupboards revealed very little that she thought would appeal to Dan. She'd offer him a sandwich and if he didn't like it, he didn't have to eat, she decided as she headed for the stairs.

As she climbed up, she could hear him snoring. It took some effort for her to knock loudly enough to be heard over the snores. Eventually he replied to her knocks.

"Okay, I'm awake. I'll be down in a few minutes."

"I can make you a sandwich for lunch," Bessie called back. "I don't have much else in, I'm afraid."

"A sandwich would be most welcome. Thank you."

Bessie returned to the kitchen and got busy making sandwiches after she'd started a pot of coffee. Dan staggered in a short while later.

"I'm not sure if I feel better or worse," he said. "I'm less exhausted, but I feel slightly hungover or something."

"I've started coffee."

"I'm sorry for everything I've ever done to upset you."

Bessie laughed. "Help yourself." She opened a cupboard so that he could get himself a mug.

"Do you want a cup?" he asked after he'd poured his.

"Yes, please," Bessie replied.

They sat down together with sandwiches, crisps, and coffee.

Dan took a bite and then sighed. "This is actually quite civilized," he said. "I'll bet you never imagined you'd be having lunch with me today."

"You'd be right."

"I should be asking you about finding dead bodies and hearing confessions. I could get at least a dozen articles out of the things that have happened to you over the past two years, and probably a good deal more than that. Instead, I'm just going to eat my sandwich and try not to think about what's coming."

"Why are you so frightened?" Bessie asked. "I know Harrison was a reporter and so are you, but there has to be more to it than that."

Dan shrugged. "Maybe the attempts on my life scared me more than I'd realised at the time. I don't know. I just keep thinking that I'm following in Harrison's footsteps, trying to get a good story. Those four men up there in that mansion, I know they all have secrets. One of them, though, has a secret he's willing to kill to keep. That scares me."

"You've confronted people with secrets before."

"And I nearly got killed for my efforts last time. Those murder attempts, though, they didn't feel quite real. Seeing Harrison's body, on the other hand, that was real. He was younger than me. He was taller and fitter, and yeah, I'll admit it, he was smarter than me. Maybe that's why I'm scared."

"You're smart enough to refuse to meet someone on a deserted beach."

"I am now, but I wouldn't have been a few days ago. If I'd been chasing a big story and someone had offered to meet me on Laxey Beach for a chat in the middle of the night, I wouldn't have hesitated. It never would have occurred to me that I might get killed. It will now, but what if the killer is smart enough to realise that? He may already be making plans for his next kill."

"I hope not," Bessie shuddered. "Some of my dearest friends live at Thie yn Traie."

"Yeah, I'd be worried if I were Mary and George. I think I'd send Elizabeth to stay with Andy, even if he is living with his mother at the moment."

"We really need to find out why Harrison was on the island."

"I wish I knew. I tried ringing his editor at the paper across, but he wouldn't speak to me."

"Did Harrison have any friends on the island when he lived here?"

"He was briefly involved with the girl who works at the front desk at the newspaper office, but only briefly. I can't imagine he's spoken to her since he left."

"But you haven't asked her?"

Dan flushed. "I didn't really think about it until now. The police asked me about Harrison's friends or girlfriends, but I didn't really give it much thought when they asked. I suppose she might know something. I'll ask her when I get to the office later today."

Bessie nodded. While she was curious what the girl would say, it probably wasn't urgent. If she actually knew anything, surely she'd have gone to the police herself. John hadn't mentioned her, which didn't mean he hadn't spoken to her, of course.

The phone rang, startling Bessie and making Dan jump.

"Hello?"

"Bessie? It's Maggie Shimmin. I saw a car in the parking area outside your cottage when I drove past. I would swear it's Dan Ross's car. It's been there for several hours now, but I don't know where Dan is. I just wanted to warn you, in case he decides to pay you a visit."

"Thanks, Maggie, but Dan is here now. We're having lunch together."

Bessie almost laughed out loud as the stunned silence dragged on.

Eventually, Maggie cleared her throat. "I suppose that's all right, then," she said. "I hadn't realised that you and Dan had become friends."

"That isn't the word that I would use," Bessie replied.

"Oh? Of course you can't talk, not with him sitting there listening to your every word. We'll talk soon," Maggie said before putting the phone down.

Bessie only just resisted rolling her eyes as she returned the receiver to its place.

"Maggie Shimmin? I'd recognise her voice anywhere," Dan said. "I shouldn't say anything negative about her because she always shares everything she knows with me, but the woman could gossip for her country."

"She has a heart of gold," Bessie said, defending her friend even though Dan was right.

"I know she does, and she's been incredibly kind to me over the years, as well. I just sometimes wish that she'd share a bit less, really."

Bessie took a sip of coffee to stop herself from laughing. Dan was right again, but she wouldn't do or say anything that might seem critical of Maggie. The woman could be difficult, but Bessie had known her for a long time and she wasn't going to give Dan the satisfaction of hearing anything negative from her about her old friend.

"She rang to warn you about me, did she? I could hear most of what she said, anyway."

"She saw your car and wasn't sure where you were," Bessie explained.

"And now everyone on the island is going to know that I spent several hours in your cottage today, even staying for lunch. People will start to think that you've lost your mind."

"I may be tempted to agree with them."

Dan laughed. "It's been a strange morning," he agreed. "But I slept very well in your spare room. It felt oddly safe and secure, and I'm starting to appreciate why people confide in you and even confess to murder to you. Not that I have anything to confess to, of course, but if I did, I think I would tell you over anyone else that I know."

Bessie wasn't sure if she felt flattered or not. She definitely didn't want to hear any of Dan Ross's secrets, that was certain. "Would you like more coffee?" she asked, getting up and refilling her cup.

"As much as I hate to say it, I need to get to Thie yn Traie," he replied as he glanced at the clock. "I can't thank you enough for your hospitality today. I was expecting you to shut your door in my face, and I probably deserved that, too. Instead, you were kind and you listened to me and even let me take a nap in your spare room. It's been the strangest morning I think I've ever had, but I'm really grateful to you."

"It's been quite unlike anything I would have expected," Bessie agreed. "But I'm glad I was able to help. I'll wish you luck at Thie yn Traie."

He got to his feet. "Are you truly busy this afternoon? I really would like to come back and talk to you about the suspects after I interview them. You don't have to say anything, just listen to me babble."

"What time do you expect to be finished?"

"Three, maybe? I can't see it taking less than ninety minutes to talk to George and then all four of his potential partners, but I can't see them giving me more than two hours, either."

"I'll be here at three," Bessie agreed.

"Thank you," Dan said, sounding sincere. "I'm going to give you my mobile number. If I'm not back by half three, please ring me. I may be in trouble." He wrote a number on a sheet of paper and dropped it on the table.

"I don't think I'll need that," Bessie said.

Dan shrugged and then took a few steps towards the door before stopping and looking over at Bessie. "I haven't hugged anyone since my mother passed away three years ago. I feel as if I should hug you, though."

Bessie wasn't quite sure how to respond. She opened her mouth and then shut it again.

Dan chuckled. "No worries. I'm not going to act on my feelings. I just wanted you to know how I felt." He walked to the door and let himself out before Bessie could reply. As the door shut behind him, Bessie sank back down in her chair, feeling somewhat overwhelmed by the way her day had started.

The phone rang almost immediately.

"What's this I hear about Dan Ross having lunch at your cottage?" Doona demanded.

Bessie laughed. "Did Maggie ring you?"

"She did. She sounded quite concerned."

"It was a very strange morning."

"I'm just finishing my shift at the station. Would you like some company this afternoon?"

"I'd love some company. You can even stay and chat with Dan when he comes back later."

"He's coming back later? Who are you and what have you done with the real Bessie Cubbon?"

Bessie laughed. "As I said, it's been a strange morning. Come over and I'll tell you all about it. Dan won't be back before three."

"I'll be there in half an hour, maybe less. I'll warn you, though, I'm going to tell John what's happened before I come. He may want to come over and find out what's going on himself."

"John is more than welcome, too, although I don't know if Dan will talk in front of him."

"I'll be there as soon as I can," Doona said, sounding concerned.

Bessie put the phone down and then shook her head. "It all does sound rather crazy," she said in a low voice. "But it isn't as odd as it sounds."

She hadn't quite convinced herself of that as she started the washing-up.

CHAPTER 8

*a*fter Bessie told Doona the whole story, her closest friend could only stare at her. "You made him tea, let him take a nap in your spare room, made him lunch, and invited him to come back again this afternoon," she said eventually. "Did I follow all of that correctly?"

"You did, but it truly isn't as odd as it sounds. He's genuinely concerned for his safety. I was just trying to help."

"Help Dan Ross? The man who has done nothing but make your life miserable for the past two years?"

"He was on his best behaviour today. He didn't try to get me to talk about finding dead bodies or anything."

"Which probably just means that he's learning to be more subtle," Doona suggested. "Don't be surprised if tomorrow's paper has a headline like 'The Secrets in Treoghe Bwaane' or something similar."

Bessie shuddered. "He wouldn't."

"You don't think so? I do."

"I hope not," Bessie said after a moment's thought. "I suppose I shouldn't have trusted him, though. I'll be more careful when he comes back."

"You should send him to John when he comes back. If he learns anything from those four men, John needs to know about it."

"I'm sure he knows that I'm going to share everything that he tells me with John."

"I hope so. He won't have any doubts about my intentions, anyway."

"You're going to stay, then?"

"Absolutely. I'm not letting that man take advantage of you."

"I truly don't think he's trying to take advantage. I think he's really scared and wants my help."

"If that's the case, then he won't mind my being here to hear what he has to say."

"He shouldn't. If he does, he doesn't have to talk to me."

Doona nodded. "Maybe you should go and stay at the Seaview for a few nights. It might be nice for you to get away from Thie yn Traie and everything happening there."

"I was thinking about that, actually," Bessie admitted. "Mostly because it's frustrating not being able to walk very far along the beach. I just get started and then I run into the police tape. How much longer will it be there, do you think?"

"You'd have to ask John about that."

"I will, the next time I see him."

A moment later, someone knocked on the door.

"We were just talking about you," Bessie said as she let John into the cottage.

"Doona told me that you've been spending time with Dan Ross. I thought maybe I should hear the whole story from you," he replied.

Bessie made tea for everyone and then settled back at the table. It only took her a few minutes to tell John about her unusual morning.

"I think you're right. I think Dan is genuinely frightened, but I'm not sure why. I suspect it's because he knows something that he hasn't told anyone, but I can't prove it," he said when Bessie was done.

"What could he know?" Bessie asked.

"Maybe something about what Harrison was doing on the island.

It's possible that Harrison rang him for information before he came over, for instance," John replied.

"Surely he must realise that he'll be much safer if the police know everything that he knows," Bessie said.

"At the end of the day, though, he still wants his headline. He'd love to solve the case before the police do," John told her.

Bessie frowned. "If he truly is withholding information, I don't want to help him."

"You may be our best chance for finding out what he knows. It will be very interesting to hear what he has to say after his interviews this afternoon. I'd really appreciate it if you'd let him tell you everything."

"I can do that," Bessie said.

"I'm going to stay, too," Doona said.

John nodded. "Hopefully, he'll still talk in front of you. I'm sure he wouldn't in front of me, though."

"He told me that the police found a slip of paper in Harrison's wallet with the words 'Thie yn Traie, Laxey' on it," Bessie remembered.

John frowned. "Did he happen to mention from where he got that information?"

"He said he has sources within the constabulary and that he was told that on the condition that he didn't publish it for the time being," Bessie replied.

"So someone in my office is selling information to Dan Ross," John sighed. "I don't know why I'm surprised."

"Does it have to be in our office?" Doona asked. "Maybe it's someone in the Chief Constable's office."

John grinned. "That's a lovely thought. I'm going to call a meeting tomorrow morning, anyway. Wherever the information is coming from, I want everyone in Laxey to know that I won't tolerate it. If I find out the source, that person will be let go."

"Dan used the pronoun 'he' when discussing his source, but that may not mean anything."

"Anything else I should know?" John asked.

Bessie shrugged. "Not that I remember. It will be nice having

Doona here for his next visit. I won't have to remember everything he says."

"Try to get him talking about Harrison. See if you can find out more about the man and his time on the island."

"Dan said that Harrison went out with the paper's receptionist, but just briefly," Bessie said.

"Really? He never mentioned that to me," John told her.

"He said that he hadn't paid much attention, but when we were discussing Harrison he remembered," Bessie explained.

John made a note in his notebook. "Anything else, then?"

Bessie laughed. "I'm not deliberately giving you the information in bits. That's just how I'm remembering it."

"And it would have been rude for you to take notes," John said with a grin.

"Maybe I can take notes during the next conversation," Doona said.

"It would probably be best if you didn't," John said. "I'd rather Dan think of you as Bessie's friend who's just visiting, rather than as a member of the island's constabulary."

"I'm a part-time receptionist, not really with the police," Doona laughed. "He needs to worry because of our relationship, not because of my job."

John nodded. "And I'd appreciate it if you didn't answer any questions about that relationship."

"There's no way I'm going to talk about that," Doona said firmly.

"Right, I'm going to get back out there. I have the newspaper's receptionist to interview, and I think I'd prefer to talk to her myself, all things considered. Ring me when he's gone and I'll come back," he told Doona.

"Unless he refuses to speak to me with Doona here," Bessie said.

"That in itself would be useful information," John told her. "If he won't speak to you in front of Doona, I'll assume he has more to hide than I'd realised and have him pulled in for another chat at the station."

Doona grinned. "Maybe we could just tell John that he didn't cooperate," she suggested to Bessie.

"You want the poor man dragged to the station and interrogated," Bessie said.

"You would have too, yesterday," Doona told her.

Bessie nodded. "Part of me still does, actually. I feel sorry for him, but I still don't like him, even after he spent the morning with me."

Doona walked John to the door, and Bessie pretended to be busy at the sink while they said their goodbyes.

"Are you going to give Dan tea?" Doona asked after she'd shut the door behind John.

"I suppose I should offer him something, although I feel as if I've had quite enough tea for today."

"Coffee?"

"We had coffee with lunch. If I drink more now, I'll probably have trouble sleeping tonight."

"Cold drinks?"

"I suppose." She looked in her refrigerator and sighed. "Except I don't have much here in the way of cold drinks. I need a trip to the shops, really."

"Tea, then," Doona suggested. "I'd offer to go and get you some cold drinks, but I don't want to risk Dan arriving while I'm away."

"Dan isn't a suspect in the case. I'm sure I'm quite safe with him."

"He could be a suspect in the case," Doona countered. "Just because Harrison was on the island because of something to do with Thie yn Traie doesn't mean that he was killed because of it, or maybe Dan killed Harrison so that he could get the headlines for whatever is happening at Thie yn Traie."

"That seems a bit far-fetched."

"John did say that he thinks Dan is hiding something."

"I don't know. I can't see the man as a killer. I've been wrong before, of course, but if he wanted to kill me for any reason, he had all morning to do so."

"Maybe he just came to see how much you know. Anyone who commits murder on this island has to be wary of you, really. Maybe he's coming back to try to persuade you that one of George's friends is the killer, all to cover his tracks."

"Let's see what he has to say, shall we?"

"Anyway, I'm not leaving you alone, not when he could be here any minute."

Bessie glanced at the clock. "He probably won't be here for another hour or more."

"I'm not taking the risk. Unless you want to go to the shops with me to get some cold drinks?"

Bessie thought about it and then shook her head. "We can drink more tea. It's fine."

She lent Doona a book and the pair sat down to read for a short while. Bessie couldn't concentrate, though. Eventually she put the book down.

"I've been working on Onnee's letters again," she said.

Doona looked up from her book. "How is she? She was pregnant again, right?"

Twenty minutes later Bessie had told Doona all about Onnee, Faith, and baby William. The knock on the door came right as Bessie finished.

"That was good timing, if it's Dan," Doona said as she and Bessie walked into the kitchen.

"Let me in," Dan said, glancing back over his shoulder as he bounded inside.

Bessie shut the door. "Doona dropped in for a visit. I hope you don't mind."

Dan glanced at Doona and shook his head. "Whatever. I assume that everything I tell you will be repeated to John Rockwell anyway. I'm sure he was here while I was at Thie yn Traie. No doubt he's now off interviewing the poor receptionist at the paper, who probably knows absolutely nothing."

"Tea?" Bessie asked.

"Sure, whatever." Dan dropped into a chair and sighed deeply. "Everyone up there, from the guy that answers the door to the four men visiting, every one of them has secrets," he announced.

"Doesn't everyone have secrets?" Doona asked.

Dan looked at her. "You do, certainly. Your second husband died under mysterious circumstances and he left you a considerable fortune. You continue to work at a low-paying part-time job in spite of your newfound wealth. Of course, you initially kept the job so that you could still be close to John Rockwell. Now that you two are, well, shall we say, intimately involved, why keep working? Are you worried that if you aren't there, he may notice the rather obvious charms of one Suzannah Horton?"

"And Bessie said you were almost charming this morning," Doona replied.

Dan laughed. "I may have been. I will be again. I'm just upset and I'm taking it out on you. Don't pay any attention to me. I wasn't honestly expecting you to answer anyway."

Bessie put teacups and biscuits on the table and then sat down opposite him. "What happened at Thie yn Traie, then?" she asked.

"The man who answers the door, I didn't catch his name, he's creepy," Dan said.

"As I wasn't there, I can't be certain, but that was probably the butler," Bessie said. "His name is Geoffrey Scott. He's only here temporarily, as the regular butler, Jonathan Hooper, is on a course in London."

Dan nodded. "I know Jonathan. I actually like him, even though he won't ever tell me anything about the Quayle family or about anything that happens at Thie yn Traie. I got the feeling that this other guy could be bought, though, although perhaps not with money."

"What do you mean?" Bessie demanded.

"He seemed the type who'd trade information for information," Dan replied. "And he seemed the type who'd use that information for his own profit."

"Oh, dear," Bessie said. "Perhaps I should warn Mary and George."

"I wouldn't worry too much about them. I'm sure they're used to such things. Anyway, I doubt either of them have any secrets, not now, not after the police investigation when Grant Robertson disappeared. I'm sure when they finished that, the police knew everything about

George, from the size of his bank balance to the size of his, er, um, shoes."

"Still, it's worrying to think that the butler might be dishonest," Bessie said.

"Oh, he's dishonest, but maybe not as dishonest as those four businessmen," Dan said. "Of course, I was expecting that from those four."

"How sad."

"Where shall we start? I'm usually the one asking the questions. What do you want to know?" he asked Bessie.

"Had you ever met any of the men before?" she asked.

He shook his head. "As far as I know, this is the first time any of them have visited the island. None of them mentioned ever having been here before, anyway. I'd heard of one or two of them before, but only because I try to keep up with business dealings in the UK if I think they may impact the island in any way."

"Which ones had you heard of before?" Bessie wanted to know.

"Edmund Rhodes, for one," Dan replied. "He's thinking of bidding on the island's ferry service, which will obviously impact the island in a major way. I asked him about his bid, but he wouldn't share any information with me."

"What did he say about the retail park?" was Bessie's next question.

"That it's a great opportunity to bring his unique talents to the island and that he's looking forward to having a chance to be a part of something that the island so clearly needs. When I pushed him for details, he didn't have any idea what shops the island needs or that might be interested in having a space in the new retail park, though. I got the feeling he met George somewhere and that when George mentioned he needed a new partner, he decided to throw his hat into the ring just for something to do more than anything else. I also got the feeling that he'll grow bored with the project and drop out within a few weeks even if he does make a deal with George."

"I hope George realises that," Bessie said.

"George may come across as slightly dim and more lucky than anything else, but he's a very astute businessman. If he does end up doing the deal with Edmund, he'll have an ironclad contract that will keep Edmund involved long after he's lost interest. I suspect, if George goes that way, it will be because he'll know that he'll have free rein to do whatever he wants once Edmund loses interest."

"You sound as if you didn't like Edmund," Bessie remarked.

"I didn't like any of them, and I think any one of them would happily have stabbed Harrison Parker in the chest simply because he was bored and wanted a bit of excitement."

Bessie and Doona exchanged glances. As far as Bessie knew, no one had said that Harrison had been stabbed. Had Dan just admitted to knowing something he shouldn't have known?

"And before you think that I killed anyone, that's another fact that I got from my friend at the constabulary. He's a veritable fount of knowledge, even if I can't actually print anything he's told me yet."

Bessie frowned. "If Edmund killed Harrison, do you have any idea what Harrison knew about him?"

"If it was Edmund, I suspect it was something personal rather than business. The man's been married three times and has had more girls in and out of his life than I think I've even met. There could be something there, if someone dug a little bit," Dan suggested.

"Did he say or do anything that made you suspect him over the others?" Bessie asked.

Dan shrugged. "Not really. He was unpleasant, but he answered my questions with all the right answers. It was clear that he'd prepared his answers, and he wasn't pleased when I went off script."

"You were given a script?" Bessie asked.

"It's just an expression, but I was told that I was to limit my questions to the retail park, and when I tried to talk to him about the ferry deal, about his wives, or about the murder, he shut me down every time."

"Hardly surprising," Doona murmured.

"Had you heard of any of the others before they arrived on the island?" Bessie wondered.

"I did some digging into Owen Oliver's business dealings a few years ago," Dan told her. "He was shortlisted on a major construction project on the island and I wanted to learn more about him. There was so little to learn that I have to believe that he's hiding a lot of secrets."

"What do you mean?" Doona demanded.

"I mean, no one that I spoke with would say a bad word about him. No one would tell me anything, either. I talked to some of his employees. I spoke to a man who'd used his company to build his home. I talked to a few people who'd considered using him but had chosen to use someone else. Everyone said the same thing, almost word for word, about what a professional Owen was and that they couldn't say a negative word about him."

"Interesting," Bessie said.

"There was an accident on one of his sites a few years ago. I rang a few people right after the accident and heard a few things, but by that time the contract for the job on the island had gone to someone else, so I stopped chasing the story. When I rang those same people again yesterday, they all refused to say anything at all."

"You can't think that he's paying people to lie about him," Doona said.

"No, but I can think that he's using his influence to make it diffi cult for people to say bad things about him and his business."

"He's that important?" Bessie asked.

"Within the community in which he operates, yes. His company is responsible for a lot of building projects and they often have a hand in other projects during the various stages of development. No one that works in construction in the UK will want to risk upsetting Owen, not even after someone died on one of his sites."

"What happened?" Doona wanted to know.

"A fairly typical accident, really. Someone was working on the roof, and either he hadn't secured his safety equipment properly or there was an equipment failure. Either way, the man fell eleven stories to his death."

"Ouch," Bessie winced.

"The company had plenty of evidence that the correct safety procedures were in place. They argued that it wasn't their fault if the man failed to follow them or if the equipment failed."

"Surely it was one or the other," Bessie said.

"You'd think so, but the evidence was unclear," Dan replied.

"Unclear or tampered with?" Doona asked.

Dan shrugged. "I have no idea. The company was fined and safety inspections were stepped up for that site for the remainder of the project. As far as I know, that was the end of it."

"What about the man's family?" Bessie asked. "Is it possible that the dead man has family who aren't happy about the results?"

"I did think of that," Dan said. "I even wondered if Harrison was related to the dead man. Maybe he came over to the island to kill Owen, and after a struggle on the beach, ended up dead himself. It would make a brilliant story, but it isn't true. I tracked down the dead man's former wife. She's happily remarried, living quite comfortably in Cornwall thanks to a very generous settlement from Owen's company. They gave her a great deal more than they had to in order to get her to go away. She told me when I rang that she and the dead man had been talking about getting a divorce anyway. She was already involved with the man who is now her husband. Then she told me that she thought I sounded sexy and that I should come and visit her to talk more."

Bessie gasped.

"Videophones would have their uses," Doona muttered.

Dan frowned at her. "Thanks."

"What did you think of Owen when you spoke to him?" Bessie interjected.

"He trotted out the same sort of nonsense that Edmund had given me. He did admit that he wasn't interested in owning part of a retail park, that all he wanted to do was buy into the deal and get the contract for building the place. He was very upfront about his plans to sell his share as soon as the construction phase was complete."

"Is that normal?" Bessie asked.

Dan laughed. "Define normal. Owen Oliver has been doing this for long enough that he can make his own rules."

"Why would George agree to something like that?" Doona wondered.

"Owen would do the work for a better price than George could get if he hired an outside firm. Owen would get a big contract on the island, one that would give him a foot in the door here, something he's eager to get, I'm sure."

"I don't understand big business," Bessie sighed.

"I spend a lot of time studying it and I'm not sure I understand much of it," Dan admitted. "The only thing I'm certain of is that just about every businessman I've met has been shady."

"Not George," Bessie said firmly.

"Not now, anyway," Dan agreed.

"What about the other two men?" Doona asked. "Had you heard of either of them before?"

"I'm sure I'd heard of Ted Pearson before, but I can't remember where or when," Dan told her. "He's very American-surfer cool, but he's a very shrewd businessman under the breezy demeanor. I wouldn't partner with him on anything, myself, but I'm sure he has a lot to offer George."

"Like what?" Bessie asked.

"He wants to bring his shop to the island. It's huge with a certain segment of the US population. Wealthy young people seem to love his clothes and the other things his shop sells. He hasn't found a spot for a shop in the UK yet. Having one on the island could actually drive some retail tourists here, something I never thought I'd say about the island."

"Retail tourist?" Doona echoed.

"Young men and women who would come over here simply to shop," Dan explained. "Ted wants to include a small boutique hotel in the retail park. Imagine people flying over and going straight to the shops. They'd shop, eat, and sleep, all within the confines of the retail park, and then fly home again."

"What a hideous idea," Bessie said.

Dan chuckled. "But it could be good for the island."

"And that's what Ted wants to do if he signs a deal with George?" Doona asked.

"In theory. I suspect he'll find a spot he likes better across, though.

He doesn't want London, but he'd be happy with just about any other major city or town in the UK. It's just a matter of time before he finds what he wants at a price he likes. I think that he'll do the deal with George and put a shop here if he hasn't found anything else in the next few months, but I think that once he finds what he'd rather have, he'll pull his shop out of the island and the entire retail park project will collapse."

"How awful. I wonder if George has any idea," Bessie said.

"As I said earlier, George is very smart. I'm sure he knows exactly what Ted is planning. And I'm sure he has plans in place to stop him, as well, if he's actually considering doing a deal with Ted, which I doubt," Dan told her.

"Someone mentioned that Ted's father had some sort of trouble with the police recently," Doona remarked.

Dan nodded. "I asked him about that, but he refused to address the issue. My research suggests that his father was paying for women to attend parties he was throwing for his business associates. His defense was that he was paying for them to be there but that was all. If the women found the male guests attractive and chose to spend the night with them, then that was their choice."

"How awful," Doona said.

"The defense didn't fool anyone, but Ted's father still got off on a technicality. When you have the sort of money that he has, you can buy technicalities, I believe."

Bessie frowned. "Did you find anything to suggest that Ted was involved in any of what happened?"

"Not at all. Ted has been living in the UK, more or less, for the past several years. He visits the US, but rarely spends any time with his father. I asked him about that, too, but he simply told me that he and his father are both busy men who see one another when time permits. When I suggested that they may have had a falling-out, he simply laughed."

"I can't see Harrison being interested in that story, then," Bessie sighed.

"No, me neither," Dan agreed.

"That just leaves Nicholas Taylor," Bessie said.

"It does, doesn't it?" Dan replied. "He owns malls, not retail parks. Oh, he said all the right things when I spoke to him. He told me how the island probably isn't ready for a mall but desperately needs this retail park, and that he was considering a number of options, including some sort of arrangement with Owen if that was what George preferred."

"You sound as if you didn't believe him," Bessie remarked.

"I didn't believe a word of it. He wants a mall, probably a fairly small one, although I could see him pushing for something substantial, again building for retail tourists. He's prepared to do a deal with George at the moment, but I can see him pushing for extending the planning permission once he came onboard."

"It's already a fairly large retail park, isn't it?" Bessie asked. "I've been told there will be shops, restaurants, and offices, and you said there might be a hotel, too."

"It will be the largest retail space on the island, but that isn't saying much, really," Dan told her.

Bessie shrugged. "What else did Nicholas have to say?"

"Nothing. He said the least, really, only doing the bare minimum of what was required of him. He gave his statement about how excited he is to have this wonderful opportunity, and that was about all."

"And you don't know anything else about him?" Doona asked.

"I did do my research, but it didn't turn up much. He keeps a fairly low profile. There were some security issues at one of his malls recently, but he threw a ton of money at the problem and it went away almost overnight," Dan said.

"Security issues?" Bessie repeated.

"Mostly just kids trying to cause trouble. Large groups of them started hanging out at the mall and there were a few issues between some of the groups. Nicholas's company put policies into place that restricted children under eighteen from even being in the mall without a parent and brought in dozens of extra security officers. The first day they made over a hundred teens leave the mall because they were unaccompanied. That was pretty much the end of the problem," Dan explained.

"I have two questions for you, now that you've met them all," Bessie said. "Which one do you think George will make his deal with, and which one do you think killed Harrison?"

Dan shook his head. "I don't know George well enough to answer the first question. If I were him, I'd probably go with Owen, at least for now. That would at least get the place built. The other three all seem likely to lose interest between now and opening day. The problem with going with Owen, of course, is that he doesn't want any part of the finished product. Construction will take at least a year, probably more. I can't honestly see any of the men I met today still being interested in it a year or more from now."

"Poor George," Bessie murmured.

"He'll be fine," Dan laughed. "He could afford to fund the whole thing himself, of course, or he could get any bank on the island to lend him some of the funding. He partnered with Alastair because he wanted to work with him, not because he needed the money. Now he's looking for another partner who can help make the project a success. He wants to limit his risk and share the workload. I suspect, if he doesn't find someone soon, he'll start thinking about selling the land and moving on to something else."

"I don't really think the island needs another retail park," Bessie said.

"And I don't think George did enough research into what the island actually does need," Dan told her. "I think Alastair was the driving force behind it initially and I suspect George would love to have an excuse to cancel the entire thing."

Bessie raised an eyebrow. "Interesting," she said.

"And just speculation that I probably shouldn't be repeating," Dan said. "It's a good thing you don't write for the *Isle of Man Times*. I'd hate to see my random thoughts in tomorrow's paper."

"I think we all feel that way, all the time," Bessie said.

Dan flushed. "As to your second question, I have no idea on that, either."

"You must have some suspicions," Bessie said.

"Not really. I didn't like any of them and I'm fairly certain none of them would hesitate to kill someone who stood in his way."

"Do you think they're all capable of doing the job themselves?" Bessie asked.

Dan frowned. "That's an interesting point. These are men who have staff to deal with life's little annoyances. Maybe, when Harrison confronted one of them, he felt as if he didn't have a choice."

"Maybe," Bessie replied thoughtfully.

Dan glanced at the clock. "As fascinating as this has been, I really must go. I have a story to finish before five. I'd love a quote, something about how devastated you are to have found another body," he told Bessie.

Bessie shook her head. "No comment," she said firmly.

Dan laughed. "And now we're back to being enemies, I suppose. It's been an odd day, but I do appreciate your time. If you could please work out who killed Harrison by the end of the day, I'd be grateful."

He'd turned and let himself out before Bessie could reply.

CHAPTER 9

"Work out who killed Harrison by the end of the day," Bessie echoed as the door slammed shut. "What a ridiculous notion."

Doona laughed. "I'm sure Dan doesn't really expect you to solve the case by the end of the day. He was just teasing."

"It wasn't funny. I knew I didn't like that man."

"Perhaps you should..." Doona was interrupted by her mobile phone. She pulled it out of her bag and then frowned at it. "I really need to take this," she told Bessie as she stood up.

"Use the sitting room," Bessie suggested.

Doona nodded and walked out of the room, already talking into her phone.

Bessie did the washing-up and then tidied the kitchen. While she heard an occasional monosyllable from the sitting room, she had no idea who Doona was speaking to or why they'd rung. Eventually, she began to poke through her cupboards, looking for inspiration for dinner. Nothing sounded good, and she thought that she would probably need to walk up to the shop at the top of the hill before she could eat.

"Sorry about that," Doona said as she walked back into the kitchen.

"Is everything okay?" Bessie asked, taking in Doona's frown.

Doona shrugged. "That was my solicitor across. He and Doncan have been working to get Charles's estate settled. It should have been done ages ago, but that's another matter. Anyway, he was ringing to tell me that things are finally falling into place. Now I just have to decide what I want to do with everything."

"Define everything," Bessie said.

"Charles owned partial shares in a number of hotels across the UK. In many cases, he only owned a tiny percentage of the property. Herbert Howe gave the shares to him whenever he hit particular financial targets in the business. It looks as if I'll now own something like two per cent of a hotel in Birmingham, four per cent of a hotel in Brighton, et cetera. My solicitor has been working with Herbert to establish a fair market value for each hotel and they've arrived at a number. Herbert has offered to pay me that amount to buy out all of the shares."

"That seems sensible, unless you wanted to keep them for some reason?"

"Not really. I mean, I suppose I'd be entitled to a share of the profits from each property if I kept them, but it all sounds as if it would be an accounting nightmare. I've never really had any interest in owning hotels and I certainly don't want any part in managing them."

"Fair enough. Did you tell your solicitor to agree, then?"

"Not yet. I want to talk to John first and I want some time to think. Once I've agreed, I can't go back and change my mind, so I need to be sure."

"Of course."

"Then there's the holiday park," Doona added. "Once everything is settled, I'll own half of the holiday park."

"That has to be worth a great deal, doesn't it?"

"Yes and no. The business isn't doing all that well, really. Harold Butler is a lovely man, but he isn't the best manager in the world. Charles was sent there to help improve the bottom line, but he didn't live long enough to make a difference. Now Harold is back in charge and profits aren't where they should be."

"I'm surprised that Herbert hasn't let Harold go."

"The court case against Lawrence Jenkins and the issues with Charles's will kept things tied up for the past year. Now that everything is about to be settled, that's exactly what he wants to do. He also wants to buy my share so that he'll be the sole owner."

"You don't sound happy about that."

"I don't know what I am. It's crazy for me to think about owning half of a holiday park in the UK. I've no interest in helping to manage it and I can't even imagine visiting more than once in an odd while, but I'm strangely reluctant to sell it, maybe just because it's my last connection to Charles."

"About whom you still care deeply."

Doona flushed. "I'm crazy in love with John, but yes, I still care about Charles. I loved him a great deal and, if I'm honest, I'm really sorry that I didn't get a chance to hear what he wanted to say to me when I saw him that last time. John and I talked about it the other day, actually. He still cares about Sue and was devastated by her death. That doesn't mean that he loves me any less, though."

Bessie nodded. She'd never stopped loving Matthew Saunders, but there had been another man in her life, years later. In the end, she'd turned down his offer of marriage because she hadn't been prepared to give up everything she'd worked so hard to build for herself, but she understood what Doona was saying. "So what are you going to do?"

"Talk to John, talk to myself, probably cry," Doona replied with a sigh. "Apparently, Doncan insisted that the two deals be completely separate, so that I can agree to sell the hotel shares and not the holiday park share, or vice versa. I think he knows me better than I know myself. If it were all one big deal, I'd have a much more difficult decision to make."

"You want to keep the holiday park," Bessie said.

"I do, but it isn't logical."

"So what? I'm sure if you change your mind in a year or two or ten," you'll be able to find a buyer. Selling lots of little bits of hotels might be difficult, but there must be plenty of people who'd want to buy half of a holiday park."

"Herbert would get first refusal, if I don't sell to him now, but I can't see why that matters. He'd have to pay me the average between three assessments of the business, so it isn't as if he could cheat me in any way. I just need to think about it, really."

"You need to talk to John, too."

"Yeah, maybe I should ring him."

"We were supposed to ring him when Dan left, anyway."

Doona nodded and then pulled out her mobile. "I'll send him a text that Dan is gone. The other issue needs to be talked about in person." She sent the text and then laughed when her phone buzzed just a moment later. "He's on his way," she told Bessie.

"That was fast."

"Maybe he was bored."

John was at the door a few minutes later. "Please tell me that Dan had something useful for you," he said tiredly.

Bessie and Doona did their best to repeat everything that Dan had said. John took notes, but he didn't look very happy when they were done.

"There isn't much there," he complained.

"I don't think Dan thought it was very helpful, either," Bessie said.

"I'm going to have to pull him in for more questioning," John sighed. "I hate that he knew that Harrison had been stabbed. We've no way to know who else he might have shared that fact with."

"It's true, then?" Bessie asked.

"Yes, it's true," John confirmed.

"Did you get a chance to talk to the paper's receptionist?" Doona asked.

He nodded. "And as she knew nothing at all, I can even talk about it."

"Nothing?" Bessie repeated.

"According to her, she and Harrison went out exactly twice. They had fun but there was no chemistry. That was about four months ago, and she never spoke to him again after he left the island," John said.

"So it's unlikely she killed him," Doona said.

"She has an alibi anyway," John told her. "She was at a newspaper event, actually. Just about everyone from the *Isle of Man Times* was there. She had to be there early, to set up, and she stayed late to help with the cleanup. Unless the coroner got the time range wrong for Harrison's time of death, there's no way the receptionist killed him."

"This event, was Dan there, then?" Bessie asked.

"Interestingly, he was notable in his absence. Apparently, he was supposed to be there, but he never arrived."

"That's something else you can ask him about, then," Bessie said.

John nodded. "I have a lot of questions for Dan."

"In that case, we should let you go," Doona said.

John looked startled. "I don't need to rush away. I was going to wait and have Dan brought in tomorrow morning. Do you think it's more urgent than that?"

Doona sighed and shook her head. "I just spent ages on the phone with my solicitor. Things are moving forward with the settlement, but now I have to make some decisions."

"And you hate making decisions," John said, putting his hand over hers.

"I don't even want to talk about the decisions," she said in a low voice.

"But decisions have to be made," Bessie said firmly. "If you two want privacy, I can go for a walk."

"No, that's okay," Doona said. "You've already heard it all anyway." She told John everything that she'd already told Bessie. "I think I want to sell the hotel shares to Herbert. There seems little point in keeping them. It's the holiday park that is the problem."

John nodded. "If you keep it, it will generate an income for you from the profits, right?"

"Yes, and a pretty decent income, too. More than I currently make working part-time, anyway," she replied.

"If you sell it, you can't change your mind later, but if you keep it, you can decide to sell later," John said.

Doona nodded. "That's what I keep thinking, even though the idea of owning half of a holiday park is insane."

"You already own it, crazy or not," John pointed out. "Why not keep it for now and see how it goes?"

Doona blurted out an amount of money that made Bessie's eyes water.

"That's what Herbert is offering for my share of the holiday park," she said. "You could quit work, too. We could travel."

"I'm not interested in quitting my job. I love what I do," he replied. "And as for travel, until the kids are through school and uni, I don't know that I'd want to go far."

Doona nodded. "It isn't as if we need the money. I'll already be getting another lump sum from the hotel shares, although it isn't anywhere near that much. Regardless, I think I want to keep my share of the park, for now, anyway."

"Do you feel better for having made a decision?" Bessie asked.

Doona nodded. "Much better, actually. It may not be the right decision, but it's the right decision for right now. Did that make sense? I'm talking nonsense now."

John and Bessie both laughed.

"I think we should go out for dinner to celebrate," John said. "I have to go back to the office to finish up some paperwork, but the kids both have other plans for dinner. Let's go somewhere nice."

"What are the kids doing?" Doona asked.

"Thomas is taking a girl from his English class out for a meal," John told her. "Her mother is driving. Thomas keeps insisting that it's just friendly, but that's mostly because Amy keeps teasing him about having a girlfriend. Amy is going to a friend's house after school. The friend's mother has promised to feed her because they're going to be working on a project for hours and hours, apparently."

"Which means they're going to be laughing and talking for hours and hours and may or may not get around to their project," Doona guessed.

"Probably," John agreed. "So, dinner?"

"Sure, why not."

"Bessie, would you like to join us?" John asked.

"That's very kind of you, but this is your celebration," Bessie replied. "I'm sure you could get a table at the Seaview."

"Their food is excellent, but it's expensive," Doona said.

"I think I can afford it," John laughed. He pulled out his mobile. "Do you know the number?" he asked Bessie.

She did, because the hotel was owned by a dear friend. "Ask for Jasper and tell him that I suggested that you have dinner there," she instructed John as he punched in the numbers. The conversation was short.

"Jasper hopes that you'll be gracing his establishment with your presence again soon," he said. "He said they have a number of affordable specials tonight. Apparently, it's their off-season."

"It is," Bessie replied.

"I should go home and change clothes," Doona said.

"You look lovely just the way you are," John countered. "But you have two hours before our booking, if you want to get more dressed up."

"I feel as if I should," Doona told him. As she started to get to her feet, John's mobile rang.

"John Rockwell," he said as he stood up. He disappeared into Bessie's sitting room, only to reappear a moment later.

"I'm not going to be able to make dinner," he said apologetically to Doona. "We have a missing child case in Ramsey."

"Oh, no," Doona exclaimed.

"I'll ring you when I can. If I won't be home by ten, maybe you could be there when the kids get in?"

"Of course I can."

"Take Bessie to the Seaview," he added on his way to the door. "You still deserve to celebrate tonight."

He was gone before Doona could reply.

"Would you like to go to the Seaview for dinner?" Doona asked.

"I'm not going to say no, although I should because I've been eating biscuits nearly all day and I'm not going to be hungry enough to truly enjoy the food. I wish John had told us more about the missing child, though."

"You know you can find out more easily enough. He was in a hurry."

"And rightly so. I'm just nosy," Bessie laughed. Her phone rang a moment later. When she put it down, she frowned at Doona.

"A little girl called Sarah Hansen didn't come out of school at the end of the day to meet her mother, who was waiting outside. Sarah is six, and the family has only been on the island for a few months. Obviously, Sarah's parents are distraught. They've searched the school and now they're searching the surrounding area."

"Those poor parents. I think I'm glad I didn't have to worry about Thomas and Amy when they were that small," Doona said.

"I can't imagine what they must be feeling," Bessie said. "I wish there was some way to help, but I'm sure the police have everything in hand."

Doona pulled out her phone and rang someone. "The police are doing a methodical search with the help of dozens of volunteer parents from the school. Right now there's nothing we can do to help."

"I'm going to feel guilty going out for a nice meal while poor Sarah is missing," Bessie said.

"But Jasper is expecting us," Doona pointed out.

"That's true," Bessie sighed.

"I'm going to go home and change. Maybe there will be some news on Sarah by the time I get back."

While Doona was gone, Bessie went upstairs and changed into a nice grey dress and low heels. The Seaview had some of the best food on the island and it was worth dressing up for. She combed her hair and touched up her makeup, and then paced around her kitchen until Doona returned.

"No news," Doona said. "I'm not sure about dinner."

"You look lovely, though," Bessie said.

"Thanks."

The pair sat and stared at one another for several minutes, until Bessie looked at the clock. "We need to go if we're going to be on time," she said.

"I know. I just feel guilty."

"Ring Jasper and cancel," Bessie suggested.

"No, let's go. There isn't anything we can do, really. I checked again before I drove back here, and they have more volunteers than they know what to do with at this point. John told me they might need more help after dark, though. Maybe there will be something we can do after dinner."

The drive into Ramsey didn't take long. Doona parked in the large and mostly empty car park and then the pair made their way into the building. They were following the long corridor to the restaurant when Doona's phone buzzed.

"They found her," she said happily.

"Oh, thank heavens," Bessie exclaimed.

"John didn't give me any details, but they found her, at least."

"I should go home so he can meet you for dinner."

"He's probably got two or three hours' worth of paperwork to do. I'll take something home for him," Doona replied.

Bessie's friend, Jasper Coventry, greeted them at the door.

"Ah, Bessie, I didn't realise you were coming this evening," he said.

"I wasn't meant to be, but John was called to work on a missing person case," Bessie explained.

"Ah, yes, I heard," Jasper said sadly. "That poor little girl and her poor parents."

"She was found," Doona told him.

"She was?" he asked, beaming happily.

"She was. I don't know any more than that, but John texted me that much."

"Oh, thank goodness," Jasper said. "I was so worried."

"We all were," Bessie said.

He nodded. "They stayed here for a week when they first moved to the island. I got to know little Sarah quite well. She has a fondness for tiny spaces and hiding herself inside them. I kept hoping that she'd simply found herself a small hiding place and stayed there without realising the trouble she was causing."

Doona laughed as she looked up from her phone. "That's almost exactly what happened, apparently. John just texted to say that they found her in the school, even though it had already been searched several times. Apparently, she crawled inside a cupboard and then fell asleep. When she woke up, it was dark and she wasn't sure where she was. One of the constables heard her crying and found her."

"I'm so glad," Jasper said. "Does that mean that Inspector Rockwell will be joining you as well?"

"He'll be at the station for at least a couple of hours, doing paperwork," Doona told him. "I'll order a meal for him for takeaway when we're done, if that's all right?"

"Of course it is, and it will be on me, as I'm so pleased that he found Sarah."

Doona tried to argue, but Jasper wouldn't be swayed.

"Now, where would you like to sit? We have a large group coming in shortly. Shall I put you on the other side of the room?" he asked.

"That sounds good," Bessie said.

"You and Mary Quayle are friends, of course. Perhaps you'd like to sit near her," Jasper said.

"Mary Quayle?" Bessie echoed, feeling confused.

"I'm not making much sense, am I?" Jasper laughed. "I'm still all discombobulated because of Sarah. Mary and George are bringing five of their dearest friends for dinner tonight. That's the large party I mentioned earlier."

Bessie and Doona exchanged glances. "Maybe we should sit near them," Bessie said hesitantly.

Doona nodded. "At least you can point out who they all are."

"Unless Mary and George are having dinner with someone else altogether."

"What are the chances?"

Bessie nodded. It seemed very unlikely that the pair would be with anyone other than the four men staying at Thie yn Traie, although she had no idea as to the identity of the fifth guest.

"How's this?" Jasper asked, showing them to a table that was behind a small screen. The larger table that was ready for Mary and the others was just on the other side of the screen.

"Perfect," Doona said.

"You aren't totally hidden back there," Jasper said as they took their seats. "I can have another screen moved over, if you want to be completely out of sight."

"No, don't," Bessie told him. "We aren't spying on them, after all."

Jasper nodded, but he didn't look convinced.

Doona laughed. "We truly aren't," she said.

He handed them menus and then rattled off the list of specials. "I recommend the chicken," he said when he was done. "It's one of my favourites, and our chef only makes it once or twice a year, mostly to annoy me, I'm sure."

Bessie laughed. "You'll have to give me time to read the whole menu before I order the chicken. Reading the menu is one of my favourite parts of coming here."

As Jasper walked away, Doona opened her menu and sighed. "Who writes their descriptions?" she asked. "Every single thing sounds amazing in the descriptions."

"I'm sure it's all delicious, too," Bessie said. "I've never had a bad meal here."

"Me neither. John and I don't come often, but it's very special to us. We had dinner here back when we were just friends, that night when Lora White discovered that all of her tablets had been switched around. He needed an excuse to show up here while you were eating with Lora, remember?"

"I do remember. I wasn't sure whom he was meeting and I was quite concerned about it, actually."

Doona laughed. "We had such a nice time that evening. We talked about nothing and everything and sort of tentatively explored the idea of maybe thinking about being more than friends. That was before Sue fell ill, of course. That changed everything."

"But things are going well now, right?"

"Almost too well. I'm afraid something awful is going to happen one of these days."

"I think you've already had your fair share of awful," Bessie said. "Your second husband was murdered. John's ex-wife died under mysterious circumstances. Your solicitor tried to cheat you out of a fortune. Shall I go on?"

"No, you're quite right, I suppose. We have had a lot of terrible things happen. That may be why I'm so afraid to enjoy things now."

"Life is too short to waste time worrying about what's around the next corner," Bessie said firmly. "You and John seem to have something very special. Enjoy every minute of it and if it all falls apart one day, remember the good and then move on."

Doona stared at her for a moment and then laughed. "Those are very wise words," she said.

"I'm a wise woman," Bessie shot back before she grinned at Doona. "Seriously, though, I'm really happy for you and John. I hope it does work out. You both deserve happiness, and so do Thomas and Amy."

"I never wanted children, particularly, but now I can't imagine my life without those two in it. I love them both so much it scares me."

"I believe that's how parenting is meant to feel."

"Yeah, like having a large portion of your heart walking around outside your body," Doona said.

Bessie nodded. "You're very brave, taking on two teenagers, really."

"I can't have John without them. He wouldn't be the man I love without them, either. It's a wonderful, weird, wacky package deal."

Movement near the entrance caught Bessie's attention. She nodded towards the door. "They're here."

Doona looked over at the group that was following Jasper towards them. "Want to tell me who everyone is?"

"I can just introduce you. That might be easier."

Doona nodded. "I already know which one is Ted. There's only one blond surfer guy."

"Owen is the shortest one. Nicholas is the bald one, and that just leaves Edmund," Bessie told her. "The other woman is Carolyn White.

She's George's assistant, but I've never known her to socialise with the family."

By the time she'd finished speaking, the group had reached the table next to them. Mary glanced over and then smiled brightly at Bessie.

"What a lovely surprise," she said, crossing to their table.

Bessie stood up and gave her friend a hug. The men were busy selecting seats around the table. From where Bessie was standing, it seemed as if everyone wanted to sit next to George.

"Leave that seat for Mary," George told Ted as he moved to sit on George's right.

"Of course," Ted said smoothly, moving down one seat.

"I couldn't take one more night at home with them," Mary whispered. "I told George we had to go out somewhere. I'm hoping that being in public will keep the conversation light and stop the arguing."

"What are they arguing about?" Bessie asked.

"Anything, everything, nothing," Mary sighed. "Mostly they're all trying to score points with George by making the others look bad. They're all upset about the murder, of course, and I'm sure they're all looking at one another and wondering if one of them actually killed a man. Tensions are high and we needed a break. Dinner here was as close as we could get to a proper break."

"Maybe the men should get rooms here," Bessie suggested.

Mary flushed. "You'll think I'm terrible, but I was hoping maybe, when they saw how lovely the Seaview is, that one or more of them might decide to move here."

Bessie grinned. "I don't think you're horrible at all."

"Mary?" George called. "Is that Bessie? Does she want to join us?"

Bessie looked at Doona and then shook her head. "Thank you for the kind invitation, but Doona and I don't want to intrude on your evening," she said. "It is nice to see you all again, though," she told the men.

She didn't bother to note who muttered replies. Instead, she waved a hand at Doona, who stood up.

"This is my friend, Doona Moore," she said. "Doona, these are the gentlemen who are working with George on the retail park."

Doona smiled and gave the men a small wave.

"Hello, hello," Edmund said. "It's a real pleasure to meet you. Are you quite certain you don't want to join us? We can make a space for you right here, next to me."

"That's very kind of you, but Bessie and I have a lot to discuss and then I have to get home to my, um, boyfriend," Doona replied, blushing on the last word.

"Of course she has a boyfriend," Nicholas said. "Beautiful women are always taken."

George laughed. "Her boyfriend is a police inspector. You'd better be very careful what you say to her. And Doona, you'd better know everyone's names, in case you need to complain to Inspector Rockwell about any of them." He went around the table, introducing each man to Doona in turn.

"It's very nice to meet you all," Doona said when he was done.

"And you must know Carolyn. She's been my assistant for years," George added.

Doona shook her head. "I don't believe we've met. It's nice to meet you, as well," she told the blonde woman, who was frowning from her seat between Ted and Owen.

Carolyn nodded and then picked up her menu.

"Are you quite certain you won't join us?" George asked.

"I don't blame you for not wanting to," Mary said in a whisper. "I'd join you if I could."

"Why don't you?" Bessie asked.

Mary shook her head. "That's out of the question, but thank you." She turned to George with a resigned smile. "Let's let Bessie and Doona enjoy their dinner while we enjoy ours. Did you order wine yet?" She walked over and took her seat next to George while Bessie and Doona returned to their seats.

A moment later waiters appeared at both tables. Bessie and Doona ordered soft drinks, while George ordered multiple bottles of wine for his table. The drinks arrived minutes later. After their waiter repeated the specials, Bessie ordered the chicken dish that Jasper had recommended. After a moment's hesitation, Doona did the same.

At the next table, two waiters were pouring wine for everyone. Bessie listened as one of them explained the specials. No one seemed particularly interested in the food as they guzzled down their first glasses of wine. Only Mary seemed to be paying attention. She ordered the same chicken dish that Bessie and Doona had ordered. The others seemed almost to be ordering at random as the waiter worked his way around the table. Before the waiter was finished, George had requested two more bottles of wine.

"They're all going to be very drunk soon," Doona remarked.

"Maybe that will make for interesting conversation," Bessie replied.

"I'm surprised how well we can hear what they're all saying."

"We're fairly close and no one is making any effort to keep his or her voice down," Bessie pointed out.

"Some of them seem to be trying to talk loudly, actually. Ted seems to be shouting."

"And George is never quiet," Bessie laughed.

CHAPTER 10

"*Y*ou have better wine at home," Edmund said to George.

"The wine cellar came with the house," George replied.

"Fully stocked?" Edmund demanded.

"I've added a few bottles, but we've also drunk quite a few," George laughed. "The Pierce family sold the house with everything inside."

"The circumstances were unusual, of course," Nicholas said. "I can't believe they didn't take the wine, though."

"Did they truly leave everything behind?" Ted asked. "What about clothes?"

"As the house was only a summer home for them, they didn't have much in the way of clothes on the island," Mary said. "They took the clothes they'd brought for their week's holiday back with them, but they did leave a few things in some of the wardrobes around the house."

"What did you do with everything?" Ted asked.

Mary shrugged. "We donated nearly everything to charity."

"Why does Ted care?" Doona whispered to Bessie.

"I think he's just being nosy," Bessie whispered back.

The waiter arrived with their starters, and for a moment the two women focussed on eating. The other table received their starters at the same time, so the conversation stopped.

"Isn't that the reporter who was so annoying this afternoon?" Ted demanded suddenly.

Bessie followed his gaze and saw Dan Ross standing in the restaurant's entrance.

"Yes, that's Dan Ross," George said. "I wonder what he's doing here."

Dan was speaking to Jasper. After a minute, he nodded and then turned and left.

"At least he didn't stay," Ted said. "I was expecting him to ask for a table near ours so that he could eavesdrop on our conversation."

"I was, too," Nicholas said.

"Maybe he's going to sneak in another way," Owen suggested, looking around the room.

"Bessie, darling, you will warn us if you see Dan Ross sneaking in somewhere, won't you?" Ted called.

"Certainly," Bessie replied.

Ted laughed. "Unless she's working with him."

Mary chuckled. "Bessie wouldn't do that," she said firmly.

Bessie glanced around the room. There was another entrance along the back wall, but there was no way that Dan could get in that way without everyone in the room seeing him.

"I wonder why he's here," Doona said in a low voice.

"Maybe he wanted dinner, but changed his mind when he saw George and his guests," Bessie suggested.

"Maybe," Doona shrugged.

"He asked me all sorts of questions that had nothing to do with the retail park," Ted complained.

"No doubt he did the same with all of us," Edmund said. "He was probably looking for material for an article about the murder investigation. That would sell more papers than an article about a retail park that may never get built."

"Now, now," George said. "I'm committed to the retail park project, even if none of you decide to come on board."

"George, the right partner can mean the difference between success and failure," Carolyn interjected.

"Of course," George replied, giving her a bright smile.

Edmund shrugged. "We were talking about that reporter. He threw out a ton of questions about anything and everything, probably hoping to get a reaction and a quote for his next article. I hope I didn't give him anything he could use, aside from what I said about the retail park, of course."

"He was very interested in my US company," Ted said.

"He was very interested in my ex-wives," Edmund told him. "And he wanted to know my plans for the ferry bid, too. I didn't tell him anything."

"He asked me about the tragic accident that happened on my building site. Of course, I told him nothing," Owen said.

"Mostly, aside from the retail park project, he asked me about the murder investigation," Nicholas said. "He wanted to talk about the victim, as if I knew the man."

"He did the same with me, suggesting that I'd met him or at least spoken to him once or twice," Owen said. "I just laughed in his face."

"I thought about telling him that I did meet him before his death, just to see how he'd react," Ted said. "I didn't because I knew everything I said would be in the papers tomorrow, which means the police would hear it and that would be awkward, as I've already told them I'd never met him."

"None of us ever met him," Nicholas complained. "And none of us killed him, but the police don't have anything better to do than harass us."

Doona drew a sharp breath. Bessie put her hand on Doona's arm. When Doona looked at her, she shook her head slightly.

"The man was wandering around on a deserted beach in the middle of the night," Nicholas said. "He was probably killed by a homeless person."

"I don't think that's very likely," Mary said.

"It's as likely as one of us killing him," Ted said. "Anyway, I understand he used to live on the island. No doubt he left some enemies behind."

"He was a reporter. Of course he had enemies," Edmund agreed.

"Let's talk about something more pleasant," Mary suggested. "My starter was excellent. I hope you all enjoyed yours?"

"Mine was good," Owen said. "Not as good as anything your friend prepared for us the other day, but good."

"I'm still determined to get that man to come to work for me," Edmund said.

"He doesn't want to leave the island," Mary said.

"Well, I'm not moving here," Edmund retorted.

"I'm afraid you'll have to live without Andy's cooking, then," Mary replied.

"I was thinking about trying to hire your butler away," Ted said. "He's a very proper English butler. My American friends would be very impressed."

George shrugged. "He's only here temporarily. Our regular butler is on a course at the moment. Geoffrey came from an agency. He'll be available again in another six weeks."

"Really?" Ted asked. "Interesting."

"I don't like him," Owen said. "He seems to be everywhere all the time."

"That's the best part," Ted laughed. "Every time I want something, there he is, just hovering, waiting to be needed. It's amazing."

"I had a butler when I was married to my second wife," Edmund said. "She thought it was posh, but then she had an affair with him."

"With the butler? I thought wives were supposed to have affairs with the chauffeur," Ted laughed.

"That was my third wife," Edmund replied. "And two or three of my fiancées, as well. After the last one, I finally stopped hiring men under sixty to drive for me."

"I've never had a butler," Nicholas said. "I don't have a lot of staff, actually. I have a team that comes in to clean once a week and a cook who makes all my meals. That's about it, aside from my driver and my personal assistant."

"That's it?" Doona laughed softly.

Bessie shrugged. "I wouldn't mind a cook."

"I could do with a team to clean," Doona said. "My house and John's."

"Surely that's what the children are for," Bessie teased.

"They actually do quite a lot," Doona told her. "John was giving them more and more responsibilities the longer they were here because he simply didn't have time to do it all himself. Now that I'm helping out, they try to get away with doing less, but I'm starting to push back."

"Good for you."

Doona shrugged. "They're going to be going out on their own soon. They need to learn how to look after a house and how to feed themselves."

"Unless they get a cook and a team of cleaners," Bessie laughed.

"I hope the police asked the butler about the murder," Owen said. "He seems to know everything about everything that happens at Thie yn Traie. He must know who was tucked up in bed when the murder happened."

"If he did, he'd also know who the killer was," Edmund argued. "The police would have already arrested someone."

"Unless the killer didn't come from Thie yn Traie, which is what I've been saying all along," Ted said.

"Maybe someone followed this Harrison Parker person from the UK, killed him, and then went back home without even being noticed," Owen suggested.

"Why are the police so certain that the killing is tied to Thie yn Traie, anyway?" Nicholas demanded. "Maybe the dead man stumbled across a drug deal on the beach that night. It seems the perfect place for that sort of thing."

Bessie made a face.

"He would probably be right anywhere but the Isle of Man," Doona said quietly.

"We could speculate all night about why the man was on the beach that night and what he might have interrupted," Ted said. "I can't see what good such speculation will do, though."

"It's interesting, anyway," Edmund said. "The possibilities seem endless and yet the police keep focussing on us."

"Not just the police. I'm sure that reporter thinks one of us killed the man," Owen said.

"I don't suppose any of you want to confess, just to make things easier for the rest of us?" Ted asked.

A few of the men laughed.

"I don't think so," Owen said. "I wouldn't be tempted, even if I had killed the man, but since I didn't, I certainly don't intend to confess."

"Of course, you'd say that even if you had killed him," Ted said. "We're all busy protesting our innocence, but someone killed him. Edmund, which of us do you think is most likely to have been the killer?"

Edmund stared at Ted for a moment and then shook his head. "What an odd question. I've not given the matter any thought and I don't intend to waste my time with pointless speculation. Let's leave the police to deal with all of that, shall we?"

"They don't seem to be getting anywhere," Ted argued. "Owen, what do you think? Who killed Harrison Peters?"

"The man's name was Harrison Parker," Mary interrupted.

Ted waved a hand. "Peters, Parker, whatever. Owen, who killed him?"

"Maybe you," Owen shot back. "Maybe he discovered that you haven't been paying your taxes in the US. As I understand it, the IRS is much scarier than our Inland Revenue."

Ted laughed. "That's what I want, ideas," he said. "I might have killed him to cover up for not paying my taxes, as well, except I am paying my taxes, sadly. But it's a start. What sort of motive can you suggest for Nicholas?" he asked Owen.

Owen shrugged. "I haven't the foggiest idea. Shady business practices, probably, but that's the same thing that reporter could have had on any of us."

"Not me," Edmund said firmly. "I keep a close eye on my businesses and I keep everything strictly legal and ethical."

"So it must have been your personal life that Harrison was investigating, if you killed him," Owen said. "Let's face it, your personal life is a mess."

Edmund flushed and then took a sip of wine. Bessie could almost see him counting to ten in his head before he replied. "My personal life is solely my concern. I'm not doing anything illegal or unethical personally, either."

"But I'd be willing to bet some of your former, um, companions would love to sell a story or two to the papers," Owen said. "If nothing else, there's probably a small percentage of the UK population that would love to hear about your prowess in bed. 'Multimillionaire Businessman's Weird Lovemaking Habits' would make a great headline."

"Too bad I don't have any weird habits," Edmund snapped.

"I'm sure at least one of your exes would disagree," Ted laughed.

Edmund frowned. "This is a pointless conversation."

As the waiters began to clear away the empty starter plates and deliver everyone's main course, Doona turned to Bessie.

"They're all turning on each other," she whispered.

"It's awful to watch."

"But we could learn something interesting."

"So far, I think all we've learned is that they all dislike one another."

"They're rivals for a business deal. That's hardly surprising."

"I don't know. It seems to go deeper than that," Bessie said. She cut into her chicken, smiling as it almost fell apart under her efforts. "Delicious," she murmured after her first bite.

"So Nicholas and I are doing something shady that the reporter discovered, Edmund has issues in his personal life, and Ted is cheating on his taxes. Did I get all of that correct?" Owen asked.

"If that was all right, then we'd all have solid motives for the murder," Ted said. "It seems more likely that only one of those things is right, though."

143

"Well, we all know Edmund's personal life is a car crash, so let's just assume that he did it," Owen suggested.

Edmund turned bright red. "That's insane. My personal life is absolutely fine, and I didn't kill anyone. I didn't know Harrison Parker. He never contacted me to ask me any questions about anything. Whoever killed him had to first know that he was here. That rules me out."

"Which you'd say even if you were the one who met him on the beach the night he died," Nicholas pointed out.

"We're just going around in circles," Edmund said. "Carolyn, where were you when the intrepid reporter met his fate?"

Carolyn raised an eyebrow. "Safely at home, in Douglas, many miles from Laxey Beach. I'm afraid I live alone, so I don't have an unbreakable alibi, but I don't believe the police consider me a suspect."

"Of course not," George said loudly.

An awkward silence fell for a moment before Edmund spoke again. "Are they giving rain for tomorrow, does anyone know?"

"Why? Are you thinking about taking a walk on the beach?" Ted asked. "I'll warn you, you can't get down there at the moment. There's police tape blocking off the bottom of the stairs."

"And you know this because?" Owen asked.

"Because I thought I'd do some exploring around the house when I was bored yesterday. Everyone has been talking about tunnels and secret doors and whatnot, so I thought I'd see what I could find. I found the tunnel that opens up in the middle of the cliff face. When I tried to walk down to the beach, though, I couldn't get off the stairs because of the police tape," Ted explained.

"How did you find the tunnel?" Owen demanded. "I went looking for it but couldn't find it."

"It isn't hard to find," Nicholas laughed. "Once you know where to look, anyway."

"And where is that?" Owen asked impatiently.

"Surely you can picture the house in relation to the cliff," Nicholas said. "Then you just have to work out where a tunnel that came out on the side of the cliff would open into the house."

"It could open anywhere," Owen argued.

"Not at all. As it happens, it opens exactly where it should, in one of the rooms along the outside wall of the house," Nicholas said.

"Have you found it, too?" Owen asked Edmund.

He shrugged. "Yes, but I simply asked the butler to show it to me. He told me that he'd made it his business to find every one of the house's secrets after the murder. He even hinted that he'd been working with the security team to make sure that every entrance was being monitored, even the secret ones."

"Interesting," Ted said. "I didn't see any cameras or anything when I went out yesterday, but maybe they're really well-hidden or disguised. Is there security on the secret exit now?" he asked George.

George shrugged. "I let my security team handle the details," he said. "This is excellent. Is everyone enjoying their meal?"

A few people muttered replies, but Bessie was pretty sure that none of them were paying much attention to the food.

"I'll bet Mary knows," Doona whispered.

Bessie nodded. It was unlikely that Mary was going to volunteer that information, though.

"What would you have done if that reporter had rung you and threatened to write a shocking story about your personal life?" Ted asked Edmund a moment later.

"Told him to publish and be damned," Edmund replied.

Ted laughed. "Of course, but seriously, can you see yourself killing someone? I've been thinking about it a lot. I'm pretty sure I couldn't actually do it, not even if someone was threatening to reveal my deepest, darkest secret."

"Then your secret isn't dark enough," Owen said.

Ted nodded. "That may well be the case. I don't actually have any secrets that would drive me to murder. I'm not sure I can imagine what it would take to turn me into a killer, though. What do you all think? What would make you kill another person?"

"This is fascinating dinner conversation," Edmund said. "Maybe we could talk about the food, which is excellent, or the latest news from the UK. I hear there may be an election coming up."

"I don't have children," Owen said. "I've heard people say that they would kill to protect theirs, though."

Ted nodded. "I don't have children, either, but I've heard the same. It might be more common in women than in men. A sort of mother bear instinct. What do you think, Mary?"

Mary looked surprised and then smiled politely. "I would absolutely kill to protect my children if they were in immediate physical danger. If someone was threatening to publish a story about one of them in the papers that would simply damage his or her reputation, then no, I wouldn't."

Ted nodded. "That's what's puzzling me. What could the man have known that would be bad enough to murder him over? I haven't exactly led a blameless life, but I've not done anything that I'm that desperate to hide."

"I've done some things that I'm not proud of," Nicholas admitted. "Things I'd hate to see dragged up in the papers, even, but nothing that I'd kill to hide."

"I'm starting to think I'd kill to end this conversation," Edmund muttered.

"You don't seem to want to talk about the murder," Ted said. "That makes me wonder what you're hiding."

Edmund's laugh was a sharp bark. "I'm hiding a somewhat squeamish disposition," he snapped. "I'd rather not talk about murder while I'm eating. It seems I'm the odd one out, though, as everyone else seems to be enjoying the conversation immensely."

"I wouldn't say that," Owen protested. "We are caught right at the centre of it all, though. I'm finding the entire situation fascinating. I've never been questioned about a murder before. I just wish I actually knew something that would be helpful to the police so that they could get the case solved."

"Don't we all?" Nicholas asked. "I keep hoping they'll discover that the man interrupted a drug deal or something similar that has nothing to do with any of us. I really just want them to make an arrest, and soon. I'm ready to go home."

"Are you, now?" Edmund asked quickly. "I was under the impression that George still had issues to discuss with all of us."

Nicholas shrugged. "I think George and I have concluded our business discussions for the moment."

"What does that mean?" Ted demanded. "You haven't signed a deal with him, have you?"

"I'm sitting right here," George said, sounding amused.

"I thought you weren't making any decisions until the weekend," Owen said.

"I'm not," George replied.

"So Nicholas is no longer interested in taking part?" Ted asked.

"I didn't say that," Nicholas said with a laugh. "It's really none of your concern. George knows where I stand on things."

"We all should know where you stand on things," Ted objected. "If George has agreed to a deal with you, the rest of us can simply give up and go home."

"Except the police aren't going to let us go anywhere," Edmund pointed out.

"Regardless, we could stop worrying and refining our offers and trying to work out what exactly George wants, if he's already signed with Nicholas," Ted said.

"I haven't signed anything and I won't be signing anything in the next three days," George said loudly. "You've all been asked to get your proposals to me by Friday afternoon. That hasn't changed."

"So Nicholas has just finished his proposal, is that it?" Owen asked.

"You don't need to worry about what I've done," Nicholas said firmly. "Focus on what you're doing and let me worry about my offer."

"As if things weren't difficult enough," Edmund muttered.

"Anyone considering pudding?" the waiter asked Bessie as he cleared away her empty plate.

She looked at Doona. "I'm very full, but I'll have a look at the pudding menu anyway."

Doona nodded. "I need to order John's meal, too."

"If you order what you want for takeaway when you order your puddings, the meal should be ready to go after you've finished your sweet course," the waiter suggested.

"Which means we really have to get a pudding, whether we want one or not," Bessie said, winking at Doona.

Doona laughed. "I don't need much persuading."

He left them with menus, promising to return shortly. At the larger table, dinner plates were being removed.

"What about pudding?" George asked.

"None for me," Edmund said. "I never eat sweets."

"I'd rather get back to the house. I need to ring some people," Nicholas said.

"I'd love dessert," Ted said.

"He's just trying to upset Nicholas," Bessie whispered to Doona.

"I can get a taxi," Nicholas said, getting to his feet.

"Oh, I don't want to inconvenience you," Ted replied, clearly lying.

"Our driver can make two trips," Mary said. "Anyone who doesn't want pudding can leave now. Laxey isn't far away. By the time the puddings have been enjoyed, the driver will be back."

Edmund stood up. "I'll go now."

"Me, too," Owen said.

"If you no longer need me, I'm going to go as well," Carolyn said, getting to her feet. "Of course, I have my own car in the car park."

She followed the three men who walked out of the room quickly as Mary pulled out her mobile. She texted something to someone and then smiled at George. "I've told the driver to take them home and then come back for us," she said. "Are you going to have a pudding?"

He shook his head. "I rarely eat puddings, but I was sure you'd want one. I thought I should stay and keep you company."

Mary smiled and patted his arm. A moment later the waiter was back, giving them the appropriate menus.

Bessie and Doona both ordered the chocolate gateau. Bessie got cream with hers while Doona opted for custard. She also ordered the same chicken dish that she and Bessie had enjoyed to take home for John.

"Well, this is nice," Ted said loudly. "I feel as if I should be enjoying having you all to myself," he told George.

"I don't want to talk about business over pudding," George said.

"No, of course not," Ted laughed. "Let's talk about murder."

"I think we've talked about that rather enough," Mary said.

Ted shook his head. "I've been trying to work out which one of those three was the killer. After tonight, my suspicions are centered on Edmund."

"Why?" George demanded.

"He was the most reluctant to talk about the case," Ted reasoned. "He also seemed like someone with a secret, although I suspect we all have secrets."

George shrugged. "I'm sure we do."

"He admitted to knowing where the hidden tunnel is, too, even if he did say that he'd found it after the murder. Maybe he just asked the butler about it in an attempt to hide the fact that he already knew exactly where it was," Ted said.

"Maybe," George said, clearly not interested in the conversation.

"The reporter must have been chasing something about Edmund's personal life, I reckon," Ted continued. "We all know what a mess it is. He loses interest in women at an alarming rate, really."

"I don't understand it all," George said, patting Mary's hand.

"I mean, I don't have a great track record with women, but I've managed to avoid marriage, and I've only been engaged twice. The first time I was only eighteen, and I got engaged mostly to annoy my parents, as well. Edmund seems to get engaged to every woman he meets."

"I can't see that leading to murder," George said.

The puddings were delivered to both tables at the same time. Ted made a face at his.

"George, would you like some of this? I didn't really want anything. I was just trying to keep Nicholas out of the house for as long as possible," he said.

"Why?" Mary asked.

Ted shrugged. "Why not? He was clearly eager to get back. That was reason enough."

"I should have had you each come across individually," George said with a sigh.

"It would have been easier, but far less interesting," Ted laughed. "Of course, it would have been obvious who'd killed Harrison Parker in that scenario. I'm sure the police would rather that you'd had us all one at a time."

"I'm certain the police will have a solution soon," George said.

Ted picked at his Victoria sponge while Mary ate her chocolate gateau. She shared several bites with George, who made a token protest before each bite. When they were finished, George waved to their waiter. Mary got up and crossed to Bessie.

"I hope you heard all of that," she said. "I don't think any of it was useful, but maybe John will find something in it."

"It wasn't a very pleasant evening for you," Bessie said sympathetically.

"No, but it was better than having the same conversation at home. At least here no one could storm out because Ted said something horrible," Mary replied.

Bessie got up and gave her friend a hug. "You'd be happiest, then, if the police arrested Ted for the murder," she suggested.

"I'd be happiest if the police find the killer, whether it was Ted or not. That's all that needs to happen for the police to tell everyone that they can go. Given permission to leave, all four of them would be gone within hours, I'm sure."

"What about the deal with George?"

"I don't think any of them really want to be involved in a retail park on the island, at least not now that they've spent some time here. The problem is, now they all feel as if they're competing with one another and they all want to win, not because they want the deal, but because it will bruise their egos if they lose. I suspect whoever does get the deal will find an excuse to get out of it within months, maybe even weeks."

"Have you talked to George about it?" Bessie asked.

Mary nodded grimly. "He knows exactly how I feel," she said flatly.

Bessie gave her another hug and then sat back down and watched as Mary returned to her table. George jumped to his feet and Ted followed more slowly. The trio left the dining room as a waiter delivered a large brown bag to Doona.

"Your takeaway order," he said with a small bow.

"Wonderful, thanks," Doona replied. "We just need the bill, then."

The waiter shook his head. "Mr. Quayle insisted that we put your dinner on his account," he said. "And Mr. Coventry didn't charge you for the takeaway order, either."

Doona frowned and looked at Bessie. "Is it worth trying to argue?" she asked.

"Not with the waiter here. I'll have words with Mary the next time I see her," Bessie replied.

"She'll probably tell you that she didn't even know that George had done it," Doona predicted as the women stood up and gathered up their handbags. "I'm sure he did it while Mary was at our table."

The pair made their way back through the building and out to Doona's car. "Can you text John while I drive?" Doona asked. "Tell him I'm taking you home now. He may want to talk to you about everything we overheard at dinner."

"Does he know that everyone from Thie yn Traie was there?" she asked in surprise.

"I may have texted him during the meal," Doona replied. "You were so busy watching the men at George's table that you didn't even notice."

Bessie flushed. "You're right about that. I am sorry."

"It's fine. I was watching them intently, too, but I thought it was worth letting John know. I'm sure he'll want to talk to you eventually, anyway. He might be too tired to do it tonight, though."

Bessie sent the text and then laughed when she got a reply almost immediately. "He's not too tired," she told Doona. "He's sitting in front of my cottage, waiting for us to get back."

Doona laughed. "We'll have to talk fast if he's going to get home before the kids do."

"If he's busy eating, he won't be able to ask any questions, anyway."

A short while later, they were sitting together around Bessie's kitchen table. John had his dinner in front of him while Bessie and Doona both had tea.

"Tell me everything," John said before he started eating.

Bessie did her best to take him through the evening. Doona helped her remember bits of the conversation as she went along. When she was done, John sighed.

"It's all interesting, but I'm not sure any of it helps," he said. "But that's always the case in murder investigations. The solutions often seem to come from odd remarks that seemed insignificant at the time."

Bessie packed up a few biscuits for John to eat on his drive home. Doona followed him out, leaving Bessie to wash up the teacups and John's plate. Feeling as if it were much later than it actually was, Bessie took herself off to bed, crawling gratefully under the duvet and falling asleep almost immediately.

When she woke at two minutes past six, she remembered that she'd been having a very strange dream. The four men from Thie yn Traie had been sitting all around her, shouting out random words. The only words she could remember now were tunnel and knife. Bessie's dreams weren't usually significant, so she tried to put it out of her head as she took a shower and made herself some breakfast. Feeling as if she needed a brisk walk in the sea air even more than normally, she put on her shoes and a jacket and headed for the door.

She was delighted to see that the tide was out, which meant there was a chance that she might be able to walk past the crime scene. Setting off at a brisk pace, she pulled her coat tightly closed against the wind and marched along the sand.

CHAPTER 11

*G*etting past the police tape meant walking right on the water's edge. Bessie rushed along, trying to avoid the waves that lapped at her shoes. It was worth it, she decided, as she reached the other side of the tape and the beach stretched out in front of her. It felt as if it had been ages since she'd been able to walk as far as she pleased. Setting the new houses as her goal, she continued on her way, ignoring the wind and the cold.

The new houses seemed to appear in front of her more quickly than she'd been expecting. Continuing past them, she reached the building site for the next lot of new houses and stopped. The sign advertising the homes now read "All Sites Sold," which was good news, really. Bessie studied the sign and then shook her head. The houses were all detached, but they were going to be awfully close together. The new houses she had just passed were also tightly packed, but these appeared to have even less space between them. They were smaller, as well. Most were described as having three bedrooms whereas Bessie knew that Grace and Hugh had four.

Feeling glad that her friends had been able to afford their lovely home, even if someone had been murdered in the dining room, Bessie turned back towards Treoghe Bwaane. She walked more slowly now that she wasn't fighting the wind. It seemed to be trying to hurry her along, and she was determined to enjoy her walk, so she did her best to dawdle. As she reached the new houses, she spotted Grace on her patio. She was rocking Aalish, who was screaming loudly.

"My goodness, she's very upset," Bessie said as she approached.

Grace shrugged. "She has a cold, which means she can't really breathe properly, so that makes her mad. Then she cries, which makes it even harder for her to breathe, which makes her even angrier. I was hoping the sea air might help, but everything just seems to make her cross at the moment."

Bessie almost laughed when she looked at the tiny angry face. Aalish was very upset about something she couldn't possibly understand. "Can I do anything to help?"

"If you could take her for one minute, I could pop back inside and get some headache tablets," Grace said. "I don't want to take her back inside because poor Hugh is trying to get some sleep. Neither one of us got much sleep last night."

"Of course," Bessie said nervously. She didn't have much experience with babies. Grace handed Aalish to her and then fled into the house before Bessie could stop her.

The baby was already crying, so she couldn't do anything else to complain about the handover. She looked at Bessie and then scrunched up her face and wailed.

"You aren't doing yourself any favours, shouting like that," Bessie said conversationally. "If you stop crying and simply relax, you'll feel much better. I'm sure your mother and father would feel better, too."

Aalish didn't look at all interested in Bessie's opinion. She continued to sob, while wiggling in Bessie's arms.

Bessie turned around and walked slowly towards the sea. "Look at the waves," she said. "If you stop shouting, you'll be able to hear them, too. They're lovely and soothing and they'll put you right to sleep, if you let them."

The walking seemed to be helping as Aalish's screams turned to softer, hiccupy sounds.

"Look at the seagulls," Bessie suggested, pointing to the sky above them. "And that's an aeroplane, way up in the sky, really quite far away."

Aalish stared at Bessie, seemingly fascinated by her.

"The water is very cold," Bessie said. "That's why we aren't going to actually go into the sea. We'll stop here, on the sand, and just watch the waves. The tide is going out and that's very good news, as it will make more room for me when I walk home."

Bessie continued babbling about everything and nothing as she walked up and down the beach with the baby. Aalish went from crying to whimpering to fast asleep before Grace reappeared.

"I'm so sorry," she said as she walked out of the house. "The phone rang, and then I had to wake Hugh to take the call, and that took ages. Then I had to wait to see what they said, because it was the college, and they wouldn't stop talking. I didn't mean to leave you alone with Aalish all this time."

"It's fine. She's fallen asleep."

"She's fallen asleep?" Grace echoed, sounding stunned. "I was so tired that I didn't even notice when I came out of the house. But she hasn't slept in ages."

"Then she clearly needs it."

"Yes, definitely, but she's been fighting it so hard." Grace stopped and blinked several times. "I'm so overtired that I'm practically crying because the baby is actually sleeping," she said, shaking her head. "Thank you so much."

"She'll probably wake up the minute I try to hand her back to you."

"Probably, but maybe not. Maybe you could keep her for, I don't know, another six or seven hours?"

Bessie gasped as Grace giggled. "I don't mean it," she said quickly. "I'll take her now if you want."

"I'll keep her for another minute or two," Bessie said, feeling oddly reluctant to return the tiny bundle. "Should I ask what the college wanted?"

Grace grinned at her. "They were ringing with Hugh's score from his maths exam. When I told Hugh that you were here, he told me that I could tell you how he did."

"And how did he do?" Bessie asked, feeling certain the results were good, based on Grace's smile.

"He scored a ninety-three. The only questions he missed were a few things that we hadn't actually gone over yet."

"Good for him. I knew he could learn the material if he tried. He's a very bright man. He just needed the right motivation."

"I'm so very proud of him. He worked really hard to learn everything he needed and then some. He even came to enjoy it, at least a little bit. He's thinking about taking an extra maths class now, along with his course. He has this idea that he's going to need to help Aalish with her homework soon."

Bessie glanced down at the sleeping baby. "Those days will be here before you know it. I'm sure it doesn't seem like it now, but she'll grow up very quickly. Children always do."

"She's already not an infant anymore. The doctor said that she'll be sitting up in no time, and she's already working on rolling over. It's exciting watching her grow and develop, but I do sort of miss my tiny baby."

"Except when she's screaming and you aren't getting any sleep," Bessie suggested.

Grace nodded. "She can be very challenging, of course, but she's also incredibly sweet, and Hugh thinks the world of her. He's finally getting more comfortable with her, too, as she seems less fragile now that she can support her own head for the most part."

Aalish sighed in her sleep and then wiggled a bit, causing Bessie to tighten her grip. A tiny smile passed over Aalish's face, and Bessie felt herself falling even more in love with her. "She is very sweet," Bessie said softly.

"And now I should take her and let you get on with your walk. You'll want to get back while the tide is out, I'm sure, so you can get around the police tape."

"Any idea how much longer it's going to be there?" Bessie asked.

Grace shrugged. "You'd have to ask John that question. Hugh doesn't tell me much, but I do know that he doesn't make those decisions. We often walk on the beach at night, and Hugh has been complaining about it to me every time we walk that way. He wants it gone as much as you do."

Bessie nodded. "I'm going to ask John about it the next time I speak to him. I can't imagine that they think they're going to find any additional evidence on the beach now."

Grace glanced back at the house and then took a step closer to Bessie. "As I understand it, one of the main reasons the tape is still there is that it's keeping the people at Thie yn Traie off the beach," she said in a low voice. "The stairs to the mansion are inside the tape, which means no one is meant to be coming down them to the beach. That means the security team at Thie yn Traie can keep track of everyone as they come and go."

"I suppose that makes sense, but it's frustrating for the rest of us."

"It is, at that."

"I'd better go, then," Bessie said reluctantly.

"You're welcome to come back and have a cuddle any time," Grace told her. "We'll be here."

Bessie nodded. "Tell Hugh many congratulations on his exam results. You should go out and celebrate."

"We might. Mum has been asking to have Aalish stay with her one night and I think I'm just about ready to agree. We'll have to wait until Aalish's cold has gone, but then maybe Hugh and I will have a night out, just the two of us."

"Plan it now, so you both have something to look forward to," Bessie suggested.

"I hate to admit it, but I'm mostly looking forward to getting an uninterrupted night's sleep. I mean, I love Hugh and I love the thought of spending some time alone with him, but I need sleep and it's been in short supply lately."

"Something you don't have to worry about, do you?" Bessie asked the sleeping baby. "You just sleep whenever you want, don't you?"

"She does," Grace laughed. "I just wish she wanted to sleep a bit more often."

Bessie carefully handed the baby back to Grace, holding her breath and hoping that they wouldn't wake her. In Grace's arms, Aalish squirmed for a moment before settling down, her eyes still tightly shut.

"I'm going to go inside and sit on the sofa with her," Grace said. "If she'll stay asleep for a few hours, I'm sure she'll feel better when she wakes up."

"Good luck," Bessie said. She watched as Grace let herself back into the house, and then Bessie turned and headed back to the water's edge and down the beach. When she reached the police tape, she felt as if she'd had a narrow escape, even though the tide was only slowly starting to come back in. She walked briskly past the tape, but when she reached the other side, she dropped back to a more leisurely pace.

"Good morning," a voice said, making Bessie jump.

"Oh, good morning," she replied, smiling at Geoffrey Scott, who was walking towards her from between the last two holiday cottages.

"It's a lovely morning for a stroll," he said when he reached her.

"It is, yes. The wind has died down in the last half hour or so and the sun is doing its best to warm everything up."

"It's a beautiful stretch of beach. I can see why you walk here every day."

"It's home," Bessie said simply.

He nodded at her. "If I were you, I'd walk on the beach at all hours of the day and night."

She shrugged. "I don't usually walk at night. Sometimes I sit on the rock behind my cottage in the evening, just to get some fresh air, but I don't usually go any further."

He stared down the beach towards Treoghe Bwaane. "And the rest of the properties are holiday cottages, didn't you say?"

"Yes, there used to be several cottages along the beach, all of which were individually owned and lived in all year-round. Thomas Shimmin started buying them years ago. I believe his original intention was to move to the beach himself, but in the end he decided to build the holiday cottages instead."

"I'm sure he'd love to get his hands on your cottage."

Bessie shrugged. "I don't know about that. I think he and his wife already have enough work to do with the cottages they already own.

Anyway, my estate will all go to my family in America. They may well sell the cottage to Thomas or someone else, but that will be their problem, not mine."

"And no one ever stays in the holiday cottages in the winter months?"

"Thomas has talked about doing off-season rentals, but he hasn't done any yet. I don't think many people would want to stay here during the winter months. It's rather bleak and cold, and the cottages are really designed for short-term stays. The furniture isn't very comfortable, and I'm not sure how good the heating is, either."

"I wonder if they'd let me stay in one, just for a few nights. Obviously, I'd pay for the privilege. What do you think?"

"I thought you were staying at Thie yn Traie," Bessie replied, feeling confused.

"I am, but I was considering staying on the island for a short while after Jonathan returns. I couldn't possibly remain at Thie yn Traie once I was no longer employed there."

"When does Jonathan return? It's already March and the rental season for the cottages usually starts in April. You may find that everything is already booked."

Geoffrey frowned. "That would be unfortunate. Tell me, the reporter who visited the house the other day, Dan something, is he good at his job?"

"Dan Ross? I'm sure he thinks he's very good," Bessie said with a laugh.

"Yes, of course, but what do you think of him?"

"I'm not fond of him," Bessie said honestly. "He's nosy and pushy and rather obnoxious, really. Why?"

"The police don't seem to be getting anywhere with their murder investigation. I was just wondering if that newspaper reporter would actually be able to solve the case."

"I'm sure the police are doing everything they can," Bessie said with a frown. "I don't imagine Dan will learn anything that the police don't already know."

"It's worrying, working with a group of people, suspecting that one of them is a murderer."

Bessie nodded. "I'm sure George and Mary would rather the foursome moved into a hotel or somewhere else, but they can hardly suggest such a thing."

Geoffrey nodded. "I don't suppose you know whom the police actually suspect, do you? They must have a favourite suspect among those four men. I'd really like to avoid being alone with the police's favourite suspect."

"The police don't confide such things to me," Bessie told him. "But you see the four men regularly. Surely you have a favourite suspect."

The man shook his head. "I have no idea who killed Harrison Parker. I do know who I hope did it, that is, whom I dislike the most of the four men, but I don't think the police are interested in my opinion."

"You'd be surprised, actually. I suspect they'd be very interested in your opinion. You've spent quite a lot of time with the men, after all."

"I don't know," Geoffrey shrugged. "I'd like to think I'm a good judge of character, but I don't care for any of the four, really, which may be clouding my judgment."

"So whom do you suspect?"

"Are you going to repeat what I tell you to the police?"

"Would you rather I didn't?"

He laughed. "Actually, I'd rather you did. I don't want to talk to them again, but the last time I was interviewed I had only spent a short amount of time with the men and hadn't really formed any opinions of them. It would be awkward now to go to the police simply to share my thoughts on the suspects, but it might be a good thing if the police knew them."

Bessie nodded. "Go ahead, then, tell me what you think of each of the men."

"Let's start with which man I'd love to see arrested, shall we?" he asked, grinning wickedly. "If the police dragged Ted Pearson away, kicking and screaming, I'd be delighted."

"Why don't you care for him?"

"He's arrogant, demanding, and incredibly American, even though he's spent a lot of his adult life in the UK. He's forever on his mobile, talking loudly about huge deals that involve vast sums of money, but I'd be willing to bet that the calls are mostly faked, just to make everyone think he's that important when he really isn't."

"Surely he wouldn't waste his time on fake phone conversations."

"He would if he thought it would help him sign the deal with Mr. Quayle. He's desperate to sign it to get his brand into a shop over here." Geoffrey blushed. "I probably know more about the retail park project than I should because everyone insists on discussing it loudly all throughout Thie yn Traie. Regardless, I shouldn't be discussing it with you."

"Do you have any reason to believe that Ted actually killed Harrison, or do you simply dislike him?"

"He doesn't like it when people ask him questions about his business or his personal life, but he does seem to enjoy prying into other people's lives. I suspect if someone did some digging, he or she would find a lot of interesting things hiding in Mr. Pearson's past."

"Such as?"

"How should I know?" the man demanded. "I'm sure he's had a lot of women in and out of his life. That would be a good place to start. I suspect his business deals would be worth investigating, too. If I ever decide I don't want to be a butler any longer, maybe I'll become a newspaper reporter. There seem to be stories everywhere."

"Except if you choose the wrong one, you can get killed," Bessie pointed out.

"Harrison Parker made a fatal mistake. The only thing that makes sense is that he met someone on the beach, alone, after dark. That was foolish. I wouldn't make the same mistake."

"Anything else about Ted?" Bessie asked.

"Not really. As I said, I don't care for him, and if he were arrested tomorrow, I'd celebrate."

"What about the others?"

"They're all far less annoying. Mr. Rhodes can be a bit stiff, but he's far less demanding than Mr. Pearson, anyway."

"Can you think of any reason why Edmund would have killed Harrison?"

"Oh, with him it would have to be something to do with the women in his life, I'm sure. He's short and not very attractive, but he's rich, so women fight over him anyway," he said with a sigh.

"I'm not sure that attracting women who are only interested in his money is a good thing."

"It isn't, of course, but it's still annoying to those of us with no money with which to attract women. There aren't any single women at Thie yn Traie, though, and Mr. Quayle isn't the sort to throw a party full of them to entertain his guests. I believe Mr. Rhodes is rather fed up at the lack of female companionship. Miss Elizabeth is distantly polite, which is appropriate but annoys him even further."

"What about Nicholas?" Bessie asked.

"Mr. Taylor is a very busy man. He owns some of the most successful shopping malls in the UK and I'm not entirely certain why he's even here."

"But what do you think of him as a person?"

"I've barely spoken to him, actually. He's usually in his room, no doubt genuinely making the sort of deals that Mr. Pearson pretends to be making all the time."

"Can you think of a reason why he'd have killed Harrison?"

"It would have to have been something to do with his business, but I do think that if he wanted someone dead, Mr. Taylor would hire someone to take care of the job, not do it himself. If that were the case, I can't see the police ever solving the murder. Whoever killed Harrison Parker will be long gone and it will probably be almost impossible to tie Mr. Taylor to his death."

"It's an interesting theory, anyway. What about Owen?"

"Mr. Oliver is a builder," Geoffrey said dismissively. "I'm quite certain he has secrets and I don't imagine it would take much effort for someone to discover them. Mr. Oliver doesn't seem bright enough to hide things successfully."

"It sounds as if you don't care for him."

"I don't care for any of them, but Mr. Oliver can be difficult, let's say. He treats me as if I were his employee rather than Mr. Quayle's, making demands on me and my time that can be quite unreasonable."

"With which one do you think George will partner?" Bessie asked.

Geoffrey sighed dramatically. "That's the question, isn't it? Everyone wants to know the answer to that. I believe each of the four men has asked me for my thoughts on the matter at least once a day since he arrived. I keep telling them that I've no idea, that it's none of my concern, and that, even if I did have any thoughts, I wouldn't share them with anyone, but none of them will listen to me. They keep asking and asking and asking."

"Do you have any thoughts?" Bessie pushed.

"I mean, I do, but I don't know that I should share them." He looked up and down the beach and then took a step closer to Bessie. "I think Mr. Quayle has already more or less agreed to a deal with Mr. Taylor, but he isn't going to finalise anything until the weekend. Mr. Taylor has been acting quite smug and self-satisfied lately, anyway."

"And what do you think of that choice?"

"It isn't anything to do with me, of course, but it seems a reasonable choice, considering the alternatives. Mr. Oliver only wants a short-term deal, to get the buildings built. I'm sure Mr. Quayle will be able to reach some sort of arrangement with him on the construction side, anyway. Mr. Rhodes will lose interest long before the project is finished. Mr. Quayle needs a partner who will actively help generate interest in the project at every step along the way."

"And you don't want Mr. Pearson to be that partner, of course."

"No, I don't," Geoffrey said flatly. "He's only interested in getting his shop on the island. It would do better in Douglas town centre, anyway, not in Mr. Quayle's retail park. If I were Mr. Pearson, that's where I'd be focussing my efforts."

"I wonder why he isn't."

"I believe that he is. He's simply doing so very quietly so that if it doesn't materialise, he can fall back on his deal with Mr. Quayle. Perhaps that was what Harrison Parker learned about the man."

"I can't imagine Ted murdering anyone just because he was going to spoil a potential deal for him."

163

"I can see Mr. Pearson murdering someone for spare change," Geoffrey snapped. "He's far too accustomed to getting his way all the time. If Harrison Parker stood between him and something he wanted, I can easily see Mr. Pearson eliminating him."

Bessie sighed. "I can't imagine murdering anyone under any circumstances."

"No, of course not. It's a horrible thing to contemplate. I almost feel sorry for Mr. Pearson. He must have felt as if he had no choice but to commit that horrific act."

"There are always alternatives."

"Perhaps the killer offered a financial settlement in exchange for Harrison ending his investigation. I would assume that Harrison refused any such offer."

"That's an interesting idea."

"I'm full of interesting ideas," Geoffrey laughed. "But now I truly must get back to Thie yn Traie. I'll be missed if I'm gone for much longer."

"How did you get down here? I thought the stairs down to the beach were still inside the police tape."

"They are. I walked down the road from the house to the car park for the holiday cottages. It isn't a long walk, really, not when you're enjoying the fresh air. I needed to get away, anyway."

Bessie nodded. "I quite understand."

Geoffrey nodded. "And now, sadly, I must get back. All four of our visitors are late risers, but they'll all want breakfast, probably at the exact same time. Such things fluster the chef, who dislikes guests almost as much as Mrs. Quayle does. I shall spend the rest of the morning rushing between the guest rooms, carrying trays and dealing with impossible requests."

"Impossible requests?" Bessie echoed.

"I've been asked to procure everything from willing women to illegal drugs in the past week," he told her. "And just about everything in between, as well. Rich men don't like to take no for an answer, either."

He bowed to Bessie and then turned and walked away, leaving her wondering what fell into the "everything in between" category. She was fairly certain that Edmund had been the one requesting female companionship, but she was less certain about the drugs. Maybe Ted, she thought as she resumed her walk. He seemed the type to dabble in such things, even if he wasn't a habitual user.

Back at Treoghe Bwaane she started a pot of coffee. The long walk had been invigorating, but the two lengthy stops had given her something of a chill. While the coffee was brewing, she dialled a number she knew well.

"Laxey Neighbourhood Policing, this is Suzannah. How can I help you?"

Bessie made a face. Suzannah was meant to be moving to a different station. Why was she still in Laxey? "It's Elizabeth Cubbon. I need to speak to John Rockwell, please."

"Certainly, Mrs. Clubby. I'm going to have to put you on hold for a moment. Please hold."

"It's Cubbon."

"Pardon?"

"It's Miss Cubbon."

"Yes, you already said that. I need to put you on hold. Is that okay, Mrs. Bubblon?"

"It's Miss Cubbon."

"Yes, you've said that several times now. I just need you to agree to be put on hold while I try to connect you with Inspector Rockwell. May I put you on hold, please, Mrs. Crumbles?"

Bessie took a deep breath and slowly counted to ten. "Yes," she said through her teeth.

The phone clicked several times and then the line went silent. Bessie frowned. Where was the annoying music that always played when she was on hold? A moment later, she got her answer as the line began to beep at her. The connection had been broken. Bessie put the phone down and paced around her kitchen, muttering angrily to herself. Although she couldn't imagine murdering anyone herself, if Suzannah had walked into the cottage just then, Bessie thought she'd be quite capable of throwing something at the girl. It took her several minutes to recover from her upset.

When she picked up the phone again, she dialled John's mobile.

"John Rockwell."

"It's Bessie. I just had an interesting conversation with Geoffrey Scott about the four men staying at Thie yn Traie," she said.

"Really? He wasn't very forthcoming when I spoke to him. Did he say anything particularly interesting?"

"He hates Ted Pearson."

"Why doesn't that surprise me? Anything else?"

"I don't know what you'd qualify as interesting."

John chuckled. "I'm sorry. I'm not trying to be difficult, but I'm rather busy right now. I'd love to hear the entire conversation, but that's probably going to have to wait until later today. Why don't we have another gathering tonight? I'll bring Doona, as I know she's available, and I'll invite Hugh. You can tell us all everything that Geoffrey said and we can talk about a few other developments in the case."

"There are other developments?" Bessie asked.

"Let's just say that I'm hopeful that there will be by tonight," John told her.

"Six o'clock?"

"That should work. I'll talk to Hugh and Doona and, unless one of us rings back, you can expect us around six. I'll bring dinner, maybe something from that Italian place again."

"That sounds good," Bessie said. "I'll make something for pudding, apple crumble, maybe."

"That sounds very good. See you later."

Bessie put down the phone and sat down at the table with a cup of coffee. The things that Geoffrey had said were interesting, but she wasn't sure that they were going to help solve the murder. Geoffrey's dislike of Ted proved absolutely nothing, even if it did reinforce Bessie's own opinion of the man.

She was heading for the stairs, ready for another session with Onnee's letters, when the phone rang.

"It's Elizabeth. We're going mad over here, dealing with our guests.

Mum and I were hoping that you might be willing to come to tea this afternoon. Andy is making cakes and sandwiches and all manner of things. He's testing a number of recipes for an event that he's catering for me next month. He'll be making enough for an army, and even with four guests, we'll never get through it all without help. Please come."

Bessie laughed. "All you needed to say was that Andy was cooking and I'd have agreed."

"He is that good, isn't he? I can't believe how lucky I am to have him in my life. He's wonderful for my business and he's wonderful, full stop."

"I'm sure he isn't wonderful all the time."

Elizabeth chuckled. "He does have his moments where he's only just good, but so far he's never been anything less than that. I'm sure we'll have our challenges, but so far it's been pretty amazing."

"I'm glad to hear that. I think the world of Andy."

"And he'll be forever grateful to you for letting him practically live with you through his teen years."

"I was happy to do it. I understood that things were difficult at home."

"That stepfather of his was the problem, of course. Andy's mum is wonderful, even if she did keep a pretty big secret from Andy for a very long time."

"She did what she thought she had to do in order to survive," Bessie said.

"Yes, I know, and so does Andy. Anyway, we've wandered way off topic. I'll send a car for you at half two or so. Tea will be promptly at three."

"I need to be home by six," Bessie told her.

"That won't be a problem, even if I have to take you myself."

Bessie realised, as she put the phone down, that she wouldn't be able to make an apple crumble if she was out all afternoon. She had plenty of time to throw together something else that didn't need to be served warm, though. In the end, she baked a chocolate sponge cake before she made herself a very light lunch. Being hungry for tea was important, as Andy was cooking, she reminded herself over her sandwich.

A skirt with a jumper seemed appropriate for tea at Thie yn Traie. Bessie slid on her shoes and combed her hair. After grabbing her handbag, she was waiting at the door with her coat on when Mary's limousine arrived at exactly half two.

CHAPTER 12

"Ah, Miss Cubbon, so lovely to see you again," Geoffrey said as he opened the front door to Thie yn Traie.

Bessie smiled. "It's lovely to see you again as well," she replied as she walked into the house.

The man glanced back and forth and then leaned forward. "I'm afraid I may have been rather indiscreet when we spoke this morning. I do hope you won't be repeating anything that I said to anyone."

"Ah, Bessie, there you are," Elizabeth said as she rushed into the foyer. "Come and tell Andy that he's crazy."

Feeling relieved that she'd escaped answering Geoffrey, Bessie let Elizabeth lead her down the corridor to the kitchen.

"Bessie is here. Let her decide," Elizabeth said loudly as she pulled Bessie into the room.

Andy looked up from what he was doing and frowned. "It isn't for Bessie to decide. I've already made my decision. We aren't going to argue about it."

"But we are," Elizabeth countered. "You can't waste that delicious cake just because it's a bit lopsided."

Andy shook his head. "It isn't just lopsided. Something went wrong somewhere along the way. It's probably not even edible."

"He won't let me taste it to find out," Elizabeth told Bessie. "I'm sure, whatever is wrong, it will still be delicious, but he won't even let me try it."

Bessie shook her head. "I've no idea what either of you are talking about."

Elizabeth laughed, and even Andy managed a small smile. "I've been baking cakes and biscuits and scones all day," he told Bessie. "One of the cakes has come out wrong. I want to bin it, but Elizabeth wants to eat it."

"I don't blame Elizabeth," Bessie replied. "You're a wonderful chef. I'm sure it will be delicious, even if it isn't perfect."

Andy shrugged and then turned around and pulled a tray out from one of the cooling racks. "It didn't rise evenly, although I'm not sure why."

Bessie looked at the cake in the tin. One side was much higher than the other. "How odd," she said after a minute. "I'm not sure I've ever seen that happen before."

Andy shrugged. "Me neither."

"You should at least cut into it to see if you can determine what went wrong," Bessie told him.

He made a face. "Once it's cut, Elizabeth is really going to want to eat it."

Elizabeth shook her head. "If it's that important to you, I won't touch it," she said, sounding hurt. "I just hope everything will be ready soon, because I skipped lunch so that I'd be really hungry for tea."

Andy sighed and then tipped the cake out onto the counter. It came out of the pan easily. When Andy flipped the pan back over, he gasped and then laughed.

"What is it?" Bessie asked.

Reaching into the pan, he pulled out a smaller pan that had been upside down inside the larger one. "I knew I had another tin somewhere," he said. "I don't know how it got inside the cake tin or why I didn't see it when I poured the batter into the pan."

"You were trying to hurry because you were running behind," Elizabeth reminded him. "And that was entirely my fault."

Andy flushed. "Maybe not entirely," he said. "Anyway, that explains the rather odd results, at least."

"We probably should taste the cake anyway, just to be sure," Elizabeth suggested.

Andy and Bessie both laughed. "As I was going to cut it into bite-sized pieces for serving anyway, you can try a bit," Andy told her. "The thin part, where the batter was on top of the other pan, is probably overcooked, but the rest should be okay."

"I like the thin side," Elizabeth said a moment later. "It's almost like a biscuit in texture, but it tastes of vanilla sponge. I like it a lot."

"It is good," Bessie agreed. "Although the other side is delicious, too."

"I'm not going to put the thin stuff out for tea, but you both know it's here if you want more," Andy said.

"I want more," Elizabeth replied quickly. "But I'm not going to have it right now. I've already put on nearly a stone since you've been home from culinary school. If I'm not careful, I'm going to have to go on a diet."

"You look great," Andy said. "You were too thin before, anyway."

Elizabeth shrugged. "You won't think that if I put on another stone, and that's a distinct possibility if you keep cooking for me."

"You were the one who asked me to put together a tea party this afternoon," Andy countered.

"Yes, I was, wasn't I?" Elizabeth laughed. "We do need to try everything for the tea party you're catering for me, though. At least this way, with all of the guests, I won't eat everything myself."

"All of the guests?" Bessie repeated.

"Oh, just you and the four men who are still here. I'm starting to think they're never going to leave," Elizabeth replied.

"I don't think they can leave, not until the police give them permission," Bessie said.

"I do wish Inspector Rockwell would hurry up and solve the murder, then. Even Daddy is tired of them being here all the time, and he's hardly ever home," Elizabeth said.

"I'm sure your mother will be happy when they can go," Bessie said.

"Mum is sorry that Daddy ever invited them, but, of course, she can't tell Daddy that. She never wants to hurt his feelings."

Bessie shrugged. She didn't really understand how marriages worked, and George and Mary's marriage was even more of a mystery to her than most. In theory, opposites attract, but in Bessie's experience, that was rarely the case. George and Mary, though, were very much opposites, and Bessie couldn't understand how boisterous George, who'd never met a stranger, and shy and retiring Mary had stayed seemingly happily married for so many years.

"Ah, there you are," Mary said as she walked into the kitchen. She smiled at Bessie. "Geoffrey told me that you'd arrived and that Elizabeth had dragged you away somewhere. I assumed it had to be where Andy was."

Elizabeth blushed. "We were just sneaking a few samples," she said. "But I think everything is just about ready, anyway. Should we go through to the great room?"

"Yes, let's," her mother agreed. "I asked the men to join me there at three. We should be there when they arrive."

"I'm going to put the finishing touches on everything now. I'll be ready to serve whenever you're ready," Andy said.

The great room was empty when the trio walked in a moment later.

"Let's move some chairs and couches together," Elizabeth suggested. "We'll want enough chairs together for eight, because Andy is going to join us after everything is served."

"Where is Geoffrey?" Mary asked. "I asked him to meet me here before three."

"One of the men probably needed something," Elizabeth said. "They can be incredibly demanding."

"Yes, they can," Mary said under her breath. "But we can't move furniture ourselves."

"Andy and I can manage it," Elizabeth said airily. "Or I'll get the first man who arrives to help. None of them have done anything since they've been here except be waited on hand and foot. It will do them some good to actually do some work."

"We can't ask our guests to rearrange the furniture," Mary said, clearly appalled by the idea.

"Of course we can," Elizabeth replied. "Or we can all sit in little clusters of two or three, the way the room is arranged now. That might be better, actually. I can sit with Bessie and Andy and not have to deal with anyone else."

"Am I early?" a voice asked from the doorway.

Bessie turned around and smiled at Edmund Rhodes, who walked into the room and almost immediately dropped into a chair near the windows.

"Tea will be served shortly," Elizabeth told him.

"Splendid," he said, seemingly unconcerned. He pulled out his mobile phone and began to tap out a text message to someone.

Bessie looked at Mary, who shrugged.

"Is everything ready?" Geoffrey asked as he rushed into the room a moment later.

"We were going to rearrange some of the furniture," Elizabeth told him. "But now the guests have begun to arrive."

Geoffrey frowned. "I am sorry. What did you want moved?"

Elizabeth and Mary had a quick chat. After a moment, they had Geoffrey combine two small seating areas into one larger one. Edmund never looked up from his mobile as Geoffrey worked.

"Was there anything else?" Geoffrey asked once the chairs and couches were in place.

"If you could help Andy bring everything in, that would be helpful," Elizabeth replied.

Geoffrey looked at Mary, who nodded. He bowed and then left the room.

"Jonathan can't get back fast enough," Mary told Bessie in a whisper. "I think we were rather spoiled by him, really."

"I'm here," Nicholas announced from the doorway. "I haven't been to a tea party in years. I'm usually working at this time of day, of course."

He walked into the room, glanced around, and then walked over to where Edmund was sitting on his own. After another look around the room, Nicholas dropped into a chair opposite Edmund and pulled out his own phone.

"Maybe we didn't need to move furniture after all," Elizabeth whispered. "It seems the men prefer to be by themselves near the windows."

"Maybe if we sit down, they'll join us," Mary suggested.

Bessie was quite happy for the men to remain where they were, but she followed Mary and Elizabeth to the area that Geoffrey had arranged. She was just taking her seat when Owen swept into the room.

"I'm not late," he announced from the doorway. He looked at the two groups and then shrugged. Bessie wasn't surprised when he walked over and joined the other two men, leaving Bessie, Mary, and Elizabeth on their own near the door.

"There are only three chairs over there," Elizabeth hissed. "Will Ted pull up another chair there or join us here?"

"We just need Andy to set up the tea trolley here," Mary replied. "The men will join us quickly enough once the food arrives."

"Are we waiting for Ted?" Elizabeth asked.

Mary looked at the clock. It was just three.

"Let's give him five minutes. If he still hasn't arrived, we'll start without him and I'll send Geoffrey to find him," Mary decided.

Elizabeth filled the five minutes with a detailed description of the meal that Andy had prepared for her earlier in the week. "So you can see why I'm gaining weight," she laughed at the end. "Everything was fabulous, but I'd probably had ten thousand calories by the end of the meal."

"It all sounded wonderful," Bessie said, starting to regret her light lunch. She was starving, and the few bites of cake earlier hadn't done much to fill her stomach.

Mary looked at the clock and then sighed. She picked up the phone at her elbow and pushed a number. "Yes, Andy, you can start serving now," she said after a moment.

Less than a minute later, Andy pushed a large tea trolley into the room. Geoffrey followed, pushing a second one. Bessie gasped when she saw the beautiful selection of cakes, biscuits, and sandwiches on the trays.

"It looks incredible," she told Elizabeth.

"I think it will be perfect for the event I'm managing," Elizabeth agreed. "It looks perfect, anyway. You need to be honest about the taste, though. Andy needs feedback on everything and I need to keep my clients happy."

Bessie was fairly certain that everything was going to be delicious. The men had all jumped up as the trolleys had arrived and they were quick to fill plates and pour themselves cups of tea before returning to their chairs near the windows. Bessie, Mary, and Elizabeth followed more slowly. Once they were all sitting with full teacups and plates, Andy took a few things and sat down next to Elizabeth.

"Geoffrey, could you please go and ask Mr. Pearson to join us," Mary said to the butler.

He nodded. "I did ask them all to be here at three, just as you'd said."

"Yes, well, he may have forgotten or he may be on his mobile and have not noticed the time. Just a polite reminder, please," Mary said.

Geoffrey nodded and then left the room.

"Everything is wonderful," Bessie said a moment later. "Everything."

"Really? I wasn't sure about the scones. I found a new recipe and I wanted to try it, but I think I prefer my old recipe," Andy said.

"The scones are good. They're very light, but I do think they could be better," Bessie admitted. "Everything else is perfect, though."

Andy laughed. "I'm sure everything else could be improved, too, but I don't think I'll have time to work on any of the recipes between now and the event. I'll redo the scones later today for Elizabeth and Mary to try, at least."

"I don't think you need to worry about them," Mary said. "There's so much beautiful food there, no one will mind if the scones are only good and not great."

"I'll mind," Andy said firmly. "What if one of the guests is a fussy eater who only likes scones? That guest deserves the best scones I can make."

Elizabeth looked as if she wanted to argue, but Geoffrey walked back into the room with a frown on his face.

"Mr. Pearson isn't answering," he said in a low voice to Mary. "I knocked several times but didn't get a reply."

"I wonder if he went out somewhere," Mary said, glancing at the other three men. "When did you see him last?" she asked Geoffrey.

He looked surprised. "I saw all four gentlemen at lunch. I served them in the dining room and invited them to the tea party this afternoon."

"Did they all eat at the same time?" Bessie wondered.

"No, Mr. Taylor and Mr. Oliver ate together, around midday. Mr. Rhodes came into the dining room as the first two men were finishing their meals. He was nearly finished when Mr. Pearson arrived," Geoffrey told her.

"No one from the house ate with the men?" Bessie asked, looking at Mary and Elizabeth.

"I was helping Andy in the kitchen," Elizabeth said quickly.

"And I was lying down with a migraine," Mary told her. "I wanted to feel well enough to enjoy the tea party, so it seemed wise to skip lunch and let my tablets do their work."

"Are you feeling better?" Bessie asked.

"Much," Mary assured her.

"Mr. Pearson didn't say anything to you about going out?" Bessie asked Geoffrey.

He shook his head. "I didn't ask him about his plans, of course, but when I told him about the tea party, he said that he would attend."

"How odd," Andy said.

Bessie got to her feet and crossed the room to where the other three men were sitting. "Did Ted say anything to any of you about going out?" she asked.

All three men were busy on their phones. Almost in unison, they looked up at her blankly.

"I haven't seen him all day," Nicholas told her. "He didn't say anything last night about going anywhere today, not that I remember, anyway. I did have quite a lot to drink last night, though."

"I passed him in the corridor after lunch," Owen said. "We exchanged maybe three words, none of which were anything to do with our plans for the day."

"He came in for lunch while I was eating," Edmund said. "We talked about the weather while I finished and then I left him eating."

"So none of you know where he might be?" Bessie checked.

"He'll be in his room," Edmund said dismissively. "He'll be on his phone and ignoring everyone and everything until he wants something."

Bessie walked back to the others. "None of them know anything. Edmund reckons he'll be in his room, ignoring everyone while on his phone."

"That's a possibility," Mary said. She picked up the phone on the table and pushed a series of numbers. As Bessie sat back down, she could hear the phone ringing on the other end. Mary let it ring a dozen times before she returned the receiver to the cradle.

"Now what?" Elizabeth asked.

"He may simply have gone out," Mary said.

"Has he been going out often since he's been here?" Bessie asked.

Mary shook her head. "None of the men have been leaving Thie yn Traie," she said. "If they wanted to go anywhere, they'd need transportation. Geoffrey, I'm going to assume that Ted didn't ask you to arrange a car for him."

"No, madam, he did not," Geoffrey said firmly.

"Does anyone have his mobile number?" Mary asked.

Bessie looked over at the other three men. "One of them must, surely."

Mary sighed. She got to her feet and crossed to the other men, with Bessie following.

"Can one of you please ring Ted?" she asked when they all looked up at her. "I'm just a bit worried that he isn't here."

"He'll be talking to his father back in America, complaining about being stuck here," Edmund predicted.

"I'll do it," Owen said. He pushed a few buttons on his phone and then held it up. "It's in speaker mode," he said.

A moment later, Bessie could hear the phone ringing. After a dozen rings, Owen shrugged and ended the call.

"He never ignores his mobile," Mary said tightly.

"I'll text him," Owen suggested. "Maybe he didn't want to talk to me. He'll reply to my text, if only to tell me to leave him alone."

Bessie watched as Owen sent the text. Everyone in the room seemed fixated on Owen's phone as they all waited for the reply.

After several minutes, Owen looked up from the device. "Maybe he really doesn't want to talk to me," he said.

Mary frowned. "It's too soon to ring John, isn't it?" she asked.

"I was just thinking that same thing," Bessie told her.

"We should check his room first, anyway," Mary said. "Will you come with me?"

"Of course."

Andy and Elizabeth insisted on coming as well. The other three men had all returned to their phones, seemingly unconcerned about Ted.

"Geoffrey, look after them, please," Mary said as she led Bessie and the others out of the room.

"Of course, madam," the man replied with a bow.

Mary led them down a long corridor and then around a corner and down another hallway. "Sometimes I do wish this house were smaller," she said softly as they reached the end of the hall. She stopped in front of a door. "Here goes nothing," she said as she knocked.

After a minute, she knocked a second time. After a third, loud knock, Mary sighed. "Now what?"

"Do you have the key to the room?" Bessie asked.

Mary hesitated and then nodded. "I don't like the idea of invading our guest's privacy, though."

"I would suggest that the other option is to ring John and let him check the room," Bessie said.

Mary frowned. "If he is just having a nap, that would be very awkward."

Bessie couldn't imagine anyone napping through the sort of pounding that Mary had done on the door. "Shall I ring John?" she asked.

"Just open the door," Elizabeth said. "He won't be there because he's out doing something, and then we can go back and have more cake."

"If he's not there, we'll have to ring John," Mary said.

"Okay, but we can have cake while we wait," Elizabeth replied.

Mary shook her head and then reached into her pocket. The ring seemed to hold dozens of keys, but Mary flipped through them quickly. She held up a key and then frowned. "I'm still not certain about this."

"Let's ring John," Bessie suggested. "Maybe he'll have a better idea."

"Ted has probably simply gone for a walk or something," Mary said.

"Then it won't hurt, just peeking inside his room," Elizabeth suggested.

"Just a quick peek," Mary conceded. She unlocked the door and then slowly turned the knob. The room was dark, and Mary reached around the doorframe to switch on the light.

"I'm not going to scream," Elizabeth said as she spun around and rushed back down the corridor.

Bessie and Mary stood in the doorway. Bessie felt transfixed by the body on the bed. Andy pushed his way in between them, crossing to the bed.

"Don't touch anything," Bessie said. "It's a crime scene."

"He's still alive," Andy announced. "We need an ambulance."

"He's alive?" Mary echoed. "Oh, thank goodness."

Bessie pulled out her mobile and punched in 999. She requested an ambulance and then asked that John Rockwell be notified as well. The dispatcher promised to take care of both things.

"I'm going to go and wait for the ambulance," Mary said. Her face was pale and she looked badly shaken, but her voice was steady.

"Andy and I will wait here with Ted," Bessie said, feeling as if Ted shouldn't be alone, even if it seemed unlikely that he knew they were there.

Mary nodded. Bessie knew that whatever had happened to Ted, the police were going to investigate, so she was reluctant to enter the bedroom, but she was curious to see exactly what they'd found.

"How bad is it?" she asked Andy as she took a step into the room.

"It looks as if he cut his wrists," Andy told her. "There's some blood, but not all that much. He's unconscious, but I don't think he's lost that much blood. Maybe he took something before he cut his wrists."

"You think it was a suicide attempt?" Bessie demanded.

"I think it's meant to look that way, anyway. There's a note."

Bessie took a few more steps and then stopped when she saw the note on the bedside table.

"I can't live with what I've done. That reporter was getting too close to finding out everything. I needed to stop him. I offered him money, but he refused. I didn't think I had a choice, but now I can't live with the guilt. It's better this way," she read out loud.

"Do you think he really killed Harrison?" Andy asked.

Bessie slowly shook her head. "I don't know what to think," she said after a moment.

A few minutes later, the room was filled with paramedics and police constables. John Rockwell arrived in the middle of the chaos. He spoke briefly to the men who were getting ready to take Ted out of the room and then crossed to Bessie and Andy, who were standing together in the corner.

"I don't suppose either of you took any pictures while you were waiting for the ambulance," he said as a greeting.

"Sorry, no," Andy said. "I hope the paramedics didn't destroy your evidence."

John shrugged. "Their first priority has to be saving the man's life.

I understand that, but it is frustrating. At least I have a pair of solid witnesses who can tell me what they saw."

"You have a note," Bessie told him, gesturing towards the bedside table.

John nodded. "One of the constables told me about that as soon as I arrived. The next challenge will be getting the handwriting analyzed, but if Ted pulls though, it won't really matter."

Bessie nodded. "Now what?"

"Now you and Andy need to go back to the great room. I'm going to spend some time working the scene before I take your statements. I'm going to have to take statements from everyone else, too. I'm going to get one of the constables to get started on the staff now. I've requested Hugh because I trust him to talk to the other three guests. I want to talk to you two, Elizabeth, and Mary myself."

"We'll go and wait in the great room, then," Bessie said.

"I'd rather you didn't talk amongst yourselves while you wait," John added as they headed for the door.

Mindful of John's last words, the pair were silent on the walk back to the great room. There they discovered a pair of constables watching over everyone. Mary and Elizabeth were back in the same seats they'd been in over tea. As far as Bessie could tell, the three men hadn't moved while she'd been gone. Geoffrey was hovering in the doorway, looking as if he wanted to be anywhere but there.

Bessie slid back into her seat and stared at the tea trolley. The cakes and sandwiches still looked lovely, but the thought of eating anything made her feel slightly queasy. When she shut her eyes, she could see Ted, lying apparently lifeless on the huge bed in the middle of the expensively-furnished room. While she hadn't spoken to him very recently, he hadn't seemed the least bit suicidal the last time they had spoken. Furthermore, he didn't seem the type to feel guilty about his decisions. If he had killed Harrison Parker, Bessie thought he'd have felt as if the murder was justified in some way. Frowning, she sat back in her seat and tried to think.

"Mr. Oliver, if I could have a word with you, please," a familiar voice said in the doorway.

Owen got to his feet and followed Hugh out of the room.

"What's going on?" Nicholas demanded. "We were having tea and all of a sudden there are police everywhere. Don't tell me that Ted had a heart attack or something."

The two constables exchanged glances. Clearly they hadn't been told to expect questions.

"Mary, what's going on?" Nicholas asked.

Mary shook her head. "I'm sure the police will explain everything," she said.

"It's something to do with Ted, then, isn't it?" Edmund asked. "Is he missing? Are they mounting a search party? Maybe he simply got lost in the house somewhere. The longer I'm here, the more likely that seems. I found another hidden passageway today and, when I followed it, I found myself in another wing of the building that I hadn't ever seen before."

Mary looked at the two constables. After a moment, one cleared his throat. "Inspector Rockwell would prefer if you remained quiet while you wait," he said, sounding incredibly young and unsure of himself.

Edmund stared at him for a minute and then laughed. "Yeah, okay," he said before sliding back in his seat.

A short while later, Nicholas was escorted out for his interview with Hugh. Not long after that, John came and took Elizabeth away for questioning.

Bessie amused herself by trying to guess if John or Hugh would finish first. She was pretty sure Hugh would be back for Edmund before John returned, but John came and got Andy a full three minutes before Hugh walked back into the room.

Mary slid closer to Bessie and then reached over and took her hand. Bessie squeezed gently and then frowned as a tear slid down Mary's cheek.

"Are you okay?" she whispered.

Mary shook her head. "I'm starting to think that Thie yn Traie actually is cursed," she said. "I love this house, but even I can't ignore everything that has happened here since we bought it."

"The first bad things happened before you bought it," Bessie pointed out, not sure if that helped or not.

Mary shrugged. "I'm just feeling…"

"I'm very sorry, but you aren't meant to be talking," the young constable said, sounding apologetic.

"Sorry," Mary said. She rested her head on the back of the couch and shut her eyes.

Bessie gave her hand another squeeze. A moment later, Hugh was back. He smiled at Bessie and then asked Geoffrey to come with him. John came for Mary a moment later.

Feeling rather alone, Bessie studied the two young constables. She was sure that she'd met the older one once or twice before. It was most likely that he'd been at Hugh's wedding. The younger man, though, was a stranger. As Bessie thought about striking up a conversation, John walked back into the room.

"Bessie? I'm ready for your statement now," he said.

She stood up and followed him out of the room. After a few steps, he stopped and shook his head. "Give me a minute," he said, before returning to the great room. Bessie could hear him speaking to the two constables, giving them their next instructions. He rejoined her a moment later.

"No point in having them stand guard in an empty room," he said.

"No, I suppose not," Bessie agreed.

"Mary is letting us use several different rooms for interviews," John explained as he ushered her into the large library. "This is my favourite."

"It's my favourite, too. Mary lets me come and browse the shelves whenever I want."

"Have you found anything good?"

Bessie glanced around the room and then made a face. "It's mostly first editions of classics, which I'm sure are worth a fortune but aren't the sort of thing I'd actually want to read. There isn't very much in the way of popular literature."

John nodded. "I suppose we should get started, then."

CHAPTER 13

"Take me through your day, starting with the time that you got up," John said.

Bessie grinned. "I wasn't expecting to be able to tell you about my morning until tonight."

"Tonight will probably have to be rescheduled. I don't think I'm going to be finished here in time."

"That's fine. At least I can tell you all about my odd conversation with Geoffrey now."

Bessie did just that, telling John everything that she could remember about her chat on the beach with the butler. Then she told him about the invitation to the tea party and what had happened once she'd arrived at Thie yn Traie.

"Why were you all so worried about Ted?" John asked when she was finished. "He's a grown man. Surely it wouldn't have been surprising if he'd decided to get out of the house for a while."

"Except he hasn't been leaving since he's been here and he didn't ask Geoffrey to arrange for transportation," Bessie explained. "Anyway, if he'd decided to go out, he should have told Mary that he was going."

"Perhaps," John said. "Geoffrey said that he'd knocked, correct?"

"Yes."

"He didn't mention trying the door or going inside the room?"

"No. If he had tried the door, he would have found it locked. Mary had to unlock it when we were there. Besides, if Geoffrey had gone into the room, he would have rung for an ambulance himself."

John nodded. "I'm just double-checking what everyone told me."

"I suppose he may have tried the door, but if he did, he didn't mention it to us."

"The other three men didn't seem worried about where Ted was, though, is that correct?"

"They didn't seem at all interested, really. They were all on their phones, ignoring everyone else."

"Which is rather rude at a tea party," John suggested.

"It was very rude, but as I didn't really want to speak to any of them, I wasn't about to complain."

"Did Mary feel as if they were being rude?"

"She wouldn't have criticized them to me, but I'm sure she thought it. I also suspect that she was even happier than I was that they were keeping to themselves. She's been entertaining them since they arrived, of course."

John nodded. "Did you suspect Ted of being the killer or of being suicidal?"

"I suspect everyone of being the killer, but he didn't seem suicidal to me, not even if he was guilty of murder. He was too arrogant to feel guilty, in my opinion."

"What do you think happened to Ted, then?"

"I can only imagine that Harrison's killer was trying to frame him," Bessie said thoughtfully. "Ted did confess to the murder in his note, after all. If it's in Ted's handwriting and Ted doesn't recover, what will happen?"

"It's far too soon to speculate about that," John told her. "We're hoping that Ted will recover and be able to answer questions in the next few days. It has been suggested that one of the other men, anxious to get off the island, simply set up the frame to get the murder investigation closed."

"Someone tried to kill Ted to close a murder investigation?" Bessie asked.

"The suggestion was that whoever it was didn't want to kill Ted, just leave him unconscious for a few days, enough time that the other men could push to be allowed to leave the island. After that, even if Ted recovered, we wouldn't be able to drag the others back, not simply for questioning, anyway."

"Was Ted drugged?" Bessie asked.

John hesitated. "At this point, I'm simply speculating, but it appeared to me that he'd been drugged or that he'd had a great deal to drink. I hope to know more soon."

"And then you won't be able to tell me anything," Bessie complained.

"Is there anything else you can tell me that might help?" John asked.

Bessie thought for a minute and then shook her head. "I don't think so."

"Let's plan on having our gathering tomorrow night," John suggested. "I'll let Hugh and Doona know that the plans have changed."

"Maybe I'll be able to make that apple crumble after all," Bessie laughed.

"That sounds good," John told her.

He escorted her back out into the corridor, where Mary was pacing anxiously.

"What's wrong?" Bessie asked her.

"I have to pack a bag for Ted and take it to Noble's," she replied. "I don't suppose you could help?"

Bessie glanced at John.

"I'll need to have someone supervise what you pack," he told Mary.

"Yes, I understand that. I was going to have Geoffrey do it, but that seems, well, wrong. Ted is my guest, well, George's guest, really, but his well-being is my responsibility. Whatever happened to him, it's my job to look after him."

"I'd have Geoffrey do it, if I were you," Bessie told her.

Mary flushed. "As much as I'd like to, I can't. You don't have to help."

"I will, though," Bessie told her.

"Thank you," Mary said sincerely.

"Give me a minute," John said. He pulled out his mobile and texted someone. A moment later, he smiled. "Hugh is available to help," he said. "He'll meet you in Ted's room."

"Wonderful," Mary said, looking slightly happier.

Bessie followed Mary back down the long corridors. It was impossible for her to imagine what it would be like living in such a huge home. "Have you explored the entire house?" she asked as they walked.

Mary smiled at her. "We were given a very thorough tour when we were thinking of purchasing the house, but we know now that we missed things on that tour. Jonathan has been having great fun in his spare time, finding secret doors and hidden rooms. I believe he's found at least half a dozen rooms we didn't know we had."

"Are they all furnished as beautifully as the rest of the house?"

"They are. Several have been bedrooms. It appears that Mrs. Pierce had a secret sewing room. And there were two game rooms full of board games and comfortable couches, with large televisions, too. I assume there was one for each of their sons."

"My goodness."

"There are a number of ways in and out of the house, as well. Those are more worrying than anything else. Our security team is doing what it can to find ways to monitor them all, but we, or rather Jonathan, seems to find new ones regularly."

"I wonder why the Pierces had the house built that way."

Mary shrugged. "I can't imagine."

Hugh was standing in Ted's bedroom doorway. "We'd appreciate it if you'd try to touch as little as possible," he said to Mary.

She nodded. "I just want to pack what he'll need at Noble's."

Hugh went into the room and opened the wardrobe door. "There are two large suitcases in here."

"Either will do," Mary told him.

Hugh took out one of the cases and carried it into the corridor. He opened it on the floor. "Empty."

"So what will he need?" Bessie asked.

"Pyjamas, slippers, underwear," Hugh said. "If you two want to stay here, I'll see what I can find."

Bessie and Mary exchanged glances. "I didn't mean to make work for you," Mary said. "John just said you'd watch me."

"I could, but, as I said, we'd like to keep the room as untouched as possible. It isn't exactly a crime scene, but it could be, if Mr. Pearson doesn't recover," Hugh replied.

Mary drew a sharp breath. "Let's hope it doesn't come to that."

"Indeed," Bessie said.

Hugh nodded. "Aside from the suitcases, the wardrobe was empty. I'll have to try the drawers." There was a large chest of drawers next to the bed. Hugh opened the top drawer and grinned. "Underwear, anyway."

"He'll need some clothes to wear when he leaves hospital," Mary said. "I'm not sure what he was wearing when he left here, but I'm certain he'll want something clean and fresh when he's ready to be discharged."

Hugh nodded. A few minutes later the suitcase was half-full with everything that Hugh could find that Mary thought Ted might need. "Check the bathroom again," Mary requested. "I think we have everything, but I'd hate to forget something."

Hugh disappeared into the large en-suite. He was back a moment later. "I've pretty much packed everything that was in there, aside from a few over-the-counter medications. He shouldn't need those in hospital, surely."

Mary nodded. "I suppose that's all we can do, then."

Hugh closed the suitcase and then stood it up on its wheels. "Let me get someone to take this for you," he said, glancing at the handful of men and women who were working in the room.

"We can manage," Mary said firmly. "It's half-empty and it's on wheels."

"Are you sure?" Hugh asked.

"Quite sure," Mary told him. She grabbed the handle of the case. "Thank you for all of your help. I felt much better letting you do all the searching than I would have doing it myself."

Hugh nodded. "I was happy to help."

Mary took a deep breath and then smiled. "How's Aalish?" she asked quietly.

"She's good. Grace told me that I should tell you that she and Aalish both miss seeing you, though," Hugh replied.

Mary nodded. "Tell her I'll be back to dropping in unannounced again once our guests leave."

Hugh nodded. "She'll be happy to hear that. She tells me all the time how much she values having a bit of adult conversation in the day."

"I remember those days," Mary laughed. "It will get better."

"I'm sure it will," Hugh agreed.

Bessie followed Mary through the corridors again. "Do you visit Grace often?" Bessie asked.

Mary shrugged. "When the weather is good, I like to walk on the beach. I don't go out every morning the way that you do, but I often take an afternoon walk between lunch and dinner. Grace and Hugh's house is just about the right distance from here for a good walk. I'd do better if I walked there and straight back, but I often end up stopping for tea and biscuits with Grace and Aalish. I love babies very much and I think my children are done giving me grandchildren, well, unless Elizabeth decides to have children one day. She's always said she didn't want children, but maybe she'll change her mind."

"I'm sure Grace appreciates the company."

"She seems to, but I appreciate the baby cuddles far more. They're very special days and they go by far too quickly."

Bessie opened her mouth to reply, but she was interrupted by Geoffrey.

"Ah, Mrs. Quayle, you must let me get that," he said, reaching for the suitcase.

"It's fine. There isn't much in it," Mary replied.

Geoffrey shook his head. "Regardless, I should take it." He took the handle and tried to pull the case away from Mary.

She held on tightly, shaking her head. "I said I have it," she said sharply.

Geoffrey dropped his hand and stepped back. "Of course. I was only trying to help."

Mary nodded. "It's fine. Bessie and I are just going to take the case to Mr. Pearson at Noble's."

"I'm sure you have better things to do," he replied. "I'd be more than happy to take care of the case for you."

"Mr. Pearson is my guest. Taking him his things is my responsibility," Mary countered. "You can look after the rest of the guests while I'm gone."

Geoffrey nodded and then stepped closer to Mary. "I'm sorry for asking, but what happened to Mr. Pearson? I know an ambulance came and that he's in hospital now, but what happened?"

"I believe the police are trying to work out the answer to that question," Mary told him.

Geoffrey nodded. "I was worried that he might have overdosed on something," he said in a whisper. "When he first arrived, he asked me if I could help him find certain items, but I had to tell him that, unfortunately, I was new to the island and couldn't help him."

"If he was requesting anything illegal, I would hope you would have refused to help him, regardless," Mary said.

"Of course," the man agreed. "I wasn't certain if I should tell you or not, but I did see some drug paraphernalia in his room, as well."

"You definitely should have told me," Mary said. "I will not have such things under my roof."

Geoffrey nodded. "I should have told you. I am sorry."

"Is there anything else you haven't told me?" Mary demanded.

"No, of course not."

Mary glanced at Bessie. "Are you ready to go to Noble's, then?"

"Yes, let's," Bessie agreed.

"I do hope that Mr. Pearson is going to recover," Geoffrey said.

"The last I heard, he was expected to make a full recovery," Bessie told him. Was it her imagination that he looked a bit disappointed at her words?

"Excellent," he said smoothly, bowing and then turning and marching away.

Mary frowned at his back. "I'm starting to dislike that man," she muttered.

"Do you think he had anything to do with what happened to Ted?"

"I don't know what to think."

They walked through the house to the large garage. A man was polishing a car and he jumped to attention when Mary appeared.

"Mrs. Quayle, did you need a ride somewhere?" he asked, sounding confused.

"Yes, please, I need to go to Noble's," Mary replied.

"Ah, yes, of course," he said, looking around rather desperately. Another man walked out from another section of the garage.

"I've got this, Stuart," he said. "Mrs. Quayle, let me take that bag for you. We'll take the black car, if that suits you."

"It does," Mary said. She and Bessie followed the man across the garage to a large black limousine. He held the door to the rear section for them before he loaded the suitcase into the boot.

"Straight to Noble's?" he asked as he slid into the driver's seat.

"Yes, please," Mary told him.

She settled back in her seat and looked over at Bessie. "Did you see any drug paraphernalia in Ted's room when we went in?" she asked in a low voice.

"No, but then I really don't have any idea what constitutes drug paraphernalia. I didn't see any tablets or any bottles of anything, but I've no idea what I might have missed."

Mary nodded and then sighed. "I have no idea to what Geoffrey might have been referring. I know nothing about drugs."

"Me neither. Did Ted ever seem to be under the influence of anything when you spoke to him?"

"Not that I noticed, but I don't know that I would have noticed. I don't care for the man and I rarely spoke to him except when necessary."

191

"Did he drink much?"

"No more than the other three men. No more than George, if I'm honest. I keep trying to get George to cut back, but he doesn't drink nearly as much when it's just us at home. When he has guests, he feels as if he has to keep up, I believe."

Bessie sighed. What was it about men, she wondered. "What do you think happened to Ted, then?"

"I'm afraid whoever killed Harrison tried to kill Ted," Mary said. "I don't believe that he was attempting suicide. He isn't the type."

"I agree, although I'm sure there isn't really a type."

Mary nodded. "You're right, of course, just as there isn't a type to be a murderer. The ones I've met over the past few years have all been very different."

"So who might have tried to kill Ted?"

"I believe everyone at the house had the opportunity," Mary said. "The four men all went back to their rooms after lunch. They were supposed to return for the tea party, but anyone could have done anything in the interim."

"Where are the other three men's rooms in relation to Ted's?"

"They were all on that same corridor. It seemed easiest to keep them all in the same wing."

"I'm sure John has asked them all what they did between lunch and tea," Bessie said thoughtfully.

"I'm afraid I don't have much of an alibi. I was in bed with a migraine, but, of course, I don't have any witnesses to that."

"But of course you didn't have anything to do with what happened to Ted."

"Thank you," Mary said. "I wish I felt as if John Rockwell believed that."

"John knows you didn't have anything to do with anything criminal."

"I hope you're right."

"I know I'm right."

The car pulled up to the doors at Noble's a moment later. "Parking can be difficult. I may have to drive around to find a space," the driver said.

"I'll ring you when we're done," Mary told him.

He got out and retrieved the suitcase from the boot. "Is there anything else?" he asked.

Mary shook her head. "We'll ring you."

"Very good."

He drove away as Mary began to pull the suitcase towards the building's doors. Bessie followed her into the large foyer.

"I'm not sure where to go," Mary said, glancing around.

"We can start with information, but they may not tell us anything," Bessie suggested. They crossed the room to the desk at the back.

"We're here to see Mr. Ted Pearson," Bessie said. "If he isn't allowed visitors, that's fine. We'll just leave his bag."

The woman behind the information desk checked her computer and then flipped through some paperwork. "I'm sorry, but I don't have any record of any Mr. Pearson here at the moment."

Bessie nodded, unsurprised. "We should have asked John where to take the bag," she told Mary. Finding her mobile in her handbag took an embarrassingly long time. When she pulled it out, she stared at it for a moment.

"Is something wrong?" Mary asked.

"I'm not sure whom to ring," Bessie admitted. "I could ring John, but I'm sure he's busy. Or I could ring Helen, who works here and knows everything that's going on, but who is also, no doubt, very busy."

"Maybe you could ring Hugh," Mary suggested. "He can probably find out what we need to know fairly quickly."

Bessie nodded. "That's a good idea. I'm sure he's busy, too, but maybe less so than the other two." She was starting to push buttons on her phone when she heard her name being called.

"Bessie?"

She turned around and gave Pete Corkill a huge smile. The man was a police inspector with Douglas Constabulary. He and Bessie had met over a dead body years earlier, and initial dislike had turned to mutual respect and, eventually, friendship. As soon as he was close enough, she added a hug to her greeting. "We were just trying to work out whom to ring," she told him as she dropped her phone back into her bag.

"John rang to tell me that you and Mrs. Quayle were on your way," he told her. "I thought I should try to catch you down here because I knew the woman at the desk wouldn't be able to help you."

"They said Mr. Pearson wasn't here," Bessie told him.

"Which is what they've been told to say," Pete told her. He glanced around the room. "Let's go and talk somewhere private," he suggested. He led the two women to a bench in a corner and then waved them into seats.

"How's Helen?" Bessie asked.

Pete's face lit up at the mention of his wife. They'd also met during the murder investigation that had introduced Bessie and Pete. Pete had been recovering from a messy divorce, and Helen was nearly forty and ready to give up on finding anyone. Bessie and John had stood as witnesses when the pair had married, and all of their friends had been delighted when Helen had recently announced her pregnancy. "She's fine, although she's having odd cravings. The midwife says it's all perfectly normal."

"Odd?" Bessie asked.

"She's been wanting to eat raw potatoes and paper," Pete told her.

"Raw potatoes? Paper? And that's normal?" Bessie replied.

"According to the midwife, it's normal, and it's even safe as long as she limits herself to just a tiny bit of each thing." He shook his head. "I've never been so glad to be a man in my life, and she's only a few months along."

Bessie shook her head. "But what about Ted Pearson?" she asked.

"Mr. Pearson isn't allowed visitors," he said. "I can take his suitcase up to him, but he's some way away from needing anything in it."

"I'd like to see him," Mary said in a low voice. "I have to ring his father later tonight and I'd like to assure the man that I've seen him."

Pete hesitated and then nodded. "You may have a quick look from the doorway," he said. "We've two constables with him at the moment, but I'll be accompanying you as well."

Mary nodded. "Whatever you want to do is fine with me."

"Bessie, would you mind waiting here?" Pete asked. "The fewer people who know exactly where Mr. Pearson is, the better."

"I'm happy to wait here," Bessie replied, mostly truthfully. She felt a bit left out, but she'd seen Ted before the ambulance had arrived and she didn't really want to see him again, not until he was recovered, anyway.

Pete nodded and then stood up. "Let's go," he said to Mary, taking the suitcase from her. Bessie watched as they crossed the lobby to the lifts at the back.

"So Mary gets to see Ted. That suggests that she isn't a suspect in his attack," a voice said in Bessie's ear.

She made a face as Dan Ross dropped into the chair next to hers.

"Don't look so happy to see me," he laughed. "I've been staying well away from Thie yn Traie for the last few days. I thought maybe you'd missed me."

"Not likely," Bessie replied.

"And you weren't worried about me?"

"I'd have heard if something had happened to you."

"I suppose so. Your network for skeet is better than anything I can put together, even with paid sources," Dan sighed.

Bessie hid a grin. Dan was probably right, though. Her sources were widespread and reliable.

"Anyway, if Mary gets to visit Ted, she must have been eliminated as a suspect. Why?"

"No comment."

Dan stared at her for a moment and then laughed. "Really? No comment? I deserve more than that."

"What makes you think Mary is visiting Ted?" Bessie countered. "What makes you think Ted is at Noble's?"

"I got an anonymous tip that Ted Pearson took a nearly fatal over-dose in his room at Thie yn Traie," Dan told her. "The caller seemed to

195

think that it was an accidental overdose or maybe a suicide attempt, but since you're here, I'm guessing it was another murder attempt."

"My presence in the lobby of Noble's doesn't mean any such thing," Bessie protested.

"Which one of the other men wanted him dead, then? Was he close to signing the deal with George? Was it professional jealousy, or does his overdose tie into Harrison's murder? Did Ted know something about that murder, or was the killer just looking for a convenient scapegoat? Come on, Bessie, you can tell me. What's actually going on?"

Bessie counted to ten before she replied. "No comment."

He laughed. "Why not? What are you hiding?"

Counting to ten again kept Bessie from blurting out a response. After she reached ten, she kept going, curious to see how long Dan would be able to sit in silence.

"Could it have been a suicide attempt?" Dan asked as Bessie reached fifty-three.

"No comment," she said with a yawn.

"Is the retail park project going to be put on hold now?"

Bessie began to search her bag for her mobile. Maybe she could pretend to be busy doing something on it until Dan got tired of being ignored.

"Maybe I should go and ask some questions at Thie yn Traie," Dan said. "Who would you suggest I talk with first?"

Wondering whom she could text, Bessie began to look through her list of contacts. Doona might be at work, but she might not. *Hello,* she texted to her closest friend.

"Ah, come on, Bessie. Don't do this to me. I thought we were friends now. I slept in your spare room. You made me lunch."

Hello? was the reply Bessie received.

I'm sitting at Noble's. Waiting for Mary. Dan Ross is annoying me, she replied.

"Was there a note?" Dan demanded. "I'll bet there was a note. I'll bet Ted confessed to killing Harrison. That will be why there are so many constables here. They aren't here to protect him. They're here to guard a killer."

Oh, sorry, Doona replied.

Mary shouldn't be much longer, Bessie told her.

"That's it, then, I'm going to have to put my life in danger and go to Thie yn Traie," Dan said dramatically. "If you find my body on the beach tomorrow, tell my mother that I loved her."

Bessie stared at him for a moment. "If you think your life is in danger, I suggest you stay away from Thie yn Traie."

"I won't have to go there if you'll tell me what's happening."

"You know I'm not going to do that."

He shrugged. "Then I have no choice."

"Are you bothering this woman?" a man in a security uniform asked Dan.

He flushed and then stood up. "I was just leaving."

"I think that's probably for the best," the guard said sternly.

Dan looked as if he wanted to say something else, but one glance at the security guard's face had him snapping his mouth shut and walking away.

"I hope everything is okay now," the guard said to Bessie.

"It's fine. He wasn't really bothering me, well, no more than normal," she tried to explain.

"I had a message from the Laxey Constabulary, asking me to check on you," the guard explained. "Someone called Doona Moore sent me."

"Well, thank you. I'll thank Doona, too."

He nodded. "If you need anything else, my office is right over there." He pointed to a door that Bessie could just see from where she was sitting.

"I'll keep that in mind." Bessie waited until he'd walked away before she texted Doona again. *Thanks for sending security over. He got rid of Dan very quickly.*

I was happy to do it, Doona replied.

Bessie sat back in her seat and thought about what Dan had said. Was he really putting his life in danger by going to Thie yn Traie to ask questions? It seemed entirely possible that he was, actually, she decided.

Dan's going to Thie yn Traie to ask questions, she told Doona. *Can John arrest him for something in order to keep him safe?*

A moment later, Mary crossed the lobby. Bessie stood up to greet her friend. "How are you?" she asked, feeling concerned, as Mary was pale and looked sad.

"He looked more alive when we found him on the bed earlier," Mary said softly. 'If they didn't have a dozen monitors tracking his breathing and everything else, I might have thought he was dead."

"Oh, dear," Bessie said.

"I only got a very quick look at him, but from what I could see, he isn't going to be answering any questions in the next day or two. I just hope he recovers eventually."

Bessie gave her friend a hug. "I got to talk to Dan Ross while you were gone."

Mary frowned more deeply. "What did he want?"

"The full story of what happened to Ted, of course, and any speculation I wanted to share about the situation."

"What did you tell him?"

"Nothing, of course. And then Doona sent security over to chase him away."

"Good for Doona. Was she here?"

"No, I texted her while Dan was peppering me with questions."

Mary nodded. "I've notified the driver that we're done. He should be here in a few minutes."

"Dan told me he was going to go to Thie yn Traie next to ask his questions there," Bessie warned her.

"I shouldn't be surprised, should I?"

"He seemed to think that his life might be in danger there."

"He may be right. Harrison is dead and Ted is in a terrible state. The curse of Thie yn Traie seems stronger than ever."

"Thie yn Traie isn't cursed," Bessie said firmly.

Mary shrugged. "I hope you're right."

Bessie's phone buzzed. She glanced at the screen. *John is going to try to intercept Dan. If he can, he'll find an excuse to keep him away from Thie yn Traie for as long as possible,* Doona had replied.

She read the message out to Mary, who nodded.

"I suppose we'll have to be happy with that, then," Mary said, sounding anything but happy.

A moment later Mary's driver appeared in the doorway. He waved and Bessie and Mary walked across the lobby and followed him outside.

"We'll take you home, unless you wanted to come back to Thie yn Traie," Mary said as the car began the journey out of Douglas.

"Do you want me to come back?"

"Yes, of course I do," Mary said with a shaky laugh. "But I'm sure you have better things to do than sit with me simply because I'm feeling a bit wobbly."

"When will George be home?"

"That's a good point," Mary said, glancing at the thin gold watch on her wrist. "He may already be home. It's nearly six. I hadn't realised."

"I hadn't, either," Bessie said. She hadn't eaten all that much at the tea party, but she didn't feel particularly hungry for dinner, either.

"We'll take you home," Mary said. "I'm sure you aren't in the mood for George tonight. Not after the day you had."

Bessie thought about objecting, but Mary was right. The last thing she wanted at the moment was to spend time with George Quayle. "Are you sure?" she asked, after an awkward pause.

"Quite sure," Mary told her.

Bessie sat back and looked out the window, wondering if Mary was also not in the mood for her boisterous husband on this particular evening.

CHAPTER 14

They arrived back at Treoghe Bwaane a short while later. "Thank you," Bessie said to Mary.

"No, thank you. Thank you for coming to tea this afternoon, and thank you for your help with Ted's things. I could have managed on my own, but it was much easier because you were there."

"I didn't actually do anything," Bessie pointed out.

"But you were there. That meant a lot to me."

"Do you have a number for Jonathan?" Bessie asked as the driver opened her door.

"Of course," Mary replied. She opened her handbag and pulled out a small leather-covered notebook. "Shall I copy it onto something for you?" she asked.

"If you don't mind."

Mary tore a scrap of paper out of the book and carefully wrote down the number that had been neatly printed on one of the pages. "He's in classes all day, but he's usually in his room in the evenings," she told Bessie as she handed her the scrap. "He has voice mail, as well."

"Thank you," Bessie said, slipping the sheet into her pocket. As she climbed out of the car, she wondered if she'd have been as forthcoming if Mary had asked her for someone's number. No doubt she would have at least asked the other woman why she'd wanted it. As Bessie wasn't entirely certain why she'd asked for the number, she was relieved that Mary hadn't asked her for any explanations.

Inside her cottage, she switched on a few lights and then sat down at the kitchen table. It took her several minutes to clear away all of the messages on her answering machine. Most of them were simply nosy friends who wanted to hear the latest on what had happened at Thie yn Traie. Bessie deleted those immediately. Doona had rung to confirm that their gathering was being postponed until the next day. There seemed no need to ring her back either. The last message was from Dan Ross.

"It's getting late tonight, but I'm going to be at Thie yn Traie first thing tomorrow morning to get some answers. If you have any idea who was behind Harrison's murder, I'd really appreciate it if you'd ring me back and give me a hint. I won't quote you or anything. I just want to know who I need to be extra careful around, that's all."

Bessie pressed the delete button and then sat back in her chair. Dan was probably being foolish, visiting Thie yn Traie. No one was going to speak to him, and it seemed likely that someone there was a murderer. He would be wasting his time, but Bessie had to hope that his life wouldn't be in any immediate danger. It seemed unlikely that he was anywhere near solving the murder.

It was already six o'clock, and she hadn't even thought about dinner. A quick search through her cupboards didn't reveal anything that sounded appealing. Wishing she'd eaten more of the delicious tea that Andy had prepared, she looked through her tins of soup, trying to muster up some enthusiasm for tomato or potato and leek. Finally, she shut her eyes and grabbed a random tin. Soup, with some slightly stale bread, was her dinner. She had tea with biscuits after she'd finished her soup, and then wondered what to do with her evening.

Onnee's letters were, as always, waiting for her, but she didn't feel up to the task of deciphering them at the moment. Instead, she pulled the slip of paper that Mary had given her out of her pocket. After staring at it for several minutes, she reached for the phone.

"Hello?"

"Jack? It's Bessie Cubbon."

"Bessie, my dear, I hope nothing is wrong."

"No, not at all. I just wanted to ask you a few questions about Thie yn Traie, that's all."

"How are things at Thie yn Traie? I do miss it and I miss the family. Mrs. Quayle rings me at least once or twice a week, just to check on me, but she won't talk about how they are doing with my temporary replacement. I do hope that Geoffrey is doing a good job for them."

Bessie frowned. It sounded very much as if Jack didn't know about Harrison Parker's murder. She hadn't expected him to have heard about Ted, but she hadn't realised that she'd have to tell him about Harrison as well. "There have been some issues," she said slowly. "Not with Geoffrey, but with other things."

"I don't like the sound of that. Can you hang on a minute?"

"Of course." Bessie heard him put the phone down and then, a moment later, a door shut.

"Sorry, we all leave our doors open in the early evening so we can talk and compare notes. I have a feeling this conversation might need a closed door."

"I feel bad telling you things that Mary hasn't shared with you."

"She doesn't want me to worry, but if there are problems for the family, I should know about them."

"I'm surprised your mother hasn't told you about everything that's been happening on the island."

"Mum is in Florida for three months. She has friends who bought a house there when they retired, so she's gone to visit them and soak up some sunshine. I doubt she's given the island any thought since she left."

Bessie sighed. "There was a murder on the beach," she began. Ten minutes later, she'd told Jonathan everything that had happened in the past week.

"I wish Mrs. Quayle would have told me all of this," he said when she was finished. "No doubt she knows that I would have wanted to come back immediately, though. She and Mr. Quayle are paying a great deal of money for me to take this course. I'm sure they wouldn't get a refund if I quit halfway through."

"How is the course?"

"Actually, it's brilliant. I've learned a lot about computers and networks, and also security. I should be able to help the security team set up all sorts of useful things once I get back. It seems as if I'll be a bit too late, though, at least to help Mr. Parker."

"What sort of security things?"

"Better cameras with night vision, motion sensors for little-used areas of the house, alarms that can be put on hidden doors and sliding panels, things like that."

"That all sounds very useful for Thie yn Traie. I never knew how many secrets it had."

"I'm fairly certain I haven't found everything. I've been trying, in my spare time, but I don't get a lot of that, really."

"I don't suppose you've ever met any of the four men who are currently staying at the house?"

"I have met Owen Oliver, actually. He was a guest in a house where I worked many years ago. He was helping them add an extension and he stayed in one of the guest rooms for about a month while supervising the construction."

"That seems odd to me."

"It was odd, but he was also having an affair with the lady of the house, so maybe that explains it."

A dozen questions sprang into Bessie's head. "If Harrison Parker found out about that affair, can you see Owen killing him to keep it quiet?"

"Oh, goodness, no. It was an open secret in the house. I'm sure her husband knew. I can't imagine anyone else caring, really."

"Can you suggest any motive Owen might have had for killing Harrison?"

"I'm afraid not. As I said, I barely know the man. The other three are total strangers."

"What about Geoffrey?"

"What about him? Can I think of a motive for him for Harrison's death? I only spoke to the man twice, once when he came for his interview and then a second time when he actually arrived on the island. We did a brief handover the day before I left for London."

"How brief? Did you take him all around the house? Did you show him all of its secrets?"

"I don't know about all of them, but I showed him a few. There were some that I knew would be useful for him, shortcuts between the wings and that sort of thing. I also showed him the tunnel that leads out to the stairway to the beach, because it's one entrance that security can't really monitor, for the moment, anyway. I put a padlock on the door and gave Geoffrey the key."

Bessie frowned. Several people had talked about that tunnel. She didn't remember anyone mentioning a padlock on the door. Grabbing a pad of paper, she made a note to ask John about the padlock.

"What did you think of him as a person?" she asked Jonathan.

"He seemed as if he'd be perfectly adequate for the job. If Mr. and Mrs. Quayle had been looking for a proper replacement for me, I don't think they would have chosen him, but as a temporary substitute he seemed, as I said, adequate."

"Only adequate?"

"He has the right credentials and impeccable references, but I didn't care for him. Maybe that's just because he went to the other butler training school, not the one that I went to, but the rival school."

"I didn't realise there were rival butler schools."

Jonathan laughed. "Only people who train as butlers or hire butlers care, I'm sure. There are probably a dozen places that offer butler training, but only two that regularly supply staff to nobility and the royal family. I went through one of their programmes and Geoffrey went through the other."

"Are they very different?"

"They're probably identical, but I prefer to believe that I received a superior education."

"Did you speak to any of Geoffrey's references yourself?"

"No, but I believe Mr. Quayle rang a few of them."

"What else do you know about Geoffrey?"

"He's just returning to work after some time off due to ill health. This is his first assignment in over a year, I believe. It's quite unusual for anyone who trained at either of the two top schools to take temporary jobs, actually. Mr. and Mrs. Quayle felt that they were fortunate to find him."

"Did they interview many others for the job?"

"As far as I know, Geoffrey was the only person who was interviewed. Mr. and Mrs. Quayle worked through an agency. I believe the agency sent information about half a dozen candidates and Mr. and Mrs. Quayle chose Geoffrey from them."

"Can you see him as a killer?"

"My first instinct is to say no, but that would probably be the same for anyone. I can't imagine how he'd even have known Harrison Parker, though. What was Harrison doing on the island?"

"No one seems to be able to answer that question. Apparently, he was chasing a story, but it wasn't one that he'd been assigned, as I understand it."

"I've no idea what Harrison could have been investigating that might have involved Geoffrey. If it was something to do with Mr. Quayle's business deal, which seems likely, then I can't imagine why Geoffrey would have been involved in any way."

"Yes, of course," Bessie agreed. The pair chatted for a few more minutes about the case and then about Jonathan's course. When Bessie put the phone down, she frowned at it. Something was bothering her about Geoffrey Scott, but she wasn't sure what it was. She paced around the kitchen for several minutes before deciding to take a walk on the beach instead. It was too dark for her to walk far, but she didn't feel as if she could simply sit still on her rock tonight.

Determined to keep her cottage in view, Bessie stayed away from the water as she walked along right behind the holiday cottages. When she reached the police tape, she stopped and glared at it. If she walked much further, she'd lose sight of Treoghe Bwaane, but she still found the tape annoying.

With a sigh, she turned back around and started for home. A

moment later, something moving caught her eye. There was someone walking down from the car park behind the holiday cottages. Bessie moved closer to the nearest cottage, trying to stay out of the line of sight of the new arrival. Whoever it was, he or she was looking around, presumably trying to avoid being seen.

Moving even further into the shadow of one of the cottages, Bessie watched as the other person approached the police tape. After a quick glance around, he or she ducked under the tape and headed for the stairs to Thie yn Traie.

As the figure moved up the steps, Bessie walked closer, trying to see if her suspicions were correct. Halfway up the stairs, a section of rock slid open and the person ducked into the tunnel that Bessie knew led up to the mansion. The tunnel was well lit, and Bessie nodded with grim satisfaction as she recognised Dan Ross just before the door slid shut again.

As she marched home, Bessie debated whom she should ring first. Wanting to warn Mary that the reporter was in her house seemed less important than ringing John to let him know that Dan had breached the police tape. She briefly considered ringing Dan's number and suggesting that he remove himself from Thie yn Traie immediately.

It was John's mobile that she tried first, in the end.

"Hello?"

"It's Bessie. I was just having a short walk on the beach when I saw Dan Ross walking down from the car park behind the holiday cottages. He ducked under the police tape and sneaked up the stairs to Thie yn Traie. He went in through the hidden door that's halfway up the cliff."

John sighed. "I was hoping to have a quiet night," he muttered.

"I'm sorry."

"It's fine. I was afraid Dan was going to do something stupid, although this seems even dumber than his usual stunts. Knowing him, he probably arranged to have the killer let him into the house and is now chatting with him or her over tea."

"That seems possible. I think you need to take a good look at Geoffrey Scott," Bessie said.

"Do you? Why?"

"I don't honestly know," Bessie sighed. "I don't care for him, but that isn't enough reason to suspect him of murder. I spoke to Jonathan Hooper tonight, though. He told me that he took Geoffrey all through the house and showed him some of the secret exits and rooms and things."

"Interesting. That isn't exactly what Mr. Scott told me, but never mind. I think I need to get to Thie yn Traie."

"Jonathan also told me that he locked the entrance from the beach with a padlock and gave Geoffrey the key," Bessie added.

"Did he really?"

"I may ring Mary and warn her," Bessie said.

"Please do, actually. I'd like her to know that I'm on my way. If you ring her, that will save me a task."

"Will I be in the way if she invites me to come over?"

John sighed. "Maybe, but you might also be quite useful. A lot depends on whether I can find Dan Ross or not."

He put the phone down and Bessie immediately rang Thie yn Traie.

"Good evening," a man's voice said.

"Ah, yes, this is Bessie Cubbon. I was hoping to speak to Mrs. Quayle, please."

"One moment, please."

Bessie found herself pacing back and forth while she waited. Geoffrey had answered the phone, which must have meant that he wasn't having tea with Dan Ross at the moment. Was it possible that Dan was talking with one of the other suspects?

"Bessie? Is something wrong?" Mary's voice came down the line.

"Not really. Are you alone?"

"No, not at all."

"Try not to react, then, please. John is on his way there. I just saw Dan Ross sneaking into the tunnel at the back of Thie yn Traie."

"Really? How interesting."

"I assume you haven't seen him?"

"No, not today, anyway."

"The worry is that he somehow made arrangements to meet with the killer," Bessie explained.

"That would have been very foolish."

"Yes, but this is Dan Ross we're discussing."

Mary chuckled. "So what happens now?"

"As I said, John is on his way. I believe he's going to want to search the house, but he'll probably need your permission."

"That isn't going to be a problem."

"I just wanted to warn you, really."

"I greatly appreciate it. Would you like to come over for a drink? I think I need one."

Bessie smiled "I'd love to."

"I'll send Geoffrey immediately."

Mary put the phone down before Bessie could object. The last person she wanted to be alone with at the moment was Geoffrey, but there seemed nothing she could do. It took her a few minutes to comb her hair and change, but she was at the door when Elizabeth's car rolled into the parking area a short while later.

"Mum told me what's happening and I offered to come and collect you," Elizabeth told her as Bessie climbed into the car. "John arrived just as I left."

"He's going to want to search the house. I hope you and your mother will be able to help him find all the hidden rooms and whatnot."

"We'll do our best. Jonathan is the real expert."

"Maybe someone will have to ring him."

A few minutes later, the pair walked into the great room. John was standing near the windows, staring down at the sea.

"Good evening," he said after he'd turned around. "I'm just waiting for everyone to join me here before I start my search. Geoffrey is rounding up the guests and the staff."

Bessie made a face, but didn't speak.

"We have men watching the beach, in case anyone tries to leave the house that way," John added.

"This is highly irregular," Owen said as he walked into the room in his pyjamas. "I was having an early night. At the very least, I should have been allowed to change."

"You should have," John agreed. "Would you like to go back to your room and change now?"

He stared at John for a minute and then shook his head. "I'd like to get this all over with. Why are we even here?"

"I'll explain everything when everyone is here," John promised.

The other two men were also complaining when they walked into the room a short while later. They were followed by a number of men and women who must have constituted the house's staff. Bessie was surprised at how many of them there were, especially since she didn't think she'd ever seen most of them before. George stomped into the room and took a seat in the corner. He looked angry at someone or something. Elizabeth joined him, and before long she'd managed to get him to smile, at least a bit.

Geoffrey was the last to arrive. "That's everyone in the house," he announced.

John looked up from his notebook. "And there isn't any internal security that tracks the house's occupants?" he asked Mary.

She shook her head. "We sometimes post guards within the house when we have guests, more to see to their needs than for security purposes, but we haven't anyone working inside at the moment."

"A short while ago, a credible witness spotted Dan Ross, a local reporter, sneaking into Thie yn Traie," John said in a loud voice. "If any of you have seen Dan tonight, I'd appreciate if you'd tell me where I can find him."

"You need better security," Nicholas told George.

He shrugged. "I thought we had good security."

"How did he get in?" Mary asked.

"He ignored the police tape and entered through the tunnel from the beach," John told her.

"I thought the police put a lock on that door after the, well, unfortunate incident on the beach," Mary said.

"The police did put a lock on that door. The lock is still in place, but Dan Ross definitely got into the house that way. That suggests that someone let him in, someone with a key or the ability to pick locks."

"If you put the lock on, you must be the only person with a key," Owen suggested.

"I don't have the key, though. The police provided the lock to block access while the police tape was in place, but we gave the key to the head of security here," John replied.

All eyes turned to look at the security chief. He shrugged. "We had the key on a hook in the office. It's gone now."

"This is ridiculous. Who cares?" Edmund demanded. "So someone got inside the house. He's gone now, or he's hiding. He'll come out when he gets bored or hungry or whatever reporters get."

"You may be right, but out of an abundance of caution, my colleagues and I are going to search the house," John told him.

"Search the house? That seems completely unnecessary," Owen said.

"We're going to ask that you all remain here while we're searching. It will make our job a good deal easier," John continued.

"Do we have a choice?" Nicholas demanded.

"Not really," John told him flatly.

Mary got to her feet. "May I have a word?" she asked John.

"Of course," he said. "Let's talk in the corridor."

"Bessie, will you come with me?" Mary asked.

Bessie nodded and then got to her feet. They followed John out of the room.

"Thank you for picking up on all of your cues," John told Mary.

"Just trying to help," Mary replied. "Can Bessie and I help with the search?"

John hesitated and then shook his head. "This really needs to be a police operation."

"You'll need me to show you where some of the secret doors are, though," Mary suggested.

"Yes, there is that," John sighed. "I'm sending constables into each wing. Your butler has given me several master keys that are meant to open every door in the house. The constables will be going into every room they can find. Perhaps you could show me some of the secret rooms."

Mary smiled at Bessie. "We'll bring Bessie, too, for good luck," she suggested.

John just nodded. "Where shall we start?"

"There are secret rooms in every wing," Mary told him. "We should probably start with the wing where our guests are staying, as they're the main suspects, are they not?"

"Or the staff wing," Bessie suggested.

Mary frowned. "Whom do you suspect?" she asked.

"There's something I don't like about Geoffrey," Bessie told her. "It may just be me, though."

Mary frowned. "We've been discussing dismissing him early, but we never imagined that he was a murderer."

"Why are you thinking of dismissing him early?" John asked.

"He's, well, he seems to be everywhere you don't want him to be, although he isn't always where you do want him to be. He seems very interested in our guests, to the point of being intrusive. I was wondering if he was trying to work out George's decision and then use that information in some way."

"How could he use it?"

"He could sell what he knew to one of the other men, giving them advance warning of what was coming," Mary suggested. She shrugged. "I don't know. When I say it all out loud it sounds rather ridiculous, but I do feel as if Geoffrey is trying to find out things that he doesn't need to know."

"Maybe he makes a habit of blackmailing his former employers," Bessie suggested.

"What a horrible thought," Mary said. "We didn't hear a single complaint against him when we checked his references."

"But who would want to admit that they were being blackmailed?" Bessie murmured.

"Let's focus on finding Dan," John suggested. "We know he hasn't left the house, unless he found another way out that we don't know about."

"Which is possible," Mary sighed. "I hope it's unlikely, though. Our security team has been around the outside of the property a number of times. They seem fairly certain that we've found all the exits, even if we haven't found all the hidden rooms."

"Hidden rooms, right, let's see if we can find anyone hiding in any of those hidden rooms," John suggested. "Let's start with the one in the wing where your guests are staying."

Mary led them through the corridors. Bessie wasn't sure that she'd have been able to find her way there, even though she'd just been to that wing several times because of Ted. When they reached the right corridor, Mary stopped in front of a section of wall. There was a large painting that Bessie assumed was a copy rather than an original.

"This is it," she said, sliding the painting to the side. Behind it was a small doorknob. Mary turned the knob and a section of the wall suddenly opened.

Behind the door was a spacious bedroom. John walked through it and checked the attached en-suite. "Empty," he announced.

"This is gorgeous," Bessie said.

Mary nodded. "It's one of the nicest rooms in the house. I've no idea why the doorway is hidden."

"How did you ever find it?" Bessie asked as they walked back into the corridor.

"Jonathan has been going through the house, inspecting anywhere where there are spaces between rooms or walls that don't match up to the exterior walls, that sort of thing," Mary explained.

"Let's see what there is in the staff wing, then," John said.

"This wasn't the staff wing when the Pierce family had the house," Mary explained as they walked. "They used a different wing, but George and I preferred this section."

"Why?" Bessie wondered.

Mary flushed. "The rooms in this wing are somewhat larger and better furnished. As we don't plan to have enough guests to fill the house, we thought it would be better to give our staff more comfortable rooms."

Again, they walked down a corridor and stopped. This time there was no painting. Only wallpaper covered the wall.

Mary ran her fingers along a section of the paper, stopping suddenly. She seemed to push on the wall before a section of it slid away.

Another beautiful bedroom was hidden behind the sliding door. John checked it quickly.

"Also empty," he said. His mobile buzzed. He pulled it out and frowned at it. "No one has found anything on the search of the rest of the house," he said.

"We have at least another four or five hidden rooms to check," Mary told him.

"I think we should try whatever is closest to the tunnel," Bessie said. "If Dan was meeting someone at the house, that person wouldn't have wanted to be seen with him."

"Good point," John said.

"There are two hidden rooms in that corridor," Mary told him. "Jonathan is convinced that there's a third, as well, but he hasn't found it yet."

She led them back through the house. Bessie now felt completely lost. All of the corridors were starting to look alike.

"This is the first," Mary said, sliding open a door by twisting a candleholder that was mounted on the wall.

"Empty," John sighed.

"And this is the second," Mary told them a moment later. This time the door opened after she'd lifted a vase on a table in the corridor. As the vase was raised, the table folded flat against the wall and then a section of wall moved backwards.

"Also empty," John reported a moment later.

"Why does Jonathan think there might be another room?" Bessie asked.

"He thinks there's an odd gap here," Mary said, pointing to the opposite wall. "It isn't really big enough for a room, but it could be a small storage cupboard."

Bessie stared at the blank wall. If there was a hidden door, there had to be a way to get it open.

"Jonathan has tried everything, but he can't find the way in," Mary said.

"The hidden door in the great room had a switch on the skirting boards," Bessie recalled.

"Yes, but every other door has a different mechanism. Anyway, Jonathan tried the skirting boards, I'm sure of it," Mary said.

Bessie bent down and ran her hand along the skirting board. There didn't seem to be any hidden buttons or levers there. John began running his hands up and down the wall.

"There isn't any wallpaper here," Mary said. "It's the pattern in the other corridor that lets you find the hidden button."

John began to tap on the wall as he walked up and down the corridor. "This section certainly sounds different," he said after a minute.

"Yes, Jonathan thought as much, too," Mary agreed.

Bessie had been staring at the wall for what felt like ages. Now she took a step forward. "There's a shadow here," she said. Reaching out, she traced her finger around the shadow. "What's making it?"

The others looked around.

"Maybe it's a stain in the paint," John suggested.

"Or maybe it's the way in," Bessie said. She tried pushing on the shadowy area, but nothing happened. Then she tried tapping it. Again nothing.

Mary frowned. "One of the doors opens when you hit a section of the wall in just the right place. You have to hit it rather hard. Jonathan found it quite by accident when he was feeling a bit frustrated."

John grinned. "I can understand how he felt."

He took a step back and then slammed the side of his fist into the shadowy area on the wall. A moment later, a panel slid sideways, revealing a small, dark space.

John switched on his torch and Bessie gasped as the light illuminated a dark figure standing in the space. There seemed to be just enough room for the person and very little else. He or she was facing away from them, and Bessie could see a rope around the person's wrists, which were behind his or her back.

"Stand back," John said as he reached forward. As he tried to turn the person around, the figure suddenly collapsed at their feet.

"Dan Ross," Bessie exclaimed as he fell.

A cloth had been stuffed into Dan's mouth. John pulled the cloth out as he rubbed Dan's face. "Dan?"

The reporter opened his eyes and moaned. "The butler did it," he choked out before his eyes rolled back in his head.

CHAPTER 15

*J*ohn already had an ambulance waiting, just in case. Paramedics were wheeling Dan away within minutes.

"I think he'll be okay," one of them told John. "I think maybe he was just overcome by the experience."

John nodded.

"What about Geoffrey?" Bessie asked.

"He's been sitting quietly in the great room while we've been searching. I've asked that he be taken down to the station for questioning," John told her.

"He must have killed Harrison and tried to kill Ted," Bessie said. "I shudder to think what he planned for Dan."

"Dan's lucky that you saw him sneaking into the house. If you hadn't raised the alarm, no one would have been looking for him until tomorrow at the earliest," John replied.

Bessie nodded. "I can't believe he wasn't more careful."

"It will be interesting to hear what he has to say when he wakes up," John said.

Mary had her driver take Bessie home. The news the next day had little to say about the previous evening's events.

"An ambulance was called to Thie yn Traie again last evening.

Police Inspector John Rockwell refused to comment," was all that the local radio station reported.

Bessie was sure that Dan Ross's next article for the local paper would contain a good deal more information. After a brisk walk to the police tape and back again and a healthy breakfast, Bessie rang Noble's.

"I'm sorry, but Dan Ross isn't currently a patient here," she was told.

Frowning, she put the phone down. Was he sufficiently recovered to have been released or were the police hiding him in the same way they were hiding Ted? She didn't get her answer until the next day.

She'd just finished a light lunch and was heading for the stairs and some time with Onnee when someone knocked on her door.

"Dan? This is a surprise."

He shrugged. "I'm told that you spotted me sneaking into Thie yn Traie and rang the police. Apparently, you saved my life."

"I'd have done the same for anyone."

Dan laughed. "Oh, I know. You weren't actually trying to save my life. No doubt you were hoping I'd be arrested for going under the police tape."

Bessie shook her head. "Not at all. I was genuinely worried about you. The more I thought about it, the more likely it seemed to me that Geoffrey was behind Harrison's murder. I was afraid you were still focussed on George's guests and wouldn't be properly cautious around Geoffrey."

"You were right about that," Dan said ruefully.

"Come in for a cuppa," Bessie offered somewhat reluctantly.

He grinned. "Thank you kindly. I will."

Before Bessie had shut the door, he was sitting at the table, beaming at her. "You want to hear the whole story, don't you?"

For a moment, Bessie was tempted to say no, just to annoy Dan, but she did want to hear the story. No doubt it would all be in the papers eventually, but she wasn't willing to wait, not if she was going to be giving the man tea and biscuits, anyway.

"Go ahead, then," she said as she filled the kettle.

"I got an anonymous tip that the killer was Owen and that my caller had proof. I recognised the voice. It was Geoffrey. He seemed to be in the right place to have found what he claimed to have found. I rang the number that had been given by the tipster. After some back and forth, he admitted who he was and invited me to Thie yn Traie. He said he'd let me in the secret entrance and that he'd give me the evidence he'd found in exchange for a large sum of money."

"And you turned him down and rang the police," Bessie suggested.

Dan laughed. "Yeah, that's what I should have done, isn't it? I didn't even give that idea any thought. I don't have a lot of money, of course, but I was desp, er, eager to solve the case, so I agreed to meet him. I thought maybe we could negotiate or something. Anyway, I sneaked up to the tunnel and Geoffrey let me in. He gave me a drink, and the next thing I knew I was on the floor with you and Inspector Rockwell standing over me."

Bessie sighed. The story was rather anticlimactic. "I was hoping he'd confessed to something," she told Dan as she poured the tea.

"Yeah, that would have been good. The police won't tell me how their investigation is going, but I do know that they still have Geoffrey in custody. I was hoping maybe you could tell me what's going on?"

"I haven't spoken to John since Geoffrey's arrest. He won't tell me anything, anyway, not until he's ready to make a public statement."

Dan frowned. "I've a good headline for today, but I need a follow-up. Geoffrey confessing would be the best sort of news."

"I'm sure if he does confess, that John will let you know eventually."

"I don't want eventually," Dan sighed. He drank the rest of his tea in a single swallow and then got to his feet. "I'd better go and start doing some digging. Maybe I can work out what Harrison knew about Geoffrey that led to his murder. If Harrison Parker could find something, I'm sure I can, too."

Bessie didn't argue as she followed him to the door. She was heading for the stairs again, after doing the washing-up, when she heard another knock.

"I am coming," she called up the stairs to Onnee.

"John, how nice to see you," she said a moment later.

He gave her a hug and then stepped inside the cottage. "I can't stay long, but I thought you should have the news as soon as possible."

"What news?"

"First of all, Dan is fine. He's out of hospital and may well turn up on your doorstep one of these days. He should, if nothing else, come and thank you."

"He was already here this morning."

John chuckled. "Okay, then, maybe none of my news will be news to you."

Bessie waved him into a chair and put the kettle on again. "I hope you have good news about Ted."

"I do, actually. He's regained consciousness. It's going to take some time for him to recover completely, but he's doing a good deal better. He's also given me a full statement, which, incidentally, started with the words 'the butler did it.'"

"Does the butler ever actually do it in books?" Bessie mused. "Everyone seems to think so, but I can't think of a single book where the butler was the killer."

John shrugged. "In this case, the butler certainly drugged Ted. Ted remembers that much, and he also remembers being told to write something. His memory is foggy, but it seems as if Geoffrey got him to write his own suicide note before putting him to bed and then slitting his wrists."

Bessie shuddered.

"He doesn't remember that part," John assured her. "The cuts were superficial. Geoffrey expected the drugs to kill him, and they would have if he hadn't been found when he was."

"That has to mean that Geoffrey killed Harrison."

"We're carefully searching Geoffrey's belongings for any evidence to tie him to Harrison's murder. I've spoken to several of his former employers and we know what his motive was, anyway."

"Oh?"

"He was blackmailing just about everyone for whom he'd ever

worked," John told her. "Now that he's behind bars, a few of his victims have shared their stories. We're certain there are more of them, as well."

"How awful."

"We think Harrison was chasing a story about one of Geoffrey's former employers and stumbled onto Geoffrey's blackmail schemes instead. We're still searching Thie yn Traie. We're really hoping to find Harrison's notebook."

Bessie nodded. "But you're sure Geoffrey killed Harrison."

"I am, but I can't take just my opinion to court."

"I wonder what George is going to do about the retail park now," Bessie said as she let John out of the cottage.

"I'm not sure if he knows the answer to that yet," John replied.

A few days later, the local paper told her everything she needed to know. As more and more victims came forward, Geoffrey broke down and confessed to blackmail, murder, and attempted murder. George decided to buy out Alastair's share of the retail park himself, promising that getting the park built was high on his agenda before he and Mary left the island for a much needed holiday in the Caribbean.

Bessie usually let her answering machine pick up her calls, but one day, about a week later, the phone rang as she was heading for the door. It was raining heavily, and she didn't need much of an excuse to postpone her walk.

"Hello?"

"Bessie, my dear, it's Andrew, Andrew Cheatham. I'm coming to the island next month, staying in the cottages near you. I have something of an interesting proposition for you."

"Really? Tell me more."

He chuckled. "All in good time."

GLOSSARY OF TERMS

House Names – Manx to English

- **Thie yn Traie** — Beach House
- **Treoghe Bwaane** — Widow's Cottage

English to American Terms

- **advocate** —Manx title for a lawyer (solicitor)
- **aye** — yes
- **bin** — garbage can
- **biscuits** — cookies
- **bonnet (car)** — hood
- **boot (car)** — trunk
- **brewing something** — catching something (a cold or flu)
- **car park** — parking lot
- **chemist** — pharmacist
- **chips** — french fries
- **crisps** — potato chips
- **cuppa** — cup of tea (informally)
- **dear** — expensive

- **estate agent** — real estate agent (realtor)
- **fairy cakes** — cupcakes
- **fancy dress** — costume
- **fizzy drink** — soda (pop)
- **flat** — apartment
- **hire car** — rental car
- **holiday** — vacation
- **jumper** — sweater
- **lie in** — sleep late
- **lift** — elevator
- **midday** — noon
- **pavement** — sidewalk
- **plait (hair)** — braid
- **poorly** — unwell
- **primary school** — elementary school
- **pudding** — dessert
- **puds** — pudding (informal)
- **skeet** — gossip
- **skirting boards** — baseboards
- **starters** — appetizers
- **supply teacher** — substitute teacher
- **telly** — television
- **thick** — stupid
- **torch** — flashlight
- **trolley** — shopping cart
- **windscreen** — windshield

OTHER NOTES

The emergency number in the UK and the Isle of Man is 999, not 911.

CID is the Criminal Investigation Department of the Isle of Man Constabulary (Police Force).

When talking about time, the English say, for example, "half seven" to mean "seven-thirty."

With regard to Bessie's age: UK (and IOM) residents get a free bus pass at the age of 60. Bessie is somewhere between that age and the age at which she will get a birthday card from the Queen. British citizens used to receive telegrams from the ruling monarch on the occasion of their one-hundredth birthday. Cards replaced the telegrams in 1982, but the special greeting is still widely referred to as a telegram.

When island residents talk about someone being from "across," they mean that the person is from somewhere in the United Kingdom (across the water).

ACKNOWLEDGMENTS

Many thanks to my editor who has stuck with me for twenty-five titles – only one more, Denise!

Thanks to Kevin for so many wonderful photographs of the beautiful Isle of Man.

And thank you, readers, for following Bessie's story for the last several years.

Aunt Bessie Zeroes In
An Isle of Man Cozy Mystery
Release Date: October 16, 2020

Aunt Bessie zeroes in on the perfect house for her friends, Elizabeth Quayle and Andy Caine.

Actually, the Looney mansion isn't anyone's idea of a perfect house. Decades of neglect have left the house in need of a complete renovation, but Andy and Elizabeth have the funds needed to restore the house to its former glory.

Aunt Bessie zeroes in on the body on the bed.

Finding another murder victim isn't all that surprising for Bessie, but the dead man's identity is a shock to everyone.

Aunt Bessie zeroes in on the suspects.

Doing what she does best, Bessie talks to everyone she knows about the victim, why he was on the island, and who wanted him dead. No doubt, before long, Bessie will be zeroing in on a killer.

ALSO BY DIANA XARISSA

The Isle of Man Cozy Mysteries

Aunt Bessie Yearns

Aunt Bessie Zeroes In

The Isle of Man Ghostly Cozy Mysteries

Arrivals and Arrests

Boats and Bad Guys

Cars and Cold Cases

Dogs and Danger

Encounters and Enemies

Friends and Frauds

Guests and Guilt

Hop-tu-Naa and Homicide

Invitations and Investigations

Joy and Jealousy

Kittens and Killers

Letters and Lawsuits

Marsupials and Murder

Neighbors and Nightmares

Orchestras and Obsessions

Proposals and Poison

The Markham Sisters Cozy Mystery Novellas

The Appleton Case

The Bennett Case

The Chalmers Case

The Donaldson Case

The Ellsworth Case

The Fenton Case

The Green Case

The Hampton Case

The Irwin Case

The Jackson Case

The Kingston Case

The Lawley Case

The Moody Case

The Norman Case

The Osborne Case

The Patrone Case

The Quinton Case

The Rhodes Case

The Somerset Case

The Tanner Case

The Underwood Case

The Vernon Case

The Walters Case

The Xanders Case

The Isle of Man Romance Series

Island Escape

Island Inheritance

Island Heritage

Island Christmas

The Later in Life Love Stories

Second Chances

Second Act

Second Thoughts

Second Degree

ABOUT THE AUTHOR

Diana Xarissa lived on the Isle of Man for more than ten years before returning to the United States with her family. Now living near Buffalo, New York, she enjoys having the opportunity to write about the island that she loves so much. It truly is a special place.

Diana also writes mystery/thrillers set in the not-too-distant future under the pen name "Diana X. Dunn" and fantasy/adventure books for middle grade readers under the pen name "D.X. Dunn."

She would be delighted to know what you think of her work and can be contacted through snail mail at:

Diana Xarissa Dunn

PO Box 72

Clarence, NY 14031.

You can sign up for her monthly newsletter on the website and be among the first to know about new releases, as well as find out about contests and giveaways and see the answers to the questions she gets asked the most.

Find Diana at:
www.dianaxarissa.com
diana@dianaxarissa.com